To Trust

Evergreen Point Book Two

by

Rasha Selim

To Trust

Contact Information: info@thewildrosepress.com

Cover Art by *Diana Carlile*

The Wild Rose Press, Inc.
PO Box 708
Adams Basin, NY 14410-0708

Publishing History
First Edition, 2022
Print ISBN 978-1-5092-4125-5
Digital ISBN 978-1-5092-4126-2
Published in the United States of America

Life was good…until a
one-night stand changed everything

His laugh warmed me, and without thinking I stood on my tiptoes and kissed his jaw. His sharp intake delightful to me. I dropped the blanket and headed to the kitchen with an extra swagger in my step.

"Want some coffee?" I asked over my shoulder.

He grunted his answer, and I giggled.

"For every action there is a consequence," he said as he stepped to the front door.

Away from his knowing eyes, my smile grew, and I made my drink. Muffled voices carried through the air, incoherent because of the distance. I listened for a minute and when no one approached, I daydreamed, looking out the window at the peaceful lake. I held the steaming mug close to my chest and inhaled the rich aroma.

"Ann Marie," Morgan yelled, startling me out of my reverie.

I headed for him, cautious of the hot drink in my grip. I couldn't see past Morgan's broad shoulders. He rested his arm against the open wood and kept the guest outside and hidden from view. His tense neck and back muscles a loud warning sign.

At my approach, Morgan shifted, and I glimpsed the man standing at the threshold. Shocked, I stumbled and dropped the mug. It shattered on the entry-way slate tile. Pieces of ceramic ricocheted off the floor and lodged into my shins. I didn't know which was worse. The pain from the hot liquid, the pain in my pierced skin, or seeing the asshole at Morgan's door.

Dedication

For Ann Marie

Author Acknowledgments

I owe a mighty thanks to several people without whom, this book would never have seen the light of day.

My awesome husband who understands my need to seclude myself to write before all the characters in my head become angry.

My three boys, although teenagers now, who bring me sustenance while I am writing (and answer questions on today's youth culture).

My Beta Readers, Jennifer and Susan. Without their input, my stories would still be a jumbled mess in my draft folders.

My amazingly patient editor, Judi.

My readers for always wanting more.

The Wild Rose Press, Inc. for putting their faith in me and my stories.

And of course, Ann Marie for answering my many texts at random times of the day. I hope I did your character justice.

Chapter One

Morgan

The alarm on my phone, sitting on the workbench, blared through the workshop speakers as I finished applying the final touches on the custom bike. I wiped my hands on the rag tucked in my back pocket and silenced my phone. The crooning, lovesick musician's voice filled the room once again.

Rain knocked against the galvanized steel roof and competed with the volume of my music. Nothing beat the solitude of working up a sweat in my own space with chrome beneath my fingers. I stepped away and admired the finished chopper before me. I spotted a smudge, grabbed a clean rag from the shelf, and shined the metal until my image reflected back at me.

I turned off the music and headed inside to the living room as my phone rang. I needed a shower and a change of clothes before walking over to my childhood home, five houses down the street. Since my family knew my dislike of unnecessary conversation, it could be one of three people. I answered, after chuckling at the new image on my screen.

"Hey, Red. Nice picture."

Her laugh boomed through the speaker, and I puffed out my chest, pleased I made her laugh.

"Don't ever change your password. I have way too

much fun surprising you."

"I could do with a little less Pax, though. Less face sucking action."

"Admit it, asshole. You're jealous." Pax said.

"Red? Give a guy some warning when you have him on speaker. I would hate for Pax to hear all our secrets. Wouldn't want your fair skin to match your hair."

Susan's red hair resembled the color of a firetruck. Ironic, considering her situation. Her fiancé, my older brother, was a firefighter. But long before she became Pax's girlfriend, she was my best friend.

Susan laughed, and Pax growled.

"Quit stirring trouble," she said around her giggles. "Anyway, we're on our way over."

"Why?"

"Duh. It's raining. Stop working and go shower."

"Rain won't hurt me." I stripped as I walked to my room and threw my sweat-dampened clothes into the hamper inside the en suite bathroom.

"Are you kidding me? It's like forty-five degrees out here. By the time you get to Mom and Dad's your twenty-seven-year-old shriveled balls will be popsicles."

I sighed and held in a chuckle. "Thanks for your concern over my balls, but I assure you they'll thaw out. They're still young." Naked, I leaned into the stall, turned on the water, and adjusted the taps for the optimal temperature. "Hey, Hulk. Tell your woman I can walk."

"Good luck. You know she's stubborn."

He was right, and with a half-hearted huff, I relented. "Give me ten."

"Perfect, that's how long 'til we get there," Susan said.

I hung up, dropped my phone on the countertop, and stepped under the streaming water. It took less time to shower since I cut my shoulder-length straight hair but left it long enough to run my hands through it.

I dried off and dressed in my most comfortable dark jeans, a white T-shirt, worn biker boots, and a black leather jacket. I strove for relaxed, predictable, and easy in all aspects of my life. I liked nothing more than those three words.

It was the reason I left my job at the garage. Contrary to common belief, men whined and gossiped at headache-inducing levels, and the constant chatter of the shop pushed at my limits.

I enjoyed my uncomplicated life. I didn't date but had a few women I visited when the need arose. I preferred my solitude. My family and Susan, the few people allowed within my domain or heart.

The fewer you let in, the less it hurt when they left.

I stood in my living room, my gaze focused outside. The trees hid my house from the road. Insulated me from the world. The infrequent times I loosened my tight hold on my sensibilities were always in the privacy of my home. When I designed, built, or strummed my guitar, I allowed my emotions to flow. The few hours I surrendered in seclusion were enough to keep me in check.

I hummed as I dressed. Yes, I could sing. A skill I kept secret, not because of the inevitable family teasing, but because when I sang, I didn't trust my discipline. The words and rhythm of a song pushed at my self-control, allowing actions and reflections to surface from the depth in which I buried them.

The loud engine of a truck rumbled down my driveway silenced at my front door. I stepped out and petted the black cat who found me working one day with the shop doors open. And he hadn't left since.

Susan and her veterinary friend checked him over when he first arrived. Over time, we developed a quiet understanding. He sat with me when I played my guitar on the dock, or he lounged on a blanket in the garage when I worked if the overhead doors stayed open. He refused entry into the house no matter what food I waved under his nose. Enclosed spaces could be scary. I understood anxieties, and I left him to deal as best he knew how with his demons.

We all had our own monsters lurking around corners, anticipating our weakest moments.

Every day was a battle, but each time I fought and won because of my family and the woman in my brother's truck jumping for joy at seeing me. I pocketed my keys and wallet, dropped my sunglasses down onto my nose, and walked to the parked truck.

****

Ann Marie

I sat in the back seat of Pax's truck, and listened to the phone conversation with Morgan, nervous and chastising myself for it. As a twenty-six-year-old founder and CEO of a design and marketing company in Seattle, not much fazed me. But the prospect of seeing Morgan again sent shivers down my back and turned me into a nervous, pubescent girl.

I met him twice before, once as an awkward twelve-year-old, visiting Susan and her dad, and the second this past summer at Susan's fundraiser in May. Tall, dark, handsome, chiseled, and tattooed to the nines. Greek statues were hideous in comparison.

His stern features portrayed no hint of his thoughts. He grumped more than he talked, yet I thrummed with excitement in his presence. Never mind the number of fantasies he starred in over the past seven months.

The pulse between my legs increased and butterflies swarmed my belly. The sensations created a duality of emotions. Excitement and self-recrimination did not go hand-in-hand.

"You're quiet back there," Susan said, without turning her body toward me.

Pax was very much into safety and he didn't tolerate anyone moving about in his car, a fact I learned within seconds of my first ride in his truck. He pulled off into a parking lot when I leaned forward and rested my chin on the back of the front seat. He scowled at me in silence. Susan giggled and waved her fingers for me to move back. Once I resettled in my seat, he eyed me in the rear-view mirror before driving again.

"Didn't want to upset the big lug. Talking about the things I'm thinking of can prove dangerous while driving."

Pax's gaze snapped to mine in the mirror and his lips twitched, his smile-not-smile telling.

"Whatever crossed your mind, let me be the first to tell you, is wrong if it involves your brother," I said and fought the urge to slap my forehead.

Pax's sparkling white teeth blinded me, and I covered my eyes.

"His brother? Morgan? What are you talking about?" Susan's side-eye gaze swiveled from Pax to me several times. "What am I missing?"

I turned away from Pax's roguish stare and focused on the trees and houses on the side of the road. "Nothing," I replied.

"Ann Marie Tosto, I call bullshit."

I smirked at my cousin, even though she faced the front.

"Fine. I miss sex."

Susan laughed as Pax choked. "Sex with someone in particular?" she asked.

"No. Just the act of fornicating in general. It's a great stress reliever. You should try it sometime."

Susan reached over and grabbed Pax's thigh, her lust-filled gaze fanned across his face as she soothed the groove between his eyebrows with a finger. "In that case, I'm the most relaxed person on the planet," she said. Huskiness deepened her voice.

"Stop talking. Your sex voice is distracting Pax," I said, glad the attention was off me.

"Don't drag me into this," Pax said, even as his eyes crinkled further. He took Susan's hand in his and kissed her knuckles. He released her and returned his hand to the steering wheel a moment later.

We pulled up to a small yellow craftsman home set behind an array of trees. An ornate arch and awning bathed the front door in shadows. A black cat lounged on a weather-worn wooden rocking chair. The cat eyed the truck for a moment before it lifted its paw and groomed itself with lazy licks.

A massive truck and trailer blocked a set of closed garage doors. A cobblestone path to the left of the house led to a dock. A deck boat floated on the waters of Lake Washington, anchored to one of the wooden posts. A swing facing the water swayed from the rafters of a covered wooden pergola. Five lounge chairs scattered across the rest of the deck. The setup made for an inviting place to relax after a long day. A place to forget the demands of clients and employees. A place to cuddle and fall in love.

I choked on the bitter taste in the back of my throat and muttered under my breath, "You want nothing to do with cuddles and love."

A booted foot stepped out onto the slate stones. The movement grabbed my attention and pushed away the unexpected and offensive thoughts. I took my time and scanned the man wearing those well-worn boots. My gaze drifted upwards and noted every detail. My mouth watered at the sight of long muscular legs encased in form-fitting jeans, the impressive bulge hidden behind the zipper, and the tight shirt showcasing his lean, muscled torso under a weathered black leather jacket. I stifled my groan as I appreciated the face of an Adonis.

By Susan's amused giggle, I didn't hide my admiration well.

Morgan stood tall at six foot two, dark hair still wet from a shower, now cut short, and eyes hidden behind a pair of mirrored glasses. He reminded me of Adam Levine.

He pulled his sunglasses to the top of his head and petted the cat. I imagined those lithe fingers running through my hair. His gaze roamed his property and then the truck. The tinted windows hid me from his view, and I continued my undetected—at least from him—appraisal.

"Close your mouth," Susan said, and I started at the

sound of her voice. "You're drooling."

I swiped the back of my hand across my mouth and glared at Susan when my hand came away dry.

Pax's gaze moved from me to Susan, and with a last glance at Morgan, he turned back and faced the front with a shit-eating grin.

I settled back in my seat and followed Morgan's approach out of the corner of my eye. I mourned the loss of his eyes as he slipped his glasses back on, and my muscles tightened as he neared.

He opened the door and hesitated. He lowered his glasses to the tip of his nose and surveyed the interior of the truck before his gaze settled on me. I held my posture rigid, made eye contact with his striking blue-gray ones, and quirked a single eyebrow. It took everything I had to keep from squirming under his extended scrutiny, thankful for my perfected boardroom skills.

"You remember my cousin, Ann Marie?" Susan's question jolted us from our stare-off.

"Yeah," he replied, voice laced with panty-wetting gruffness.

I nodded and turned away before I did something impulsive, like jump in his lap and declare my unrelenting desire to fuck him.

Dual failed-to-convey indignation huffs rewarded Susan's snicker, and she muttered, "This ought to be good."

Chapter Two

Morgan

The tinted windows of Pax's truck obstructed my view, but as I approached, a silhouette moved within. I figured it was our cousin, Kate, and did not hesitate. I flung the door open and was hit with a familiar sweet smell. My chest and cock reacted on instinct. From scent alone, one embedded in my brain against my will, I identified the final occupant.

Unprepared, I came face-to-face with the woman who stirred my blood like no other. My memory of her luscious figure, red lips, and mischievous eyes played on repeat in my fantasies over the past few months.

Ann Marie Tosto did not fit into my uncomplicated life, but I craved her with a tenacity. A fact I loathed. Her tongue licked her lips as I settled in my seat, and my dick grew harder. I shifted and adjusted my pants.

Her gaze tracked my hand and the corners of my mouth twitched.

"I'm too much for those little hands to handle." Inappropriate? Yes, but I didn't care. It was either be an asshole or show vulnerability.

She studied me for a second then smiled. The twinkle in her eye prophesied trouble.

"Who needs hands when my tongue does the work?"

My pants tightened and cut off my circulation. I stifled a growl and scowled. I refused her any emotion other than irritation.

Her phone rang and saved her from my retort. With a huff, she pulled it from her purse and scrunched her eyebrows as she stared at the display. I turned away and fought the temptation to check the screen.

She sent the call to voicemail and held it face down against her leg. It rang again. With vigor, she stabbed the red icon and declined the call. A quick flip later, she shut off the volume.

The flash of hurt in her eyes enough to goad my long-ago buried instincts. My need to fix almost overpowered my need to stay away from Ann Marie.

"Was it him again?" Susan asked.

"Ugh, he's a pain in my ass," Ann Marie said and kept her gaze on the houses outside her window.

"Next time he calls, answer it."

"No. I already told him we're done."

"That simple, huh?" I said, against my better judgment.

"Excuse me?" Ann Marie asked and placed her hands on her hips, then angled her body toward me.

Pax chuckled, and I smirked at him in the rear-view mirror. Her indignation didn't scare me.

"He fucked someone else without protection. He knew the rules from the start," Ann Marie said.

I snorted, and her laser focus gaze scathed me.

"What? Got something to say?"

I shook my head.

She scrutinized me. "It's simple. No relationship. No fucking without a condom. Break either rule, no seconds. I don't take risks with my body or my h…"

She had my full attention at her near slip, surprised we had similar philosophies. I raised my hands in surrender.

"Nothing to say?"

"Not my business," I said.

Susan turned in her seat, annoying Pax, and patted his forearm. "Lovers' first quarrel. How cute," she said. She laughed at our matching glares. "I knew it. This is going to be so much fun."

"Stop being an asshole," Ann Marie said to Susan, and I nodded in agreement.

"Whatever. Scott's a douche, you know? Want Pax to beat him up for you?"

Ann Marie snorted. "Yeah, he is and no. I can fight my own battles. Besides, Scott's not worth my boob sweat. He was good in bed, though. He just hates I ended our arrangement, not him. Well, he can go suck it."

Ann Marie turned away, ending further conversation. I used her distraction to my advantage and raked my gaze over her exquisite body. With her long, wavy brown hair, styled to perfection, purple nails, and a hint of makeup, she was gorgeous. Her tight five-foot four little frame, covered in a purple sweater and black painted on jeans, a seduction all its own. I licked my lips instead of her skin, and imagined her taste, sweet, like her perfume.

She hopped out of the car and broke me from my trance. With a shake of my head and internal reproach, I exited and led our group up the stone-paved path to the wrap-around porch. Without knocking, I entered the house and sought my dad. He sat on one of the two large brown leather sectionals, surrounded by my brothers and cousins. Different versions of hello rang out, although their collective attention remained on the pre-game show.

"Hey, Dad. Got a minute?" I called out as I took my jacket off and hung it on the coat rack by the door.

He lifted his gaze from the TV, and with a little shove to my brother, Foster, I settled in beside him.

"Are you kidding me? Am I fucking invisible?" Foster asked.

Ma, exited the kitchen, stepped behind us to greet me, and smacked him as she said, "Language."

I chuckled as Foster rubbed the back of his head.

"Sorry, Mom," he said, his cheeks pinked.

Ma leaned over the couch and kissed me on my presented cheek. A concession I didn't make for just anyone. If it made her happy to smother me with love, who was I to deny her?

"Hey sweetheart. Are you getting enough to eat?" She reached over my shoulder and patted my stomach.

"Yep. Thanks for the casserole."

Living near my parents afforded me several advantages.

"I wondered where my dinner went." Dad bellowed.

He could bluster all he wanted. She fed him more than she did us. He enjoyed teasing her, and they had a solid, loving relationship. As role models for love, my brothers and I could not have asked for better. But their relationship wasn't the kind I wanted.

I rubbed the phantom pain in my chest and forced a smile. "It was damn good, Dad. Next time you're hungry, come over. Ma filled my fridge with her cooking."

"Stop needling your father," she said, and kissed the top of my head. She rounded the couch and enveloped Susan in a hug. "Girls, relax here or in the kitchen. Up to you. Ann Marie, it's so good to have you."

"Thanks, Mrs. Anderson. Susan didn't want me to spend Thanksgiving alone, but my parents needed this trip. I'm glad they could get away."

"Yes, Susan told me what you did. It was sweet of you gifting them a cruise."

I listened with covert attention. Susan would badger me if I showed any interest.

"It was the least I could do. Mom's had a tough couple of years. Now she's in remission, and she's always wanted to go on a Mediterranean cruise."

I closed my eyes and warded off my nausea. Death was a topic I never discussed.

Ever.

"What kind of help did you need?" Dad asked.

I shook my head and dislodged any lingering dark thoughts. It was not the time or place for me to think about my aunt and uncle and the role I played in their demise. I swallowed back bile, closed my eyes, and focused.

"I'm working on an image for this guy who loves boats, water, and his wife. He wants waves painted on the side of the bike with his wife riding a surfboard." I pulled out my phone and opened the design app.

Dad leaned over, took my phone, and studied the hand-drawn image.

"You drew that?" Ann Marie voiced from behind me.

She moved around the couch and sat on the arm

beside my dad. "This is fantastic. Did you free-hand?"

"My son can draw," my dad said. His voice dripped with pride.

"He sure can," she said, surprising me with the awe in her voice.

I grunted.

She quirked an eyebrow. But I didn't offer an explanation. After a careful examination of my detached expression, Ann Marie turned to my dad, and they bent their heads together. I paid attention as they critiqued my art and threw concepts back and forth.

I sat back, listened, and took mental notes. My thoughts were my own. No need to behave any different, even if their exclusion pissed me off.

A beer danced before my eyes, and I grabbed it with a nod of thanks to a grinning Parker. I twisted the top, took a long draw from the bottle and ignored my accelerated heartbeat.

****

Ann Marie

I couldn't believe the perfection of his work, my shock apparent in my voice. I traced the design careful not to touch the screen and spoke with his dad. My gaze flitted to Morgan's tattooed arms, my curiosity over their design urged an overwhelming desire to run my fingers along the many intricate details of his ink. I clenched my fists and stopped a hairbreadth from reaching out.

"Ann Marie, come hang in the kitchen with us," Susan yelled from the doorway.

With one last glance at the image, I handed the phone to Mr. Anderson and stood. I hid my unease at

Susan's request with a downturned face. Speaking designs was my happy place. Spending time with a group of women was not. I preferred the company of men, and not just for sex. Susan was the exception.

I joined Mrs. Anderson, Susan, and the youngest sibling, Kate, in a kitchen designed for cooking for an army. I chopped the salad—my assigned task—at the island where I had a perfect view of the living room and the men. Although they offered their help, Mrs. Anderson sent them away. My gaze drifted to Morgan on their own accord. He didn't appear happy or sad. Just content.

His flexed biceps as he drank his beer sent a thrill through me, and I imagined his arms around me as he brought me close to the edge. I closed my eyes and anticipated his work-roughened hands sliding down the sensitive skin of my belly, rubbing me in all the right places as he ventured below my panty line.

"You like?" he asked, and I hummed in response.

His long fingers reached in and played me as a guitarist does his strings. My body—in reality and fantasy—broke out in a sweat as I envisioned my breath growing ragged, my lungs needing more oxygen for the blood rushing south in preparation.

I painted a picture of his heavy weight holding me down.

"I've wanted a taste of you from the moment we met," he whispered, further fueling the fire he ignited within me. My imaginary hips flexed, and I sought more of his touch. More of his heat. More of his lips on my skin. More…just more.

With a gasp, I pulled out of my sex-fueled fantasy. I blinked and cleared the haze from my vision. Susan stood before me. She talked, but I heard nothing. Through concentration and breath regulation, I calmed my thundering heart and brought the room and conversations back into focus.

My face heated, and I staggered back, the veracity of my daydream unnerving. Like a kid caught dipping my hand in the cookie jar, I yanked my gaze away from her amused one. She giggled. Her finger hovered in a circle over my reddened cheeks. I snagged her hand out of the air and twisted.

"Ow, woman. Stop hurting me."

"Don't you dare say a thing about what you're not seeing," I said through gritted teeth. She laughed harder. Curious stares bore into me, but the heat of a particular one percolated through my veins.

Pax's gaze veered from the TV. He studied our interaction and amusement lit his face.

"Baby? Need some help here," Susan said to Pax as she wiggled in my hold.

"Nah, I think you've got it under control." Pax laughed and returned his attention to the game.

"Look at who's making googly eyes at each other," she whispered, and her gaze darted between me and the living room. "And let go of me you psycho."

"Shut up, weirdo. Who says googly eyes, anyway? And I'll let go if you don't voice whatever moronic thoughts you have going through your head."

She stifled another giggle and nodded. I shoved her away. Within seconds, she broke her promise and stepped into my space.

"You should turn up the 'I'm available' charm," Susan said in my ear. I braced my hands on her shoulders and held her back.

I scoffed but considered her proposal as the idea took a strong foothold. I didn't live in Bellevue, so having a one-night stand with Morgan wouldn't affect my relationship with Susan. It would scratch the itch I'd had since Susan's fundraiser in May.

"We'll see," I said by way of response and turned. "Mrs. Anderson, the salad's done. What can I do next?"

"Grab a cold platter and put it on the table, please. I'll have the boys bring out the hot food when it's ready." She flitted about the kitchen and pushed us out. "Go relax, watch the game."

Susan skipped to Pax and settled in his lap. He wrapped his arms around her waist and nuzzled his nose into her neck. She squirmed, giggled, and buried her face in his chest. But not before I spotted her pinked cheeks. What they had was nice, but not for me. I was happy for Susan, but I didn't believe in the fallacy of love.

Kate sat on the floor, leaning back against the couch. With two seats open, I took the empty one beside Morgan. He didn't shift as my hair flicked and hit him in the face. I raised my legs and tucked my feet under me, dipping the cushion so I rested against him. Morgan's arm jerked beneath me, and I stifled the hum threatening to escape.

"Oh, what snacks do we have here?" I asked. My breath fanned across his ear, before I leaned over his body and reached for the table.

In the new position, my breasts rubbed against his forearm, and I used the contact to wiggle more than necessary against him. His breath hitched and his chest inflated, producing an array of pleasurable sensations within me. He spotted my hardened nipples, and his eyes darkened as his gaze roamed over my breasts. My stomach muscles tightened under his perusal, and my panties dampened.

Sex. Desire. Lust. Those I could handle. And from what Susan told me so could he.

Relationship. Commitment. Long-term. Those words were not in either of our vocabularies.

I plucked grapes off the tray. I resettled, our bodies still touching. Heat permeated wherever we connected, but despite the warmth, I shivered. He pulled his arm from between us and rested it on the back of the couch behind me. He dipped his hand toward me, and every few seconds I felt a caress against my neck, my hair, my shoulder. I tapered my reaction, but by his smug look, my attempts proved futile.

"Tease," he said with a whispered breath.

"Are you calling me a tease?" I asked.

He shrugged his shoulders.

"You haven't seen nothing yet." I leaned back and took myself out of his father's view. I kept my gaze locked with his as I wrapped my lips around a grape and sucked, hollowing my cheeks. His eyes hooded, and he shifted in his seat, the movement brought us closer. I bit into the grape, closed my eyes, and hummed as the liquid burst between my teeth and cooled my throat.

Morgan shifted, and I peeled my eyes open to find his gaze fixated on a grape he held against my mouth. I wrapped my lips around his offering and rolled my tongue against both fruit and skin.

He growled low. The vibrations resonated within my heated core. His gaze fastened on mine, and he pulled his fingers out. I bit down on the grape and the juice ran down my chin. His lust-laden darkened gaze tracked the liquid, keeping me mesmerized as his thumb swiped my lip, then lifted it to his mouth.

"Dinner," Mrs. Anderson yelled from the kitchen and the room erupted with noise.

"Your timing couldn't have been more perfect. Any longer and we would have been treated to some ill-timed porn," Jesse mumbled, as he stopped next to us on the couch. He eyed his brother as Morgan adjusted his pants. "Bedroom's upstairs," he said with a pointed look before he walked away.

Alone in the living room, Morgan and I stared at each other for a heated moment. "Jesse never misses a thing," he said.

"You think?"

Morgan placed his hand on my lower back and guided me toward the table. I should have moved away, but I craved the warmth seeping through my skin and the assuredness of his movements. A longing I hadn't felt in a long time.

Mr. Anderson stood at the head of the table with his wife seated to his right and Pax to his left. Susan sat beside Pax, and next to her two available spots. We approached and to my surprise, Morgan held a chair out for me and scooted me in before sitting beside me.

I scanned the table, prepared for more of Jesse's comments, and spotted Mrs. Anderson's wide smile. Heat rose to my cheeks again. I tilted my head and hid my unexpected reaction. I took a steadying breath, then another, and willed my heart to resume a normal beat.

"Caden is coming home Christmas Eve. He called to confirm last night," Pax told his beaming mother.

"Jesse? How about you?" Mrs. Anderson asked her

second youngest son. Earlier Susan filled me in on the family. Jesse was busy completing his pediatric surgery residency at the hospital.

He sat further down the table, and I couldn't ignore his confident presence. The Anderson and Jackson men had square shoulders, but Jesse held his back without the cockiness you'd expect. Younger than me by a few years, yet his demeanor made him appear older.

"I'll be here Christmas. Christmas Eve, I'm on duty until eight. I'll do what I can to get out on time." No matter his posture, his face warmed as he spoke to his mother.

Conversations flitted across the table, some rowdier than others. The ones between the boisterous Parker, Dustin, and Foster the loudest. Jesse spoke with Kate. Susan and Pax with his parents, leaving Morgan and I guarded and quiet.

I shrugged and thought of something to say. "How's business?"

Chapter Three

Morgan

Her voice blasted through my lewd musings. Her grape sucking display boiled my blood and ways to get her alone consumed my thoughts. A rapid succession of scenarios played through my mind. Taking her against a door, a wall, any flat surface would do. What little I knew of her; sex would not be a gentle coming together of two bodies. No, it would be a battle zone. A war of epic proportions.

"Good," I responded.

"Good? You don't say much, do you?" she asked.

"Nope."

I rested my forearms on the edge of the table and held in a chuckle at the flair of her nostrils.

"Don't mind him. He's thinking of his bikes or jet skis," Pax said as he straightened his spine, raised his head higher than either of the women between us, and wiggled his eyebrows. "I'm sure if you ask, he'll give you a ride."

I cursed the image he planted in my brain and schooled my features before directing a heated gaze at Ann Marie. I bit back my smile, even though a deep satisfaction hummed through my veins.

She wasn't immune either.

My body—cock—demanded I haul her over my

shoulders, take her away, and sink into her over and over again. Lust clouded my vision, but I didn't miss her narrowed rich chocolate brown eyes. With a chin lift, she threw down an invisible gauntlet. I smiled, unable to contain my delight. I accepted her challenge with a wink. Around us, my family continued their conversations, but we existed in a bubble filled with sexual tension.

She moved in her seat, edged closer, and rubbed her thigh against mine.

"Hey Susan, we might want to turn down the thermostat. It's getting kinda hot in here," Pax said loud enough for us to hear.

Ann Marie's head snapped in his direction, and I leaned forward. He smiled at us before digging back into his food.

"I don't think it is," Susan said, confusion marred her face until understanding dawned as she looked between Ann Marie and me.

Susan elbowed Pax in the ribs and hid her snicker behind her hand.

I flung my arm across the top of Ann Marie's chair and flipped off Pax. I grazed my fingers across her nape much to Pax's amusement. His laugh turned everyone's attention toward us.

Dad's gaze pinged between Pax and me. "Now tell me about the new design you showed me," he said after a slight shake of his head.

My family fell silent, and I moaned. After years of trial and error, they discovered my Achilles heel. I could wax poetic about a bike's beauty, performance, and just about anything to do with it.

"My client is paying homage to his wife. I worked

off her portrait on a surfboard and gave it a note of pin up."

"Are you using a more traditional surfing wave or Asian stylized one?"

"He wants a classic. I've done two designs, but I like the surfing wave more."

"And there's your choice," Ann Marie said. "Part of your job is taking your clients requests and guiding them to the best option for that design."

I shifted in my seat, brought her into better view, and quirked an eyebrow.

"Go with your gut. Although, the Asian wave is a romantic image. Using the other one will make her pin up pose stand out more. The design you showed us earlier is beautiful, but her bathing suit should be red. What color is the background?"

"Black."

She raised her eyebrow in return. "Of course."

"My bike is red," Pax said, "And it's not because I'm a firefighter." He pulled Susan to his side and rubbed her hair. "It's because red is my favorite color."

Susan's cheeks reddened. She pushed up from her seat and kissed my brother on the cheek, as everyone around us either awwed or gagged.

"Let me guess. Your favorite color is black," Ann Marie asked me.

I shrugged my shoulders. "And yours is purple."

"Just because I'm wearing purple now doesn't mean it's my favorite." Ann Marie's gaze traveled down her own body.

"You wore purple at the fundraiser. Had purple extensions in your hair. You painted your fingernails purple, and I'm sure if I removed your socks, your toenails will be some shade of purple."

An eerie silence enveloped the room, quiet so deep you could discern the individual heartbeats. I stiffened in my seat but didn't pull my gaze away from hers. The sheer number of times I thought of Ann Marie in the past few months boggled my own mind.

"Didn't you also get a new custom build order?" Pax asked, breaking the tension in the air.

I hid my trembling hands under the table, rubbed my palms against my thighs, and counted to ten. I forced my butt to stay seated when every muscle in my body screamed at me to run.

"Yes," I said and took a deep breath.

"I know how much you love building from scratch," he continued.

I acknowledged my brother's distraction with a nod. "I've started building Susan's."

"Yeah? That's fantastic. I'm looking forward to teaching her, but I understand you've got a lot of work."

Dad's eyes twinkled with pleasure. "I'm proud of you. If I was any younger, I would have commissioned one, so I could whisk your mom away for long weekend rides," he said and leaned over for a chaste kiss from Ma.

Several groans and snickers spread across the room. "Just say the word, Dad. I'll build one for you guys."

"Maybe I will," Dad said as he grasped Ma's hand in his. Their love for each other made me happy—yet sad.

Emotions destroyed lives. I was the living poster-boy. After the accident I made a vow, and I never wavered from my set path. I didn't want a love like theirs. Being guided with your heart was a recipe for disaster.

It took effort, but I swallowed the bile in my throat. I picked at my food, exhausted from my family's focus, and hoped they grew bored and moved on. Conversations continued, and laughter rang out through the air. Yet no matter how I tried to ignore it, a lingering sense of unease lay just below the surface.

Ann Marie's hand squeezed my thigh. An unexpected and unwelcome comfort. With a jerk, I looked around to find the table emptied and plates cleared. I pushed back, the screech from the chair legs against the hardwood floors painful to my ears.

I mumbled, "Bathroom," to Ann Marie's questioning stare and left without a backward glance. I hustled up the stairs to the second floor, to my childhood bedroom.

I stood at the apex of the room. My breath caught in my throat. I stared at the picture of my entire family, including Aunt Karen and Uncle Dustin, on my nightstand. The image a reminder of what I had done to my family. Years ago, I turned it face down, but could never pack it away.

It was face up.

I pivoted and bolted to the bathroom, shut and locked the door behind me. I sat on the edge of the bathtub and rested my elbows on my knees. Feeling light-headed, I dropped my head in my hands. I couldn't breathe from the tightness in my chest. I swallowed, closed my eyes, and willed down my visceral reaction. Emotions threatened to explode out of me. Emotions I buried deep the day we laid my aunt and uncle to rest.

****

Ann Marie

Morgan left the room, and I tracked his exit. I didn't have any other choice. I don't know why I reached out. Touching him. But the glimpse of a little-boy-lost look in his eyes called out to me. In the short time I had known him—fine, two meetings didn't make a friendship—he smiled little, laughed less. There was a story behind his unrelenting control. One I wanted to uncover.

I ignored my foolish desire and focused on my baser needs. Those I could handle without contemplation. I thought about chasing him down and giving both of us an outlet for this crazy chemistry we had. A quick, onetime surrender to our physical pull.

Susan's rapt attention bore a hole in the back of my head, and I turned to her. I met her quirked eyebrow with an impassiveness I hoped impervious. She thought she knew me so well, but my truths would drive her to hate me. So I kept my secrets. Although selfish, I learned long ago I needed her strength and enormous heart in my corner. I couldn't bare her disappointment.

The family scattered. Most returned to the living room for the game. Their distraction a perfect opening, I slipped past them and out of the room.

My heart thudded against my ribs, as it always did at the acquisition of a new contract. I treated my actions as an attainment and nothing more.

I prowled up the stairs, my footfalls quieted by the soft fibers of the rug. I stopped at the top and considered my next move. Left, or right? I went left and crept down the hallway, my hand gliding along the wall. Doors stood open, revealing each room's secrets, but none exposed Morgan.

The smell of soap and an underlying scent of motor oil assaulted my senses seconds before brawny arms wrapped around my waist. He pulled me close, and his breath feathered across the skin of my neck.

"What are you doing up here?"

"Would you believe me if I told you I was looking for a bathroom?"

"No."

I shrugged and leaned back. His grip tightened, fingers digging into my skin. "How about if I told you I was looking for you?"

"Better."

He shifted, maneuvered us, and trapped me with the wall at my front and his chest at my back. His erection rubbed against my lower back, and I closed my eyes, enjoying the feel of him.

"I know you want to fuck me, and the way I figure it, we should get it out of our systems," I said, my voice steady.

His rumbling chuckle turned my insides molten. "You have a dirty mouth."

"I do when the situation warrants it."

I turned in his arms, reached around his neck, and pulled his face to mine. He didn't fight, and I crashed my lips to his. He was soft and compliant beneath me, but it wasn't enough. I pushed at his closed mouth, and his growl reverberated against my lips. His hold on me tightened, firing my synapses. His tongue dipped in. Explored. Learned. Coaxed brazen noises from me.

He nudged a leg between my thighs and rubbed me

through my jeans. I whimpered as the friction brought me close to orgasm. I giggled, and he pulled back and eyed me with a raised eyebrow.

"I was a teenager last time I got off from dry humping," I answered his silent question.

He nodded and almost smiled. His eyes lost focus and with quick moves he fisted my hair. He angled my head and exposed my neck for his ravishing mouth. His other hand skimmed down my side, over my hip, and cupped my ass.

"Wrap your legs around me," he ordered and tapped my butt as he anchored me against him.

The new position lined his cock with my center, and he rubbed against me. Whimpers I had no control over echoed against the walls as he moved us down the hallway.

He angled my hips and my thighs cinched around his waist. He let go of my ass and trailed his calloused palms under the hem of my shirt. Long, rough, lithe fingers squeezed my breast to the point of pain. I arched my back. My shoulders dug into the wall. My body sought more.

He grunted and pinched my nipple before soothing it with swipes of his thumb. I buried my face in his neck, drowning my moans. The combined scents of musk, sweat, and a hint of gasoline shouldn't have been a turn on, but it was. I inhaled. Let the fragrance wash over me. Used it to keep a toehold in reality. I couldn't lose my head. A feat a hell of a lot harder than expected.

I pulled away as the click of the bathroom door lock reverberated against the tiled walls. So lost in euphoria, I didn't notice our final destination. I shuddered in his hold. My body temperature set to boil. Parched mouth made swallowing difficult, and I closed my eyes, hiding any uncertainty reflected in them.

"Tell me what you want."

I seized his husky demand and used his words to focus. "I want you. Quick and hard. No strings. Just here and now."

Morgan nodded and lifted me with ease and sat me on the edge of the counter. Pulling my legs apart, he aligned his cock at my core. "I'm going to fuck you now. You have to be quiet."

"Hurry," I said, my voice hoarse with need.

"Strip," he ordered, and toed off his untied boots. They thudded to the floor and we stopped. With no evidence of someone searching for the cause of the noise, he was on me again. He pulled off his shirt one handed, and I grew wetter. He scrunched his eyebrows, and his gaze swallowed me whole before returning to mine. I understood his silent command and yanked my sweater over my head.

I reached for the clasp of the bra, but he stopped me.

"Purple? Leave it on," he said, his voice deepening.

My nipples pushed against the lace, but I did what he asked—demanded. I unbuttoned my jeans, braced my hands on the counter, and raised my butt an inch or two. He fisted the fabric and pulled them over my hips. My boots hindered his progress, and with a shrug, he dropped to his knees.

He lifted my right leg, lowered the zipper, and ran his finger along the length of my calf. He released my boot and repeated the motion on the other side. With firm hands, he tugged my jeans off and adjusted my heels, resting them on the edge of the counter.

Stepping back, his gaze roamed over me and stopped at the visible wet spot on my panties. He growled, threw his wallet next to my hip, and reached for my underwear. Confident fingers pulled the fabric aside, and my head fell back as he rubbed my seam with feather-light touches.

I whimpered and my body moved on its own accord, seeking a stronger stroke. I grabbed the waist of his jeans, pulled him closer and sealed my lips over his. I pushed my core against his palm and with a chuckle, he teased my entrance before flicking my clit. He repeated the cycle until my hips gyrated, desperate for more.

I pulled away, fighting for breath. "Fuck me, already."

His fingers skimmed my entrance in answer.

"Open your eyes. Watch."

I didn't hesitate. My gaze focused on our point of contact. Giving up control not a usual occurrence for me, yet his demands freed me. Exhilarated me. I took what he offered and surrendered for the first time in nine years. My body was his to play.

He entered me without preamble. I gasped. Shocked. He pulled out, then did it again with two fingers. He thrust, turned his digits into hooks, found my G-spot with ease, and rubbed his palm against my clit. Too heavy to hold up, I dropped my head back.

"Watch," he commanded again and fisted my hair, pushing my head forward. He held me in place with a strong yet tender hold.

I screamed as he coerced an orgasm from me. His mouth swallowed the noise. White bursts of light danced on the inside of my closed eyelids. Like never before, I floated through a euphoric out-of-body experience. In the recess of my mind, I feared he ruined sex for me. Without penetration, he gave me the best orgasm of my life. Nothing compared before, and I worried nothing would compare in the future.

With slow, deep breaths I came back to reality. My hips moved with the rhythm of the fingers still inside me. I unclenched my stronghold on the counter, hooked my hands through the belt loops of his jeans, and pulled at the fabric. He dropped his pants and boxers. I watched, fascinated, as he gripped his cock, stroked it hard before pulling a condom from his abandoned wallet.

He held the packet to my mouth, and I bit the edge as he ripped it open. With quick fingers, he readied himself and lined the head a fraction away from my entrance.

I grazed my nails against his exposed abs. His answering moan music to my ears. A tune I would never forget. Eager to hear more, I wrapped my hand around his erection. He jerked and groaned loud.

"Put me inside you," he said, his voice hoarse with tension.

I directed him closer with a gentle tug and separated my folds with my other hand.

"That's so fucking hot," he said and with a single push he embedded himself inside me.

I bit his shoulder and kept my scream from reaching the people downstairs. I succumbed to his relentless pace as my body stretched, accommodating him, and from one breath to the next, with one thrust after another, pain turned to pleasure. Morgan filling me was my new version of heaven. Or hell. Depending on how I looked at it.

Chapter Four

Morgan

Shit. Shit. Shit.

The word played on an endless loop in my mind as I pumped my hips.

She felt too good.

She felt too right.

She felt like coming home.

As each thought surfaced, I shoved it down.

My orgasm loomed, and I fought back. I wanted one more from her before I surrendered. I craved another of her stifled screams and her teeth in my flesh.

I nuzzled closer, rubbed her scent over me, and set a ruthless pace. A pace aimed to rock her world. To destroy her for other men. A desire I had no explanation for.

Ann Marie rocked her hips, meeting my every thrust. Her breath heated my skin. She sunk her teeth into my shoulder and followed it with a lick and a kiss. Her tongue licked away the pain from each bite. I fisted her hair, yanked her head back, and held her gaze captive with mine as I pounded into her. My need for her animalistic.

She closed her eyes, moaned and sucked in her lower lip, turning it white. I tugged it loose and pushed my thumb into her mouth. She drew it in with a groan.

"Look at me," I demanded through a clenched jaw.

Her eyes flew open, and her gaze returned to me. She looked at me through lust-clouded eyes. Her uninhibited responses fuel to my growing hunger. My need to devour her. Taste her. Claim her.

I leaned forward and licked her nipple. Teased it with my tongue. I bit the swollen peak and held it between my teeth. She moved faster, out of control, and I sucked more of her into my mouth. I clamped down, unrelenting, shooting a sting of pain through her. She bucked and her nails dug into my shoulders as I fisted her other breast and squeezed. Her body convulsed, her inner walls clenched around me, almost to the point of pushing me out.

I drove deeper, harder. Held her steady as her contractions milked my cock. The tingling at the base of my spine intensified, and I lost my grip on my release. I rotated my hips, braced my dick inside her, and with a feral moan I came in the depth of her heat.

"Fuck," Ann Marie whispered.

Sweat dripped down my forehead, burning my eyes. I clasped her to me. My legs shook the longer I stood. Yet, I wasn't ready to let her go. But I had to move away, regain control over my body. My senses. Her pulsating walls hardened me once again within her.

I stepped back, untangled my fingers from her hair and pulled out. The immediate sense of loss overwhelming. I removed the condom, tied it, and wrapped it in tissue before disposing of it in the trash. Beyond that, my muscles refused to move. Ann Marie lowered her legs, closing herself off. I itched to grab her knees and pull them apart again. Demand she stayed open for me.

She patted my chest and gave me a slight shove. I backed further away, forsaking the discontent running through me. She swiped wet tissues along her center, picked up her pants, and smirked at me as she put them on, sans underwear.

I spotted her panties in the bathtub. I reached for them and slipped them into the pocket of the jeans pooled around my ankles. We redressed in silence. The finality ringing through the air left me confused. The initial quiet contentment replaced with a craving for something I couldn't identify.

I turned away from her and my wondering thoughts. I faced the mirror and examined my skin for any lipstick imprints. Ann Marie hip-checked me and turned on the tap, wetting her hands. I bit back my moan as she patted down my hair.

"What?" she asked, an eyebrow quirked high on her forehead. "Now you don't look like you fucked in the bathroom."

I held in my laugh and motioned to her hair. "You look…satisfied."

She fluffed the strands and smiled. "I do, don't I? There's no fixing this mess." She gathered it back and secured it with an elastic band. Her exposed neck played notes of a siren song I found hard to resist.

"I'll go down first," I said, shook my head, and fortified my resolve.

"I can go down now," she said and bent her knees.

I grabbed under her arms, staying her upright position. "Not surprised you can't get enough."

She cocked her head. "Did you think I meant…?" She waved her hand between us. Her lips twitched, but she restrained her smile.

"It's exactly what you meant. Don't play coy. It's not who you are."

Her eyes narrowed. "And you know me so well?"

"Nope."

I hungered for her comeback, but none came. Disappointment made the compact space grow heavy with tension.

"Behind you in five," she said.

"Oooh, never done that before."

She chuckled, normalizing things between us again. She smacked my chest and turned away, but not fast enough to hide the twinkle in her eye.

I checked my clothing one last time and walked out of the bathroom. Once the lock clicked in place, I took a deep breath. It was for the best.

One time, no strings attached. Two consenting adults. Itch scratched.

Residual feelings and desires pushed away. My perfected role back in the forefront.

Nonchalant. Quiet. Solitary.

****

Ann Marie

I shut the bathroom door before sinking to the floor and used the wood behind me for support. It took every ounce of self-control I had to stop from reaching for him. My satisfied body hummed, but it also screamed for more.

Shit on a nutcracker.

Amazing sex. He got me off faster than I ever imagined. He played my body with sure and exacting hands. The best I ever had. Even better than Scott, my fling, until a week prior.

I ended my arrangement with Scott after discovering he hid his new girlfriend from me. His deceit pissed me off, and I hated cheaters. I hated relationships. Relying on others was not something I allowed. For the past four months, he hinted at wanting more. My flings were monogamous, yet uncomplicated. I didn't want the difficulties and the neediness of a partner.

I stood on shaky legs, and the returning blood flow to my limbs tingled. My flushed face greeted me in the large bathroom mirror. I drifted my fingers along my lips and imagined Morgan's mouth doing delicious things to mine. I could still taste him on my tongue. I could still feel the decadent itch his stubble created against my jaw. The length of him filled me to the point of pain, and I wanted a repeat.

I clamped a screeching halt to my libidinous thoughts. He may have given me the best orgasms and used my body to reach his without apology, but I refused to give him more.

It was a onetime thing. A curiosity satisfied. Wham-bam-thank-you-ma'am. In this case, wham-bam-thank-you-hot-damn.

After a few minutes, my pulse slowed, and my skin lost its rosy hue. I adjusted my clothes and smoothed out the creases of my jeans at the top of my boots. With a quick splash of cold water across my cheeks, I was ready to face the crowd downstairs.

I didn't care if people judged me, but I didn't want Morgan's parent's disappointment. For whatever reason, I wanted their approval, something I never sought. I valued who I was and what I'd done to get there. I was tough as nails and a force to be reckoned with, if clichés were the best way to describe who I had become.

A loud knock on the door jolted me from my self-promoting.

"Ann Marie? Are you okay? You've been up here a while," Susan said from the other side.

"I'm good. I'll be down in a minute."

"Bull. You're being too nice. No foul language, or disgusting innuendos about what you're doing in there. Open up."

Sometimes it sucked having people in your life who knew you so well. She spoke the truth. I would have made a remark about my position on the toilet, or something else vulgar. With a deep sigh, I unlocked the door and backed up, anticipating Susan's hasty entrance.

"What the actual..." she said as she set foot into the bathroom.

I leaned against the vanity and played it cool. I tilted my head and urged her to continue.

"You're flushed. Do I need to ask why, or do I already know the answer?"

"I don't doubt for one minute you know, so let's not beat around the bush."

She paced the three steps the room allowed, shook her head, and fought back her grin.

"I knew it," she said. The sudden and loud projection made me jump, and I almost tripped over the rim of the bathtub. Quick on her feet, she grabbed my arm and steadied me.

"Keep your voice down."

"You like Morgan, and he likes you," she said as she ignored my demand.

I held my hand up and halted her wayward thoughts. "No one said anything about liking. Attraction and sexual compatibility? Yes. I mean, look at him, all decked out as a bad-ass biker, in his leather jacket and scuffed boots. What woman in her right mind wouldn't want a piece of that?" By the look on her face, I failed in my attempt at normalcy.

"So what? You bang him against the bathroom door and walk away?"

"It was on the vanity, and yes."

"Holy shit, Ann Marie. Seriously? If I wasn't so in love with Pax, and Morgan was a stranger rather than my best friend, I would do everything I could to be with him. He's an exceptional guy. There's so much more to him under that tough exterior, you just need to take the time…"

Oh, hell no.

"Stop! I'm not in the market for a relationship. I don't want a steady guy. I don't want to unearth whatever fucking outstanding qualities a guy might have underneath all the layers. Besides, I live in Seattle. Last time I tried a relationship, he lived two blocks away and look how that turned out. Some of us aren't built that way."

"Bull. Stop living in the past. The asshole-who-will-not-be-named is not worth this. You're better than this," she said, and swung her arms indicating the bathroom. "Giving up on love is not the answer."

What she said came from a place of caring, but it still angered me. She had no right focusing on my slip up into my history. Besides, it didn't influence my present. Yet I couldn't stop the words.

"Just because you found a way to Pax, doesn't

mean the rest of us need to do the same. You want love, marriage, babies, and the white picket fence. Well, you got them. Now leave me the fuck out of your delusional dreams," I said, at once regretting my remarks.

Susan opened and closed her mouth several times, hurt clear on her face. It dug deep into my belly. She didn't deserve my hateful words or the belittling I dealt. Reaching for her, I prepared my apology. She didn't give me a chance, huffed, turned, and walked out of the bathroom.

I sagged back against the vanity, rubbed my face, and emitted a soulful sigh. Susan was my sister by all intents and purposes, and the last time I hurt her we were in middle school. She was my sounding board, and I was hers. I hated hurting her and putting a chink in her golden heart. With a final deep breath, I left in search of my cousin and her forgiveness.

****

Morgan

I returned downstairs to Pax's curious but silent stare. I sat on one of the two brown leather couches between Pax and Foster and focused on the football game. I devised a simple plan.

Eat pie.

Keep my cool.

Leave as soon as possible.

I ignored Pax's vibrating body next to mine. If I were a braver man, I would have faced him and addressed whatever issues he had. And it wasn't the right time to confirm or deny his suspicions.

"Later, man. Not here."

It was bad enough I abused my parent's trust in

their home. I didn't need to rub it in their faces.

"Susan went looking for you and Ann Marie," Pax said. "You couldn't hold off?"

Both his tone and words pissed me off.

I inhaled deep and willed back the desire to slug my brother. I scanned the room and noted Susan's absence. Before I could answer, Susan bolted through the room, on the verge of tears. Pax's deepened scowl shifted away from me to the fridge door behind which Susan hid.

We sprang from the couch and jostled our way to the kitchen. We made it to the island, but his size prevented me from reaching Susan first. He shoved me back, and I tripped over my boots. Pax's face lit up. And although I wanted to punch the smugness out of him, I acquiesced.

He pulled her into a hug, and I stepped behind her without touching and offered my quiet presence.

"Baby, what's wrong?" Pax asked her.

Susan shook her head against his chest and shifted to bury her face in his shirt, hiding her tears. We stood for a few moments. He kneaded her back, and I provided my support. After a time, she relented and relaxed against him. Assured she was okay, I stepped away.

I rubbed the ache in my chest. Her reliance on my brother a stark reminder of my losses. I was never in need of company, but I valued my friendship with Susan. With her, I made no pretense. She accepted me, gruff and quiet as I was. And losing her to my brother reaffirmed what I already knew. Loss didn't hurt. It devastated.

Although she was still my best friend, things had

changed. I hardened my heart, wrapped it in barbed wire, and threw away the cutters. There was no place in my life for love.

Ann Marie appeared, catching me off guard. She ignored both Pax and I and reached for Susan. Pax relinquished her to Ann Marie's hold and came to stand beside me. Ann Marie whispered in Susan's ear, while Susan either nodded or shook her head.

They conversed and didn't share any of it with us. Susan stepped back and smiled as Ann Marie cupped Susan's cheeks. They laughed and Pax relaxed.

My tension, on the other hand, escalated as soon as Ann Marie appeared. I had an idea what upset Susan, and it made me angry. The double standard unacceptable. I had given her my blessing to be with my brother. I hoped for the same.

I grabbed my jacket from the coat rack and walked out of the house without saying goodbye. I would call my mom later and apologize for my abrupt departure, but I needed breathing space.

Space to figure out why the fuck my heart and mind were warring. The walk home would give me what I craved.

Solitude.

Instead, all I felt was lonely.

Chapter Five

Six months later—April
Ann Marie

My work no longer held the appeal it once had. Designing was a passion. Working with new companies, building their brand, that's where my heart beat. Or at least it used to. But since I returned home after Thanksgiving I'd been restless. My soul trickled out of my body with each passing day filled with the grind of running a business and the relentless Seattle rainy season.

It took little for my new distraction—fine, obsession—to work its way into the forefront of my mind. My life altered by a certain someone and the unexpected news handed to me by a doctor three months ago. What a difference nine years and maturity could make. This time around, I was stronger, richer, independent. This time I was in control.

"Come in," I said, answering the knock on my door.

My business partner and longtime friend, Lian, walked into my office. She sat in a chair across from my desk and folded her hands in her lap.

"So I've been thinking…"

I quirked an eyebrow at her hesitation. She cleared her throat and scooted forward.

"You need to get away." She held up her hand when I opened my mouth in protest. "Hear me out. I know something's going on and you aren't happy. You don't need to share, but as your partner and friend, I'm telling you, you need time off. Take a few months, go away. The beach, the mountains, a lake. It doesn't much matter. Rejuvenate. Come back stronger."

I bowed my head. She wasn't wrong.

"I can't just leave you to handle things here."

"Yes, you can. Besides…" She nodded and sat closer to the edge of the seat, I feared she would fall. "I've been with you from the start. I know this business. I won't let it crumble under my watch. You make sure you're okay. Hustle and Heart Media, your staff, your clients, we'll all be here when you get back."

"What if…What if I don't want to come back?" I whispered, saying the words aloud for the first time. Yet once I did, I knew the truth of my statement. I wasn't happy.

Lian took a deep breath before she answered. "We cross that bridge if we come to it."

I looked out my office window and caught a hint of the Space Needle, visible in the gap between two buildings, and sighed. The last time I felt lost was my senior year of high school. My boyfriend walked away without a backward glance. My parents lent me their strength, but I made a promise the day my heart shattered. I would become stronger, independent, and rely on no one but me. I took a month off from my life then, came back with a commitment in mind and pursued it with a vengeance. This was no different.

"Okay," I sighed out. "I'll take two weeks off and re-evaluate then."

"Three months."

"One month," I countered.

"Two months."

"One month. Take it or leave it."

Lian stood up and extended her hand. "Deal. One month. No contact with the office. Don't check your email. You are off the work grid."

I stuttered. "Hey, no. I just said I'll take a month away. Not go incommunicado."

Lian shook her head and hid her smile behind her palm. "Nope. You agreed to a month. Totally off."

I couldn't help my smile. Weight lifted off my shoulders relieved the tension I hadn't acknowledged.

"Fine. I agree to your terms," I said, and accepted her hand.

"Any ideas where you're going?"

I weighed my options. Although a quiet beach sounded perfect, there was one place my mind nagged at me to go. Reality and the hand life dealt me had to be a priority.

****

My stomach clenched as I crossed the Evergreen Point Bridge. Whether my ever-changing body caused the nausea, or the idea of seeing Susan and telling her, or because with each mile driven, I got closer to Morgan, I couldn't tell. Making it over the mile-long floating roadway and back on dry land before my need to vomit overwhelmed me was all that mattered.

The spring sun warmed the interior of my car, and I cranked up the air conditioner. The cool blast chilled my sweat covered skin. For three days I sat in my apartment and binge watched the superhero movie series—in chronological order—working up the nerve to call Susan. I didn't call her or finish my bender, but instead packed my bags and left for Bellevue. I planned my arrival for the middle of her workday, Pax's absence a necessity.

I even drove in the middle of the nightmare inducing morning rush hour, Seattle's gray streets locking me in the early morning. I crossed the expanse of Lake Washington with the car windows rolled down and imagined the wind whispering its encouragement.

Once back on land, I avoided turning right and circumvented Morgan's road and house. I headed downtown toward Susan's rescue animal shelter, Kisses and Paws. Bellevue, similar yet different from Seattle's urban jungle, surprised me with its budding flowers having already replaced the bright green leaves on the trees lining the streets.

I pulled into the parking lot and gathered my courage until my bladder screamed for a bathroom break. The super-sized drink I gulped down on the way hadn't helped. I ignored my body's needs, took a minute longer and finger combed my curls. I opened the mirror on my visor and added mascara and red tinted lip gloss. I made sure I appeared flawless. Anything less would worry Susan. I left my purse on the backseat and covered it with my spring jacket.

With a smile, albeit a fake one, I hopped out of the car and locked it behind me. I stepped into a gardenia scented comfortable and cooled waiting area.

"How can I help you have a barking wonderful day?" the receptionist asked.

I almost gagged in my mouth. Her chipper attitude and ridiculous greeting caused a fresh bout of nausea.

Tamping down the bile, I reinforced my smile.

"I'm looking for Susan."

"Do you have an appointment?" Miss Chipper moved a mouse across the pad by the keyboard.

"I don't need one," I said and rested my elbows on the high counter of the reception desk.

Miss Chipper looked up, perplexed, but kept smiling. "I'll see if she's available. You are?"

"A surprise. Let her know her 'one and only' is here," I said around a sardonic grin.

"Okaaaay? Have a seat. Give me a minute and I'll be right back."

She left me standing and rushed through an exit to the right. Frantic and excited barking filtered through the open doorway for the few seconds it took for the door to click shut.

I used the bathroom and returned to the waiting room before she did. I studied the hand painted logo hanging behind the reception desk and smiled. It was my design. One of my best.

The door swung open and thudded against the wall. Susan came hurtling through it, screaming my name as she rounded the counter and pulled me into a tight hug. I wrapped my arms around her and giggled into her hair.

"This is an awesome surprise. Why are you here? Not that it's not great, but I'm curious. Is everything okay?"

I stepped back and held her at arm's length. "Take a breath and let's go into your office."

Her gaze darted across my face. I let her study me, not shuttering my emotions. She saw something and her eyes softened. She took my hand in hers and led me away from Miss Chipper's prying stare.

****

Susan sat beside me on the old dilapidated, yet comfortable teal couch. With her foot tucked underneath her butt, she turned and faced me.

"Although, I'm happy to see you, I know your visit isn't out of the blue. What's going on?"

I closed my eyes and took in a lungful of air.

"I'm pregnant."

She gasped before a smile blossomed on her face. She jumped and pulled me into a hug. After some time, we settled back down, and her gaze drifted to my belly. I tugged my shirt tighter against my abdomen and gave her a better view.

"Dang, woman. You're barely showing."

"Are you kidding me? Look at this," I rubbed my hand on the bump. "I'm huge and growing bigger every day."

"Okay, whatever." She sighed and fell silent for a moment. "To be honest, I'm not sure you're happy or sad."

"Happy," I blurted. "I'm happy. Scared and a little lost, but happy."

"Then, so am I." She leaned in and hugged me to her side. "Knowing you, you have a plan. Let's hear it."

I snorted—an unladylike move, but me nonetheless. "I'm raising this baby on my own. But for now, I'm visiting my favorite cousin for an indefinite number of days…" I took a deep breath, "maybe weeks."

"You mean your only cousin."

"Fine," I huffed, "whatever bitch. Doesn't mean you're not also my favorite."

"Agreed. Want to talk about it?" She waved her

hand in the general direction of my abdomen.

"Not really, but I should." She waited and clasped my hands in hers. "I'm six months along, but I found out a few months ago. For most of December and into January, I was tired and my stomach was off. I figured it was stress from work. My head was out of the game for a while. Being at the office became a burden. I fainted and Lian insisted I see a doctor. They ran some tests. *Surprise! You're pregnant!*"

"Are you feeling any better? I hear they have stuff for nausea that's safe."

"I have good days and bad days. I'm still pretty much tired all the time, but now I know to take naps and get my sleep at night."

"How…How?"

"I had sex, you dimwit."

"Duh. I know that," she said and smacked my arm.

"Cut it out. You can't hit a pregnant woman."

"Oh, shut up. It wasn't that hard." She shifted in her seat, and I knew she struggled with holding back her questions.

"My IUD failed. It expelled. Fell the *f* out. As luck would have it, so did the condom. His sperm must have superhero powers."

"What's Scott saying about this?"

"He's being a douche as always, but the thing is…" I swallowed the rising bile. "I'm not sure he's the baby daddy."

Susan jumped from the couch, halted mid reaction and lowered. She bit her lip and eyed me for a minute.

With a sigh, I told her the rest. "It could be one of two guys."

Her gaze remained on mine. Steadfast. Patient.

"I slept with both of them within a week of each other. But in my defense, Scott and I were over before I was with the second guy," I continued when she remained silent.

She waved her hand in dismissal. "That's not the least bit of my concerns. Who you sleep with and when, is your choice. Besides, Scott slept with someone else before you called it off."

"I just...I don't know. I hate these pregnancy hormones. I haven't been this...unsure, since...since my senior year."

She squeezed my hands. "Listen. I'm glad you came. I'm here for you. We can get through this together."

"I was going to go to a beach, but figured you'd kill me if I went without you."

"True story."

We huddled and laughed as we remembered the promises the younger versions of us made many years ago. Susan sat up, and her features grew serious. I let go of her hands and put a little distance between us. Her gaze bounced across my face, and unable to acknowledge her disappointment, I reached for my bottle of water. I fumbled and dropped it to the floor.

Susan bent down first and grabbed it before it rolled away. She spoke as she straightened. "Is the second guy you slept with in a committed relationship?"

I closed my eyes and took a steadying breath. "No. At least not when we hooked up."

"Did you tamper with your contraception or his to get pregnant?"

Reeling back, I clutched my chest over my heart.

"Fuck, no."

"Sorry," she said, looking sheepish. "You would never do that. So the way I see it, this pregnancy was meant to be. You're going to be an amazing mom."

I smacked her shoulder. "Shut up. Every time I think about being a mom, I break out in hives. I have no idea how to do this. What if I mess this kid up? What the hell do I know about being a mother?"

Susan giggled, took my hands back in hers, and pulled me close once again. "Seriously? You're going to be a wonderful mom, and when we move you to Bellevue, Aunt Susan and Uncle Pax will help."

"I didn't say I was moving."

She waved her hand at me again. "We'll talk about that later. Now we celebrate. Come on, let's get home so we can tell Pax."

She rounded her desk and closed several folders and her laptop. She came back and reached for me. Linking her arm in my elbow, she maneuvered us through and out the door as she yelled her departure for the day to Miss Chipper.

At my car, she stopped and tilted her head. I braced, knowing.

"Who's the second possible baby daddy?"

I didn't know where to look, but since I never cowered, I looked her in the eye and quirked an eyebrow. Realization flickered across her face, and she gasped behind her hand.

"Shit. You left Scott the week of Thanksgiving," she whispered. Her eyebrows scrunched as she put two and two together. "Oh, my God," her hand snapped back to her mouth, "Morgan."

Chapter Six

Ann Marie

I followed Susan back to her house, replaying our conversation in my head. When she figured out my secret, she nodded, kissed my cheek, and walked to her car. She didn't speak, nor reveal her thoughts. Her quietness frayed my nerves. I hated when I couldn't read people.

I slept with her best friend, yelled at her to mind her own business, and we never talked about him again. She was a better person than I. If the roles were reversed, I don't think I would have been as calm.

She pulled in and parked beside Pax's truck, and I behind her. I breathed a sigh of relief when she exited her car with a beaming smile. Before I cut off my engine, she approached the driver's door and yanked it open. She took my arm and hauled me out and into a hug.

"Damn, woman. Such violence with a pregnant lady. That's twice now."

"Oh, shut up. I'm sorry I freaked out back there."

My shoulders slumped, and for the first time in months I breathed with ease. "Please don't apologize. I was so scared you'd be mad at me."

"Fuck, no. I'm not. I hope Morgan's the father. You can move here and become a family, and we could double date. I'll have my two best friends close. Your little human will call me Auntie Susie, and…"

I held up my hands, stopping her, but couldn't hide my smile. "Whoa, whoa, whoa. Let's not get ahead of ourselves. I have a lot to consider. I hoped I could shack up with you for a couple of days. Use the time to figure out how I want to move forward with this." At the look of horror on her face, I hastened to reassure her. "I'm keeping the baby. There is no doubt of that."

"Good. We'll get through this together. Have you told Morgan yet?"

"No. But I'm planning to while I'm here. Come on, I might have peed at the shelter, but I need to go again."

I popped my trunk, and we each grabbed a bag.

"Glad to see you've packed enough for a year." She lifted the larger of the two, feigning a struggle.

"Ha ha. You're such a goofball. Two suitcases cover a month, at the most."

Susan smacked her forehead. "Oops. I forgot who I was talking to."

I swatted her arm away from her face as she giggled.

"Let's get you settled and then bring out the good stuff."

"I can't have alcohol or caffeine."

"I know that. I meant ice cream and a hot tub."

"Can't do hot tubs either."

She stopped and turned and faced me. Shock filled her eyes. "Shut up. No way. I'm never getting pregnant. I live in that tub, more so when Pax is home."

She blushed, and I had an excellent idea what they did there. I was no longer saddened I couldn't indulge.

"You keep it up, you are so getting pregnant. But I

don't need to hear about you two bumping uglies. I've been celibate for six months, and pregnancy hormones make you horny. All. The. Effing. Time."

"Who's horny?" Pax asked, appearing from nowhere.

Susan jumped, dropped my bag, and clutched her chest. "Shit. Stop doing that to me. I don't know how someone as big as you can be so quiet."

"You like how big I am, especially…"

Susan silenced him with a hand on his mouth and a blush on her cheeks. Pax pulled her to his side and kissed her, not caring he had an audience. I looked away, not out of embarrassment, but because a part of me coveted what they had. It was a fancy I forbid. Relying on a man was not in my playbook. A relationship meant sacrificing who you were. Ceding your independence. I was in love once. It ended with heartbreak. That kind of love and commitment were not for me. No thank you.

"Hey, Ann Marie," Pax said and took in my luggage. "What's up?"

"Ann Marie is visiting us for a while," Susan answered for me.

Pax ran the hand not wrapped around Susan's waist through his short hair. "Shit, did I forget she was coming?"

I stepped closer and laid my hand on his forearm. "No. I've come unannounced. Sorry."

He shook his head and looked toward the house. "No need to apologize. Come on, let's get inside." He took the bag from me, picked up the one Susan dropped, and led us through the open front door.

"Wow, the place looks fantastic."

"Yeah." Susan sighed. "Pax is working hard to get everything done. With the dining room finished, he's started on the spare bedrooms. Next is the basement."

Darth, Susan's black, now scattered with gray fur, dog meandered across the hardwood floors after maneuvering down the stairs. He bumped his head on Susan's hip, and she petted him.

"Give me twenty minutes and I'll have a place ready for you," Pax said.

"Huh? We need to throw clean sheets on the bed. That won't take twenty minutes." Susan looked bewildered.

"Yeah, that." Pax again appeared uncomfortable and rubbed his hand along his nape. "I just moved all the furniture in from the second room into the third one. Morgan's here, helping me with the reno. I can move the stuff back."

Susan's gaze pinged my way, and I suppressed my potential freak out. I wasn't ready for Morgan. My heart pounded against my ribs, threatening a cardiac arrest. The appearance of a pair of scuffed up biker boots hitting the steps sent it into overdrive. Riveted to the figure attached to those boots, from the lean muscular legs, to the shirtless, tattooed, sweaty chest as the most gorgeous man came into view.

I swallowed back the knot in my throat, straightened my shoulders and waited. Like I did all things in my life.

Show no weakness.

You control your destiny.

Reach out and take what you want.

I replayed the long-standing mantra in my head as Morgan came further into the room. I called upon my inner strength to appear unaffected by his presence, but the sweat dripping down my back threatened to give me away. I held myself steady by sheer determination and took four breaths in, held them before releasing them on another count of four, then smiled.

Morgan approached and pulled Susan out of Pax's arms for a hug. He kissed the top of her head, done with ease considering his six-foot-two frame to Susan's five-foot-five stature. His striking gray rimmed deep ocean blue eyes settled on me before long. He stiffened, much the same way I did, before collecting himself. His impassivity gave nothing away. I mimicked his greeting and clasped my hand behind my back.

Susan stared at us with crinkled eyes and covered her mouth with her hand. Not at all successful in holding back her laughter. Pax stood by her side with raised eyebrows, focus uncertain until a light sparkled in his eyes.

And before I could control it, I cringed.

"That's okay. I don't want you or Morgan to go to the extra trouble. Ann Marie can just stay at Morgan's," Susan said.

****

Morgan

I contained the hiss on the tip of my tongue at Susan's asinine remark. I lived alone for a reason.

However, at one time or another, a sibling stayed with me. I cohabitated, but only with family. Not with someone I wanted to fuck. Having Ann Marie in my house, my domain, a sure test of my willpower.

"I don't…" I said at the same time as Ann Marie spoke.

"No way," she yelled. "I don't know Morgan well enough to stay with him. Besides, I came here to see you. If you don't have the space for me, I can get a hotel room or go home."

Susan huffed at her cousin, took her hand, and pulled her to the couch. They exchanged silent looks, communicating far more than I could decipher.

"I should have called, but it was a spur-of-the-moment kind of thing. I'll find a place."

Ann Marie's continued protests pissed me off, and I forced open my clenched jaw. "You can stay with me," I said with a mental punch to the gut.

Pax sucked air as Susan bounced on the cushions, clapping her hands. I clamped my mouth shut.

"If you're sure." Pax broke the quiet tension and slapped a hand on my shoulder.

"I am," I answered.

I wasn't.

"No. I'll be fine in a hotel." Ann Marie stood and grabbed her suitcase.

I stepped forward and blocked her path to the front door. "I said you can stay with me. It's not an offer I make lightly."

My gut revolted.

"Then don't make it. And I said I will find a place," she said through gritted teeth.

She hauled her bag against her chest, like a shield, side-stepped around me and lost her balance. I grabbed her elbow, holding her steady. I bit the inside of my cheek. The instant pain a distraction from the searing heat at our point of contact.

Pax and Susan, snuck over to the kitchen but stayed close enough to hear us.

Ann Marie yanked her arm out of my grasp, stumbled and took me with her. I dug my heels into the floor and grabbed her hip, pulling her to my side. The jerky move brought our bodies closer.

I grew hard in my jeans. Her breath hitched, and I couldn't hide the effect she had on me. Her chest rose and fell in quick succession. Eyes closed to half-mast. She licked her lips, and I wished we were alone. I wanted another taste

I squeezed her hip and growled. "You're not staying in a hotel. You're staying with me."

She shivered under my hand. I smirked and enjoyed her returning glare.

"Why would I do that?"

Because one time wasn't enough. Because this time I want to lick you to orgasm. Because my cock is starving for you.

"Susan will worry about you. She'll make Pax move everything, delaying work even more."

"No, she won't. I live and travel alone all the time."

"Not when she knows you need a place to stay."

I goaded her to say yes. Masochistic of me. I wanted her close yet would deny my desire for her.

Ann Marie's gaze roamed my face before she nodded. "Ugh, you're right."

I smiled, and she slapped my hand where it rested on her hip.

"Don't let that go to your head."

I smothered my laugh and released my hold. My hand heavy without her soft curves beneath it.

She spun, faced the kitchen, and fake-grinned at Susan. "Fine. I'll stay with him," Ann Marie said, pointing her thumb over her shoulder toward me, "for two days. Will that be enough time to finish?"

Susan nodded as Pax shook his head. His smirk an unspoken proof of their ulterior motives.

"Well, I guess it's settled then," Susan said.

"How about an early dinner?" Pax asked.

"That sounds great, baby," Susan said.

"Awesome. Now, let's get some food. I'm starving." Ann Marie tapped me on the chest before moving away.

My skin flamed and blood boiled at her touch, but I suppressed any overt displays of lust.

In the eighteen years since the accident, I learned to bury my feelings behind a door I preferred to stay closed. In the six months since the bathroom incident—yes, I called it an incident—I mastered denial. I shut my eyes. Checked my emotions. I willed my dick down and braced for impact.

Chapter Seven

Ann Marie

My living arrangements settled, I made a quick trip to the bathroom. I relieved my bladder splashed water on my face and neck, reapplied mascara, and lip-gloss, and fluffed out my curls

Leaning closer to the vanity mirror, I inspected my teeth and laughed. I never procrastinated. And yet much to my chagrin I lingered in the bathroom.

I shook my head, took a deep breath, let it out, and then ran my hands down my outfit. I ensured my shirt was loose around my midsection and exited the bathroom.

Voices filtered down the hallway, and I stopped and listened.

"I'll call you down when the food gets here," Susan said to what I assumed were the men.

"Want a beer?" Pax asked.

Morgan grunted before two distinct sets of boots clomped up the stairs. I waited for the telltale creak of the wood flooring above and rounded the corner into the kitchen.

"Hey, we ordered Mexican."

I bounced on my heels, eliciting a giggle from Susan. "My favorite."

"Duh. Anything for the mommy-to-be."

I flattened a palm across Susan's lips, twisted, and gave a quick backward glance. "Shush." Susan's eyes glinted. "Ew. You licked my hand." I yanked it away, and she stuck her tongue out.

"Then don't cover my mouth."

"Then don't talk so loud," I whispered and wiped the wetness on my jeans.

"Then you better get it together and tell him." Susan cocked a hip, rested against the multi-colored reclaimed wood island, and tapped her nails against the surface.

"Then give me a few freaking minutes to get my bearings."

"Then…then…Shit, I've got nothing," she said, and we fell into a fit of giggles. Being with Susan, acting like we did when we were kids, was a balm to my stressed-out soul. For the first time since I learned of the baby, my shoulders relaxed, and I took a full and satisfying breath.

"We haven't done that in a long time," I said. "You've lost your touch. Last time we battled it out for what, twenty minutes?"

"Something like that." Susan pulled me into a hug, and my eyes stung.

I bit my lip, holding back tears. I didn't cry. Tears, both mine and others, rendered me useless. I never knew what to say to comfort them.

"I missed you, Queen Bee," she said.

"I missed you too, Bubbles."

The doorbell interrupted our moment. I hustled and reached the door with money in hand and paid for the food, much to Susan's irritation.

"You're the guest," she said and waved money in

front of my chest.

"We're family. Your house is my house," I said with an exaggerated eye-roll.

"Careful, there. You roll those eyes anymore, you'll see the back of your head," Susan said, giggled and poked my forearm. "Next time, it's on me." She turned and yelled, "Food's here."

Feet stomped across the upstairs hallway. Morgan led the way down the stairs and took the bags from my hands. I suppressed a retort and followed them to the kitchen, helping him unload the many containers.

"Quit making out and help," Morgan said to Pax.

Pax stopped kissing Susan but didn't unwind his arms. He pulled her flush to his chest and rested his chin on the top of her head.

"Jealous?" Pax asked his brother.

Morgan snorted and turned to me. At the sight of his misty eyes, I widened my smile. I couldn't deny what the glimpse of his vulnerability did to me. For a moment he wasn't the steadfast, even-tempered Morgan, and it twisted something deep inside.

My gaze softened. The motorcycle, tattooed, badass had a heart.

"Are we eating?" he asked with a scowl, ending the sliver of my budding hope.

"Yes," I said. My inflated enthusiasm drew Morgan's attention. "Better be enough food. I'm hungry."

"Let's hope so. Susan needs her energy for later," Pax said, and led her to the island. He drew out her stool and waited until she sat. He kissed her again and fisted her hair.

"Gag me now." I pantomimed throwing up.

They pulled apart, and I laughed at Susan's blush.

"Whatever." Susan shrugged, reached for the closest container and fumbled with the lid. "I can call you tomorrow with details. Might get you through your dry spell." Her high pitch belied her attempted aplomb.

"Hey." Pax took the to-go box from her and snapped off the top. He held it out to her, pulled back when she reached for it, and puckered his lip and waited until she kissed him. "There's a no kiss and tell policy in this house."

"Oh, please," she said.

"If he told me about your sex life, I'd have to deck him," Morgan said.

Pax's boisterous laughter filled the room, and I smiled, happy for my cousin.

"We'll keep the details from you, but Ann Marie would love to hear all about our bed—or out of the bed—tango."

"Ew." I scrunched my nose and shook my head. "No. Just, no."

"Whatever. You are the most sexually open-minded person I know. You love to experiment."

Morgan choked on his food, and Pax's eyes twinkled with mirth.

"Shit, Susan. You can't say stuff like that around a single heterosexual male, especially while he's eating. You could have killed him," Pax said and slapped Morgan on the back several times.

I waited for Morgan's coughs to subside, aided by several gulps of water before I spoke.

"You're right. I am very open-minded, and I'm not opposed to trying new things. A good visual is very effective when flying solo, but it still doesn't mean I want to hear about Pax's knob and how he uses it. I might get seasick if you tell me about the motion of the ocean."

I suppressed a giggle, Morgan's renewed coughing music to my ears.

Pax covered his mouth with his hand. A useless attempt at keeping his drink from escaping his lips and flowing down his arm. His face reddened, and I laughed, delighted at the Hulk's speechlessness.

"Ann Marie, leave my man alone." Susan wiped a towel across Pax's skin.

"Thanks," he whispered, and kissed her forehead.

I picked up my burrito, took a big bite, and smiled at her.

The rest of the meal, Pax, Susan, and I spoke while Morgan contributed guffaws, snorts, or one-word answers. Although I wished for more than his simple responses, his countenance captivated me.

"Renovations await," Pax said, once we were finished with our food, and rose with his empty container. Morgan followed suit. They rinsed them at the kitchen sink before tossing them in the recycle bin by the door.

Morgan waited behind me as Pax doubled back to Susan for a kiss. I wriggled on the seat of the stool, but a hand on my hip stilled me. Heat seared my skin through my pants, and I sighed, leaning into the touch. Realizing my mistake, I jerked away from Morgan and ignored the low rumble coming from him.

As the men climbed the steps, I shook off my unsettling reaction and focused on Morgan's fantastic, quarter-bouncing, tight ass. My fingers itched to squeeze the two perfect globes. Better yet, I yearned to watch them in a mirror as he pumped his cock into me.

Susan squeezed my thigh, and I groaned at the intrusion.

"Wipe the drool away," Susan said, and waved a napkin in front of my face.

I snatched the napkin, scrunched then tossed it at her. Susan chuckled when it landed on the countertop.

"Imagining some Morgan induced 'O's' are you?" Susan asked.

"Who needs my imagination when I have vivid memories." Susan laughed, and I raised my hand to stop her. "There will be no Morgan and Ann Marie hanky-panky. I'm here to tell him, figure out my shit, and return to Seattle. Get your mind out of the love gutter. Me and him?" I waved my hand between me and the stairs, "That ain't happening."

"Yeah, right. What's another few weeks when I've waited six months to see you two back together? I can hold my breath, 'cause I know it won't be long," Susan said and formed a circle with one hand and used the index of the other to—well, no further explanation needed.

I reached across the table, and she leapt away, cackling. I succumbed and let go my own belly laughs.

****

Morgan

Pax followed as I climbed the stairs at a slow pace. I listened to the soft giggles coming from the kitchen and fought a smile. I didn't want or need Pax questioning me and sighed in relief when he kept his thoughts to himself.

I was quiet throughout dinner. I took in the

conversation and observed Ann Marie. She smiled and laughed with Susan. But underneath it all, I sensed disquiet.

I lost count of the number of times I almost reached for her. I wanted her beneath me again, her fingernails digging into my scalp as I fucked her with my tongue. I missed my chance the last time. An oversight I needed to correct.

I stopped at the threshold of the room.

The idea had merit.

Pax slid past me and headed for his tools while I hovered, fixated on images of Ann Marie running through my head. Her moaning. Her eyes glazed over with lust. The taste of her lips. The slide of her skin under my palm.

Pax tilted his head in question the longer I stood immobile.

"Need a lesson on screwdriver uses?" I asked.

"Shut up, butt-head. I know how to use one." He circled the air with the tool in his hand. "I was just thinking about the look on your face. Wondering if you're giddy or freaking out about your new roommate."

"I don't do giddy."

"Then freaking out it is."

I glared at him, and he snorted, holding back his laugh.

"I don't do that either. Quit fishing."

"Where's the fun in that?"

"And she's not my roommate. Two days is all you get, then I'm dumping her on your front steps."

"I might need more than two days to get this done. I'm thinking more along the line of two weeks. Susan has a lot of demands for this room."

My brows pinched as I studied him. After several seconds of observation and stifled snorts, he laughed, bent over, and clutched his stomach.

"Whatever, man. Hope you choke on your spit." I slapped the noise-canceling headphones on my head and grabbed the sander and powered it on. His continued amusement grazed against my skin even as I turned away. I moved across the floor, not caring about the dust I created. The sooner we finished, the sooner Ann Marie's irresistible body would leave my house.

I shut my eyes, but it didn't help. Ann Marie's presence obliterated any chance I had of keeping her buried in the past. I dug deep and used skills I learned in childhood. I ignored Pax's bemused stare, tuned him and my surroundings out. Willed my mind to slow down and focus on one task.

Pax acknowledged my shut down. He witnessed it many times over the years. He set about dismantling the closet doors and carried them out of the room before repeating the steps two more times.

A mask and safety goggles appeared before me. I took the equipment, nodding my thanks to Pax and placed them on my face before I continued sanding the hardwood floor.

When my cousins first moved in with us after their parents' death, the increased noise level in the house just about drove me insane. Worse yet was the crying. I shared a room with my younger brother, Jesse, and more often than not, our toddler cousin Kate. She snuck in, too scared to sleep alone in her own room. We built forts and slept huddled on the bedroom floor, held and soothed her as she wept, and I tried keeping the guilt from swallowing me whole. I learned to be a protector, of her and the rest of my family.

I also became a silent observer. Ma and Dad often talked in the kitchen while they prepared dinner. I sat with my drawings in the living room and became the fly on the wall. Ma cried and Dad held her, rocked her, played with her hair until she stopped. I hated seeing her sadness over the loss of her sister. But I fought the sludge of guilt and observed my dad. I wanted to be like him. I vowed to protect my siblings and cousins. I had my duties, and there was no place for anyone else until Susan bulldozed her way into my life.

The older I got, the better I became at tuning out the world and shutting down my mind. I channeled my thoughts. I homed in on my creativity and focused on my art. My introspection often stole pieces of time and provided me strength to face another day.

Pax's hand on my shoulder pulled me from my thoughts, and I powered down.

"Come on, we're done for the day. Let's grab a beer before you go home."

I nodded and placed my safety gear down in the box by the door. "Thanks."

"What for? Giving you the space to get your head together? You forget. I know every little detail about you, brother."

I smiled at him. "Not everything."

"Stop talking shit. Ever since you've started me on that meditation stuff, I'm more aware of things." He shrugged and rubbed his palm against the back of his neck.

"That's good."

"I'm learning to observe. It's helping me when I

respond to a fire call."

Pax, a firefighter, loved serving people. His job terrified me. Keeping him safe always at the forefront of my mind. I taught him how to calm his thoughts and hoped when faced with life and death, he would use them to keep himself alive. He knew the risks, but he never wanted another family to hurt like ours. His vow to protect led him to be a first responder. Maybe if my aunt and uncle's accident had a quicker response, they would have lived. Truth be told, if I hadn't distracted my uncle, the disaster may never have happened.

Although Pax and I had similar drives, our executions differed. I vowed never to be a nuisance. Keep my feelings buried. Never be a burden.

"Come on, you've been in your head long enough today." He pulled me into a light choke hold and noogied me, as an older, bigger brother would do. Dust rained down around us.

Ann Marie and Susan lounged on the couch, heads canted toward each other. They talked no louder than a whisper and giggled often. At our approach, they turned and faced us.

Ann Marie scrunched her nose and laughed. "You need someone to teach you how to handle your wood?"

Pax chuckled beside me.

"You offering?" I asked and arched a single eyebrow.

She swallowed, but her expressions didn't change. "You wish."

Yes, my mind and dick screamed.

"Nah, I get what I want. No wishing needed."

She gulped, and I held back a chuckle.

"Whatever," she huffed, and shimmied further into

the couch cushion. "But me handling your wood would be a travesty to the next girl. Those experiences will never compare to what I can do."

"Prove it," I said and shifted before my cock performed a Houdini act.

Susan and Pax's gazes ping-ponged between us, and with a slap on my shoulder, Pax broke the sexual tension in the room. "How about that beer?"

Chapter Eight

Morgan

I beat Ann Marie to the driver's side and held out my hand.

"What are you doing?" she asked.

"Driving."

"This is my car. I'm driving."

"Where's your truck, Morgan?" Susan called from the porch.

"Pax picked me up before going to the hardware store."

I jiggled my out-stretched fingers. Ann Marie stood with her hands on her hips and refused to move. Pax and Susan snickered, but I couldn't take my eyes off the pissed off beauty before me.

"Ann Marie, let the idiot feel important. Besides, aren't you tired of driving today?" Susan said.

Ann Marie took in a deep breath, focused a glare at her, and counted backwards from ten. Silent but for her lips moving, enthralling me with her mouth and tongue. She was cute when angry.

"If this is some show of male ego bullshit, I'm telling you right now to cut it out. I'm not living with you for the next two days if you think you can order me around because I'm a woman."

"Only place I order a woman around is in the

bedroom."

She stared at me, muttered curses, rounded the car, and yanked the door open.

A wink and a sly look later, she settled in the passenger side. Her intentions clear. I pulled the handle of my door seconds before she pushed the lock button.

I held back my smile at her growl and contorted my body into the car. I pushed the seat back, accommodating my long legs.

"Don't mess up my settings."

With my finger on the button, I continued adjusting the seat and held back a snicker at her over-the-top huffing. Satisfied, I held my palm out again.

"When we get to your place, fix my seat." She dangled the keys, daring me to snatch them from her. "And just so we're clear, I'm letting you drive because you know the way."

With quick moves, I wrapped the keys and her fingers in mine and took pleasure in her surprise. Images of kissing her fingertips, sucking them into my mouth, flashed before my eyes. Show her what I could do with my tongue.

"Your cousin's waving like a lunatic. Think she's trying to get your attention," I said.

Ann Marie scoffed, turned to the house, and wiggled her fingers at Susan.

I started the engine and hated the confinement of the small vehicle. If I had to be in a cage, I preferred it to be big.

Ann Marie rested her head against the window and remained quiet throughout the drive. I let her be. I appreciated the silence.

I maneuvered us through the streets of Bellevue,

back to Medina and my home. Once there, I grabbed her luggage and walked to the front door. She followed me up the stairs and to the bedroom. The one on the opposite end of the hallway from mine.

"The bathroom on this floor is all yours. If you need anything, I'm sure you'll find it," I said and placed her bags on the bed.

Ann Marie stood in the doorway and surveyed the space. I kept the two guest rooms clean and the beds made. Not that I had much overnight company. Ma's lessons ingrained in me.

"Not what I expected," she said.

"Not up to your standards?" I asked. Her judgment grated on my nerves. I bit back any further retort and looked around the room.

Plain white sheets and comforter lay on the queen size bed. A dresser stood across from it beside the closed closet door. Two nightstands held chrome lamps. An area rug soft enough to sleep on protected the deep cherry hardwood floor.

"That's not what I meant. I don't know, I assumed the worst, and this is…nice."

"Kate spends the night sometimes. She stays during finals."

Ann Marie tilted her head. Her gaze studied me. I moved to the French doors and tugged the sheer curtains back.

She walked over, pushed the doors open, and stepped outside with a gasp.

"I have the same view from my room." I rolled my neck and willed myself to shut up.

I never filled the quiet with useless words. Unnecessary chatter was pointless. Yet something about Ann Marie pulled at my control.

Ann Marie rested her palms against the balcony railing, and I followed suit, leaving four feet of space between us. She inhaled, closed her eyes, and stretched so she faced the moon. The white skin of her neck tempting. The metallic moonlight turned her light-colored shirt transparent, exposing her curves through the fabric. My fingers tingled with need.

I looked away from the unintentional seduction.

Lake Washington ebbed and flowed, the water shined, black in darkness of night. In the distance to the right, the floating bridge twinkled with its multitude of lights. And across the waters the high rises of Seattle visible. My house sat in a small inlet on the lake, granting me distance and privacy from the crowds, motorboats, and weekend water sports enthusiasts.

Ann Marie sighed and leaned over the railing and breathed in the warm April night air. Her expression morphed from anxious to contented. Riveted, I couldn't look away, and edged closer when she lifted herself on the lower rungs of the balustrade.

I stepped behind her, careful not to touch. I closed the distance between us, not sure if I wanted her to hold on or slip so I could catch her.

"It's beautiful."

She was.

I nodded, a motion she couldn't see. "It's why I bought the house."

"The peacefulness of this place must feed your creative soul."

I shut my eyes against an onslaught of emotions.

"Yeah, sure," I said once I calmed my racing nerves.

She turned her head, accentuating the line of her neck. I wanted to lean down and lick it. She eyed me with curiosity but said nothing.

She turned and leaned over the edge. Without thinking, I reached for her. I hugged her to me. I secured my forearms underneath the curve of her breasts and my hands reached the opposite ribs.

She stiffened, and I loosened my hold until her body sagged against my chest. My cock jumped to attention, and I pulled her closer. I rubbed my thumbs along the underside of her bra. The heat of her skin imprinted on mine through the flimsy fabric of her shirt, and I lowered my arms down over her belly.

One moment she was in my arms, the next she stood in the bedroom's doorway. She stepped out of view, and I spent another minute getting my body under control before following. Ann Marie sat on the edge of the bed. Her stuttered gaze met mine as I stepped inside.

"Thank you for the room," she said in a strong, clear voice.

"No problem."

I walked across the floor to the door and reached for the handle.

"This is exactly what I needed. I have a lot to think about, and I want you to know I appreciate you sharing your home with me. This can't be easy for you."

Her hushed utterance stopped me mid step. I didn't turn. I didn't know if I could handle or even want to handle looking at her in that moment.

"No problem," I said.

Take whatever time you need, I thought, the words a shock yet true.

"Mind if I use your kitchen? Cooking helps me de-stress."

I turned at the playfulness in her voice. Her smile unearthed mine and eased some of the tension from my shoulders. "Depends."

"On?"

"Are you going to make something sweet?"

"Why? Do you have a sweet tooth?"

"Nah. I just like whipped cream on my pie."

To my satisfaction, she blushed, and I left the room with a hard cock and aching cheeks.

****

Ann Marie

With a cup of decaffeinated tea in hand, I sat on the balcony and enjoyed the bug free warm air the slight breeze created. The moon's reflection distorted on the lake's miniscule waves, quiet and peaceful. The serenity of nature surrounded me. Humans and traffic seemed as far away as the bridge in the distance.

I munched on crackers and hoped for a reprieve from my morning—more like night—sickness. I focused on relaxing my lungs, but my stomach still revolted. There was no use fighting it. I placed the mug down and, in my haste, almost dropped it.

I hustled to the bathroom seconds before my dinner made a reappearance. Finished, I lay on the tiled floor. The cool ceramic calmed my heated skin. I yearned for a washcloth on my neck but didn't have the energy to move.

Lost in my world of discomfort, I missed the footfalls and the opening door. Morgan kneeled before me and ran his hand across my back.

"What the fuck are you doing on the floor?"

"Fish funeral," I said, more squeak than eloquent.

"Ha ha. Here, let me help you up."

Morgan reached for me, but when I stumbled, he wrapped his arms under my shoulders and legs. He lifted me with ease. He carried me to my room and placed me on the bed. His gaze scanned my too short boxers and my favorite oversized sweatshirt hanging off one shoulder.

"Always wear that to bed?" he asked. He accompanied his snark with a head gesture.

"No. Funeral, remember? I sleep naked," I replied, my voice gaining in strength.

His Adam's apple bopped and his eyes darkened. He took a slow perusal of my body, and my skin tingled. I clenched my thighs. A shift he noticed with a smug smile. I disliked my body's reaction to him, but again, I didn't have the energy to dwell on it.

"Don't move. I'll be right back."

Morgan's tone held a hint of huskiness, leaving me hot and bothered as he sauntered to the door.

"Wouldn't dream of it."

"You always have to have the last word?"

I tilted my head and blew him a kiss. "Yep," I said, popping the p.

He left, but I swore he chuckled.

Morgan returned with a bottle of water and a wet washcloth. He handed me the drink, and I gulped it down. I relished the soothing effects of the liquid on my throat. I closed my eyes and laid back against the pillow.

"Better than an orgasm?"

I opened one eye and stared at him in confusion.

"The moaning," he said.

"What moaning?"

"The one's coming from your mouth."

"Huh? Didn't realize I moaned."

"You did."

"Oh-kay?"

He ignored me and sat on the edge of the bed. I was shocked when he reached over and with care tucked my hair behind my ear. His fingers lingered along my cheek, and I fought to appear unaffected.

"Here," he said. He waved the wet washcloth and nudged me to move. "This should help."

I shifted to face him, laid on my side, and gave him access to my nape. His weight dipped the mattress, and I rolled closer to him until my thighs rested along his lower back. The heat from his large hand penetrated the towel, warming my skin and body. Desire replaced the subsided nausea.

I rubbed my legs together and staved off the urges running through my veins.

This time, he kept his features neutral, and I couldn't tell if he noticed my sexual discomfort.

"Feeling better?" he asked.

"Much."

"You're still a bit green. I'll stay until you fall asleep."

He got up, rounded the bed, and sat. I envisioned him, with his back rested against the headboard, and his legs stretched before him.

"Go to sleep. I'm going to check my work emails for a few minutes. Once you're asleep, I'll leave. Do you prefer the light on or off?"

My eyes drooped. Exhaustion pushed at the edges

of my consciousness. I said, "Off," in answer.

He reached across my body, and for a moment his heated chest cocooned me in comfort. He turned off the lamp on the nightstand and settled into his spot on the bed.

His intent blew me away. The whole turn of events stumped me. We weren't friends, yet he welcomed me into his home, helped me through my sick bout, and offered his steadfastness as I fell asleep. I turned onto my back for a better view. With his phone screen turned off, I took in the angular structure of his jaw by the moonlight coming in through the window. His eyes, light by day, were dark by night.

"You don't have to," I said, after dragging my gaze away from his face. Where they landed wasn't much safer. His tight T-shirt framed his chest and muscles. A tiny expanse of skin showed at the hem of his shirt and waist of his gray sweats. I itched to rub my fingers along it. My brain wanted to know if it was smooth or rough. Feel his abs contract as I trailed my tongue on his belly and up his torso.

My gaze, at his growl, drew away from his stomach and straight to his amused stare. For a person who didn't blush often, my face heated. Thankful the dark hid my reaction.

"Better if I stay. Don't want you puking on my sheets." His smirk playful, yet his eyes told a different story.

If I wasn't so tired—nauseous, horny, whatever—I would have disregarded his knowing look. But in my state, with my defenses down, I read far too much in it and let my heart want what I denied it.

The protection and adoration of a man.

Morgan exuded danger in more ways than I cared to consider. Unbeknownst to him, he could crumble the walls I spent nine years building, to penetrate deep into me—not in the biblical sense—and find a way into a heart I sealed off from love.

"Come on, I'm kidding."

I rolled over, hid my smile, and closed my eyes. I may not have known him well, but I guessed he didn't show his funny side to outsiders. "I know," I whispered. His dry humor ignited a threatening flame inside me.

His proximity forestalled my sleep, but I concentrated on matching my breathing to his, and it wasn't long before I relaxed. The blue light from his phone shone across the ceiling, and his shadow moved within it, providing me an odd comfort.

Enticing images of Morgan held me like a warm blanket wrapped around us against the wind, as we listened to the small waves on the shore of the lake. I drifted off and hoped Morgan wouldn't bear witness to what I knew my dreams that night, and many like it before, would include.

Chapter Nine

Morgan

I laid on top of the covers and scrolled through my phone with Ann Marie curled up and tucked in beside me. Her soft snores filled the air, and I leaned my head back against the wall. I closed my eyes in reflection. My mind sifted through the events of the evening.

My chest hurt when I found her shaking on the bathroom floor. Seeing her distraught touched a part of my heart I repealed many years ago. Although a knight in shining armor I was not, I couldn't leave her in her distressed state.

I picked her up with ease considering she weighed a buck and nickel soaking wet, surprised when I felt an unmistakable bump. I stumbled but corrected, tugged her closer, and walked through the bathroom door. Her moans vibrated through my chest. Her arms wrapped around my neck and her head rested on my shoulder. Her body shivered, and I didn't want to let her go.

Surprised at the gentleness I didn't know I possessed, I laid her on the bed. I debated slipping in behind her and holding her through the night. But her frayed sweatshirt rode up and revealed her abdomen. And my priorities changed. I offered her my company. A small comfort. A simple gesture, yet one I didn't make carelessly.

It didn't take long for her to fall asleep. I stayed and fought the urge to open the web browser on my phone and research, instead of my email. She shifted and faced me. Her arm landed on my lap, inches from my cock, stirring him to life. I eased away, tucked the sheets around her again, stepped out of the room, and left the door ajar.

I hurried to the deck outside my bedroom, far enough she couldn't overhear, and powered up my phone. Unsure of Jesse's schedule because of his residency, I sent him a text.

—*Are you awake?*—

—*Just got out of emergency surgery.*—

—*Need to talk.*—

—*Give me ten.*—

Seven minutes later, an incoming call vibrated the phone. I answered without looking at the screen.

"Hey," he said, his voice quiet and laced with exhaustion.

"How was surgery?"

"It went okay. The kid's tough, he'll pull through."

I didn't envy my brother his profession and his passion for it. Working with sick kids was not for me, but I understood his drive. The first few years of his life were taken from him. His history with his personal battles played a major role in his decisions. He wanted to give back what his doctors gave him, and I was damn proud of his accomplishments.

"So what's keeping you up?" he asked, pulling me from my thoughts.

"Can someone get morning sickness at night?"

Jesse remained silent for a moment, and I imagined him running through scenarios where my question wasn't odd.

"Every woman is different. Some get sick in the morning, while others all day. Some get it like clockwork, no matter the time of day. Why? Are you pregnant? Medical miracle?"

I snickered. "Shut up, you dumb fuck. I'm not pregnant."

I needed a minute to come up with an answer. Something I should have thought about before texting him in the middle of the night. "I'm asking for a friend." I groaned at his exaggerated gasp. I, after all, had one friend.

"Shit, does Pax know? Susan needs to see a doctor immediately if she thinks she's pregnant. Prenatal health is vital for both her and the baby."

"Stop. It's not Susan. It's…it's someone else."

"One of your hook ups? Shit, mom's going to…"

"No, not one of my regulars." I sounded obnoxious even to my own ears.

"So who is it?"

"It's not important. I have more questions. You going to keep giving me shit?"

"No," he said followed with a deep sigh.

"When can you see the baby bump?"

"Huh? Again, depends on the woman. Some can show as early as three months, while others don't until seven months. The woman's size, the baby's size, the way she carries. There's no one definitive answer."

"But how can you tell if the bump is a baby or just the woman gaining weight?"

"Is she gaining weight elsewhere?"

"Not that I can see."

"Is she a good friend? Can you ask her outright?"

"Not sure asking her would be the best thing. She doesn't like me much."

I stood and paced and examined my options for the most pragmatic one. Raking my hand through my hair and down my face, I took in several deep breaths of fresh midnight air.

"Look," Jesse said, after a prolonged silence. "I'm not sure what's going on, but I can make a pretty good guess. I say ask her. Maybe she's said nothing to you because she's afraid of your reaction."

"I'm scared of my reaction."

"Whatever you believe it's going to be, remember this is as much your doing as hers. Be an honorable man."

"Fuck, Jesse. If she's pregnant with my baby, of course I'll do the right thing. I'm just fucking scared. This isn't what I wanted in my life."

"Whether it is or isn't, if she's pregnant…then remember the wise words from our dear mom…"

"Yeah, yeah. 'If you're mature enough to sleep with someone, then you're mature enough to deal with the consequences.' What if I ask and she says she doesn't know?"

"Don't take just her words into consideration. She'll tell you more with her body and eyes. Listen to your gut. When are you going to talk to her?"

"Not sure. Tomorrow? I'll sleep on it tonight. Figure out a way to ask her without risking my balls."

Jesse laughed. "Protecting your balls is an excellent idea," he replied, before turning serious once again. "Whatever you decide to do, get it done. Don't drag your feet and for the love of God, if she is pregnant, make sure I'm around when you tell Mom and Dad."

"Fuck off, asshole," I said, my smile evident in my tone. "I'll be Ma's favorite again, considering this would be her first grandchild."

"Yep, you do have that. Goodnight, big brother."

"Goodnight, little brother. Thanks."

"Anytime shithead."

I hung up, chuckling at our long-running departing words.

****

Ann Marie

I woke to the smell of coffee and the morning light penetrating through the balcony curtains. I stretched, spread-eagled my arms and legs, and rubbed them against the cool soft sheets, making temporary snow angels in the fabric. With a groan, I lifted off the bed and rummaged through my bags for an oversized shirt and a pair of shorts. I forewent makeup but brushed my teeth and tamed my hair then headed downstairs to an empty kitchen.

I spied a single serve coffeemaker on the counter with a mug, several kinds of pods—including decaffeinated ones—and cream and sugar nearby. I smiled at his thoughtfulness and made a cup. With my decaf doctored to perfection and the ceramic mug brushed against my lips, I meandered around the bottom level of the house.

His sense of style, although masculine, impressed me. A space free of clutter, yet walls adorned with numerous framed photos of him and his family. I stepped from one to the other. Inspected them, smiled and laughed at the ones including Susan. Tears welled in the corner of my eyes as I studied a large print of his parents and who I assumed were his aunt and uncle in a small rowboat. Susan had shared the story about their death with me.

I moved away before their grinning faces swallowed me into an abyss of hormonal induced illogical emotions. A picture of the sole female sibling in the family sandwiched in between her brothers and cousins drew my attention. A recent photo taken at Susan's fundraiser when Morgan's long hair reached his shoulders. And just like then, I wondered how silky those strands would have felt along my skin. I trailed my finger over the image.

A smiling Morgan hugging his mother with his lips on her forehead in the next frame spiked an unfamiliar sensation deep in my chest and a hitch in my breath. I stepped away from the images and the unwelcomed emotions they evoked.

I stroked the supple, soft suede of the couch, leaned down and rubbed my cheeks on it. Then I opened my eyes to the most spectacular view.

I gripped my mug closer to my chest, straightened and walked to the retractable glass doors facing the deck and Lake Washington beyond it. My jaw dropped as Morgan pulled himself onto the dock with practiced ease and muscular arms. I ogled the dark haired, tanned Adonis, sculpted to perfection, covered in tattoos I wanted to inspect closer, with my fingers, mouth, and tongue.

Water dripped down his chest. I wetted my lips and imagined licking the droplets off his skin. He grabbed a towel and see-sawed the material against his body. The muscles in his back contracted with each push and pull.

He set it on the railing and rubbed his hands through his hair, the untamed strands not detracting from his sex-appeal.

I stood transfixed by the sway of his "V" and the trail of hair from belly button to inside his swim trunks. I couldn't take my eyes off him. My neglected vagina woke up and pulsated.

"See something you like?" he asked. His nearness surprised me, and I jumped.

He held out a steadying hand, cupping my elbow.

I shrugged, and as best I could, controlled my pitch. "Just admiring the view," I said and waved my hand indicating the water's edge.

"Yeah, okay. Hungry?" he asked, his smugness telling me he saw through my lies.

"I can eat."

"There's cereal, oatmeal, or toast in the kitchen. Figured with the stomach troubles you had last night, you wouldn't be up for much more."

"Nah. Nothing bothers my stomach in the morning, even after hurling all night," I said without thinking.

He tilted his head. His gaze roamed down my body, stopping at my belly. My breath stuttered, and I knew the time had come.

"Actually, can we talk?" I gestured toward the outdoor table and chairs.

"Sure. Let me make a cup of coffee, and I'll join you on the deck."

"Yes, of course."

I sat on a wicker chair and waited, sipping my drink, taking in the water and the hazy silhouette of Seattle in the distance. Morgan stepped out onto the deck. I didn't turn to face him, yet my body attuned itself to his every move.

"I have something to tell you," I blurted before his butt hit his seat. I threw my shoulders back, trained my gaze on the lake, and took a calming breath. "I'm pregnant."

He didn't respond, and I chanced a quick glance to find his gaze on me, with quirked eyebrows and lips pinched tight. His tense stillness suffocating, and I dared another peek. He stared into his mug, steam billowing across his face.

I tucked my feet under me and couldn't wait any longer. "Say something."

He tilted his head—a trait I found endearing—and his gaze rested on my abdomen. "I guessed."

Surprised his first words weren't an inquiry of paternity, I sat back with a nod.

"Last night, when I picked you up, I felt the firm roundness of your belly," he said, answering one of my unasked questions. "When I put you in bed, your shirt rode up. Along with the vomiting, I drew some conclusions."

"Oh."

"Is that why you're here. In Bellevue?"

I nodded and gazed at the water.

"I'm the father?"

I gulped the rising bile and placed my mug on the table between us. "I don't know."

In silence, Morgan stood and walked to the edge of the deck. He leaned across the railing and dropped his head. "How many possibilities are there?" he asked, his voice muffled by his chest.

"Other than you, there's one more."

His shoulders drooped.

I approached and mirrored his position.

He didn't look my way but straightened to his full height. His six-foot-one stature towered over my five-foot-five.

"Does the other guy know?"

"Yes. I told him before coming here." His lack of response set my nerves on the fritz. "Look, I'm not asking for anything. It wasn't right for me to keep this from you. I have money. I can take care of myself and the baby. Last time…"

After a moment, he shook his head and turned. "Last time?"

I waved my hand and hoped he didn't sense my unease. "Nothing."

Tilting his head, he studied me, and I fought the urge to fidget. A move I liked a minute ago now set me on edge. Unbearable apprehension engulfed us as he placed his mug on the table and walked to the open door.

He stopped with one foot inside and the other on the deck. "I need a minute to process. I'm going for a ride," he said to the empty room.

Minutes later, the rumble of a bike disrupted the quiet. I waited for the roar to grow distant and grabbed his mug before retreating indoors. Exhaustion, both physical and mental, pulled at me. I welcomed the sweet oblivion of sleep but slugged through to the kitchen. Although I lacked an appetite, the baby's health was more pertinent than my desire to curl up in a ball. I made a bowl of cereal, retrieved a prenatal vitamin out of the vial in my handbag, and sat at the island. Alone.

As the day wore on with no sign of Morgan, I filled

my time with work until Lian sent several text-yells, chastising me. I gave up my half-assed attempts at answering emails and reviewing spreadsheets. Realization dawned. I didn't miss my office or the company I created.

Hoping to improve my melancholy, I retrieved my yoga mat from my car and settled on the boat dock for exercise and fresh air. I played a workout designed for pregnant women on my phone until I grew sweaty and tired. I laid on the sun-warmed wood. My mood much better and dangled my feet over the edge. The tips of my toes caressed the cool lake water.

By nightfall, Morgan hadn't returned. My nightly routine of eating and throwing up sapped the last of my energy, I readied for bed. I lay awake, restless, until a rumble came up the driveway. His safe return eased the tension in my shoulders and with a sigh, I closed my eyes and fell asleep.

Chapter Ten

Ann Marie

Over the course of the next three days, Morgan and I established a serendipitous routine. He worked from early morning to late at night in his garage. I spent time with Susan, and he hung out with Pax or alone. I cooked dinner, and he didn't join me. He ate his warmed food hours after I ate alone. I watched mindless TV while he showered and hoped he'd join me after. He never did. Instead, with a simple nod, no shirt, and damp skin, he shut himself away on the back deck.

Exhaustion an ever-present state of mind, I retired for the night but my hormones ruined the first hour of sleep. Morgan found me sick in the bathroom, carried me to bed, and took care of me until I fell asleep again.

Loneliness pulled at the edges of my psyche. I sat on the dock and dangled my feet over the edge into the water. A light sheen of sweat cooled my skin as the sound of laughter drifted across the water. I needed a reprieve from my pity party and dialed Susan's number on my phone.

"Hey," Susan said, answering on the first ring.

"I'm going out of my mind," I said, my voice hoarse from lack of use.

"Wow. Why, hello to you too."

"Let me repeat. I. Am. Going. Out. Of. My. Mind."

"Morgan being an ass?" she asked. "Don't answer, that. I'm coming over to wring his neck."

Her vehemence made me smile. "Get in line. Doesn't matter, anyway. I'm moving to a hotel."

"What? Why? No. You can't. Pax is working on the bedroom, I swear. He's been on shift. Comes home today. I don't want you on your own."

"I'm a big girl. Been living alone in Seattle for years. I can handle being in a hotel." Although I hated the idea.

Susan sighed. "Not the point. Morgan told Pax how sick you've been and…"

"Are you kidding me? The idiot won't say a word to me, but he's blubbering on to his brother? What the actual fuck?"

I stood. My wet feet dripped water onto the wooden boards as I stormed toward the house, ready to lay into Morgan.

"Stop." Her shout halted my steps. "Whatever you're about to do, don't. Morgan didn't kiss and tell, I swear. Morgan went to the firehouse the other night and Pax badgered him until he talked."

"That's just great. Everyone knows."

"No. Pax has told no one. I saw him yesterday, and he couldn't look me in the eye. I knew he knew. He's not good at keeping secrets from me, and he told me about their conversation. He's not telling anyone. I promise."

Listening to her brought up a mix of tears and laughter. "God, we sound like we're in high school."

"Just hang in there. I know Morgan."

My heartbeat stuttered, and I struggled to keep my feet beneath me. Jealousy was not an emotion I experienced—well, ever. I hated she knew him better. A foolish thought. But the burning desire to yell at her there none-the-less. I controlled my erratic breathing and rubbed at the burning in my eyes.

"He needs time to think," Susan said. Her voice grounded me although seconds ago it ignited my fury.

"He can take all the time he needs, but I'll be more comfortable if I didn't feel like I was invading his space."

"I get that, I really do. He can be broody at times…"

"At times? Try all the time," I said, interrupting her.

She snickered. "He's not that bad."

"Yes, he is."

Susan chuckled, her voice faint, and I realized in my frustration I had swung my arms. I brought the phone back to my ear. "His silent treatment's messing with me. And to top it off, I'm horny morning, noon, and night."

"Pregnancy hormones or are you going through withdrawal?"

"Yes," I shouted. "Morgan's walking around all day without his shirt on, all greasy and oiled up from the bikes. I want to jump him. All. The. Time. If I'm not exhausted, puking, or on the verge of tears, then I'm freaking turned on. I'm so mad I didn't bring any of my toys with me."

"You've already told me that. Several times, actually. You can always ask Morgan for the hot beef injection."

"Seriously, with the dirty jokes? There's no way I'm asking him to rummage in my root cellar. I'm craving a roll in the hay, but I'm not that desperate."

"Bullshit, besides, I'm betting he's good at dunking the dingus."

"Oh, he is, but no matter my thirst, I'm staying away from any horizontal refreshments."

"Who said anything about drinking? Laughter is what you need. Ask him to tickle your tummy from the inside."

I snorted and laughed so hard.

"Wait? I'm hungry. Maybe I should ask him to make a magical sandwich?"

"Or…or, how about, he fills your cream donut?"

"Ew, that's gross," I said around my giggles. "Stop, I'm going to pee my pants."

"Okay, okay," she said on a wistful note. After a few sighs, she continued. "Okay. So…why not sleep with him again? It's obvious you're attracted to each other. Being with him isn't necessarily a terrible thing."

"You know I can't. What happens when I go back to Seattle? What if this baby is his, and I have to see him because we share custody, and I think of how good he was, is, and we end up in bed every time we trade off Henry? Then before you know it, we have a second baby on the way because he has super sperm, and those little buggers penetrate through concrete walls, and now we have Henry *and* Seb, because he wanted to name the kid Sebastian, but I hated the name, so we compromised on Seb, and now we have to live in the same town because we're both sick of the drive and…"

"Shit, woman. Shut up." Susan's laughter rang through the phone line. "I didn't suggest you make more babies. Just get to know each other, see where things go."

"I'm not built that way. I don't want or need the love of a man."

"It's been nine years…"

"It's not about him," I said, cutting her off before thoughts of my past put more of a damper on my day. I didn't have the energy to deal with the emotions those memories summoned.

"Okay, we won't talk about him."

Little did she know there was more to the story than just him.

"Thank you."

"Pax wants to try."

"Try what? Improve his performance?"

"Oh, shut up. You know what I mean. He wants us to have a baby, and he thinks it would be fun if we had babies together. I agree with him. If I get pregnant, we could have our babies a few months apart. You'd have to move here. We can raise them like siblings."

I huffed out a laugh. "Yeah, ain't gonna happen. I'm not moving anywhere."

"Why not?"

"My business is in Seattle."

"So? You've already said how unhappy you are. Start something new. Design again. You can do that from anywhere, besides…"

The clack of keyboard clicking came through the phone and Susan stopped talking.

"Hello? What are you doing?"

After a few more seconds of silence, Susan came back.

"Sorry. Just got a notification on a package I'm expecting. Now, where were we?"

"You were telling me about this move that Pax

does."

"Oh, yes. He does this thing when he first…wait. That's not what we were talking about. You tricked me."

We both laughed.

"You're so easy, though."

A clomp behind me drew my attention away from the water. I turned in time to see Morgan retreating into the house. With his hand on the door jamb, he stopped, twisted, and faced me. His eyes difficult to see from this distance, but I felt his focused penetrating gaze.

For a minute or two we stared at each other. Neither of us made a move. Out of the blue he extended a simple wave, smiled, stepped inside, and closed the door behind him.

I waited on the dock, stunned. A wave and a smile might not have meant much coming from others, but from Morgan it was an olive branch.

****

Morgan

The delivery truck parked in front of my garage. Its loud approach on my quiet street pulled me out of the dirty fantasies my mind conjured when I saw Ann Marie on the dock with her feet dangling off the side, and her hair flying in the wind. The sight of her a picture I couldn't resist. Her laughter rang through the air, and I stopped. Took the notes of vibration into me. The overheard conversation, although one-sided, put a smile on my face and created a tightening in my pants.

I sighed. The truck's ill-timed arrival a blessing in disguise. Given the opportunity, I would have hauled Ann Marie to me and kissed her senseless. Her hot little shorts and the glimpse of ass cheeks when she stood, the belly-revealing crop top, and her sultry laughter all sent my blood boiling and straight to my cock.

I hustled to the garage as Mike, the delivery man, exited. With a flick, he opened the roll-up door, stepped inside, and emerged with several packages. I took them, moved them to my workshop, and left them by the door. I returned and repeated the process two more times.

"That's all of them," he said, handing me the tablet for my signature. "What are you working on now? That last bike you built was beautiful. Thanks for letting me see it."

"Sure thing, man. Anytime." Mike and I discovered our mutual love for bikes, and whenever I finished a custom build, I showed it to him before I delivered it to my clients. Once, he had me autograph a magazine cover displaying my bike with its new billionaire owner. My family got a kick out of it when I told them.

"I better be going. More deliveries and all."

"Thanks. See you next week." I returned to the workshop and started my music.

I pulled out a blade and unloaded the packages. I inspected each piece of chrome or accessory as I extracted it. In the last box, I wrapped my hand around something long, round, and pliable.

I tore the black bag and laughed, searching the box for the address label, and froze in panic. The box was labeled to Ann Marie, and the contents—an oversized pink dildo, batteries, and a bottle of lube—were not items I expected nor imagined she would appreciate me finding.

With a shrug, I owned my mistake.

I took the giant silicone and stepped into the house. Ann Marie lay on the couch. Her eyes drooped whether from boredom or exhaustion I couldn't tell. Ever since our discussion, I flipped between happiness, confusion, and fear. From one moment to the next I wanted the baby, Ann Marie, and fatherhood, and then I didn't. My uncertainty headache inducing, and until I figured out my shit, I stewed in solitude.

I shook off my apprehension and walked to the end of the couch. "Hey, you got a delivery," I said, brandishing the pink monstrosity.

Ann Marie's gaze drifted to my hand. "What the fuck?" she said and jumped. She bolted toward me. I lifted the penis in the air and turned my back on her.

She bounced on the balls of her feet, unable to gain enough height.

"Give me that."

I spun and dodged her, surprised by her tenacity. She stepped onto the couch, scaled my back, and wrapped her legs around my waist and arms around my neck. Between her heels digging into my groin and her choke hold, I stumbled, almost dropping her. I grasped her ass and held her in place with one hand and kept the dildo out of her reach with the other.

We fumbled across the space, and with a jerk I hit my knee on the coffee table.

"Ouch, fuck. Get off me, woman."

"No, not until you give me that."

She stretched an arm and wiggled her fingers for the vibrator. She squirmed against me, making the situation in my pants harder, and I slid into a side table. I knocked over a lamp and grunted in pain.

"Give it to me."

"Okay," I answered, and squeezed her ass.

She bit my ear, and I spun in place, dislodging her teeth from my flesh. She licked my skin and the wet heat demanded a response from my body. With all my oxygen traveling south, I loosened my hold, needing to adjust the crotch of my pants.

She tightened her arms around my neck. "Don't you dare drop me."

"Difficulty breathing here," I said, the scratch in my voice in line with that of life-time smoker.

"Good. Get your hand off my ass."

"Can't. I let go, you'll fall."

"Stop touching me, you pervert."

"Quit climbing me for your oversized fake penis," I said with a growl.

"It's not mine."

I stopped mid-step, leaned forward, and alleviated the pressure on my airway. "Why are you fighting me for it, then?"

She went still, and I held her against me with my ass-bracing hand.

"I don't know." Ann Marie released her hold on my throat, and I took in a deep breath. She unwrapped her legs and slid down, guided by my grip until her feet planted on the floor.

"They addressed the box to you."

"Then why'd you open it?"

"I thought all the packages were mine. I don't look at labels."

She stared at my hands, and my gaze followed hers. I held the penis in one hand and pumped its girth with the other.

She burst out laughing. "Oh my God. Are you sure it isn't yours? Looks like you need the practice."

I tightened my grip. "Want to teach me?"

She belly-laughed. Her response warmed me from the inside out. Wanting more, I continued rubbing the shaft. I increased the tempo and enjoyed her unbridled joy at the spectacle.

The dildo lit up, and I threw my arms in surprise. The device flew from my hand, arching through the air. I tracked its trajectory and although the moment played out in slow motion, I wasn't quick enough to stop it from reaching its destination. Ann Marie's gaze followed its descent and flinched as the head of the penis slapped her in the eye before landing on the floor.

Ann Marie flung her hands to her face. I stepped closer and grasped her wrists. I pulled them away and leaned down before staggering back.

Her tears unnerved me. They dug deep. Pulling at desires buried long ago. The need to hold her. Protect her, overwhelming.

A deep breath, followed by a few more, and I had my primeval instincts tamped down.

"Are you okay?"

She laughed, doubled over and fell onto the couch.

Shocked. Amused. Relieved. I plopped down next to her. Our legs touched from hip to knee. Heat seared through the thick layers of our clothes. I remained silent and savored her unadulterated happiness.

After a few minutes, she inhaled and exhaled. She settled down with a sigh.

"I haven't laughed that hard in forever."

Her head rested against the back of the couch, but she turned to face me. Her eyes shone, and for a moment our gazes held. Her tongue licked at her bottom lip. I clenched my hands, pushing my knuckles into my thigh.

Avoidance. Denial. Hunger. Whatever I called it; I couldn't deny how my unwelcomed attraction to Ann Marie invigorated me.

I picked up the offending member and held it out for inspection.

"It lit up," she said, reaching for it. She wrapped her hands around it, and I groaned, imagining her small, nimble fingers on me instead.

"It did," I said, after taking a deep breath.

"You hit me in the eye."

"No. I threw it. It landed on your face. I wasn't holding onto a glowing alien penis."

She snuggled further into the couch cushion and focused her gaze on the ceiling. I copied her position, comfortable in the tense-free silence. And for the first time since my childhood, inciting a reaction from someone didn't break me out in a cold sweat.

"I think you just gave a whole new meaning to being eye-fucked," I said, and her laughter, intermixed with snorts, was music to my ears.

Chapter Eleven

Morgan

Ann Marie turned her a mischievous stare my way. I lost the battle and grazed my fingertips against her cheek. I tucked her hair behind her ear.

She closed her eyes, and her breath hitched. My heart stuttered the longer I looked at her, my breathing irregular as I struggled to take in enough oxygen.

I bit the side of my tongue. The pain centered me, and I spoke without growling. "If it's not yours, why is the box addressed to you?"

She shook her head. "I don't even know your address to have something mailed to me here. Was there an order slip?"

I rose off the couch and retrieved the box from the garage. I took my seat beside her, close enough our bodies touched. I handed her the lube and batteries and rummaged through the packing material until I found a discrete, blank, white envelope. I ripped it open, pulled out the card stock, and laughed.

I offered it to Ann Marie. She hesitated. Her head cocked to the side as she studied me. With a shake and a wan smile, she took the cardstock and read the message out loud.

Dear Desperate,
A little *snicker* something to tide you over and

make you happy. Hope he lights up *snicker* *snicker* your night.

Love, a concerned bestie.

Her snorts filled the room. Her uninhibited laughter comforting while I mulled over the words in the note.

"Are you not happy?" I asked.

Ann Marie shifted so she sat sideways on the couch and tucked her feet under her. She rested her head on her hand, and her gaze flitted across my face before she answered.

"You should smile more often. It looks good on you."

I scrunched my eyebrows and took a moment digesting her words. "Thank you. Why aren't you happy?"

"You're not letting this go, are you? No?" She closed her eyes and sighed. "Fine. I've told you about the baby. It's my main reason for coming to Bellevue. But I've been feeling like a ship adrift since the doctor told me the news. Actually, no. It's been going on a lot longer than that." She waved her hand. "Doesn't matter. My plan was to take time off, make some decisions."

"Are you being purposely elusive?" I retrieved my phone from my pocket. "I'm sure Susan can tell me."

Ann Marie lunged. "Don't you dare call Susan. At least not about this. Give me a minute to explain. I promise I'll give you an answer."

I nodded.

"Susan said something the other day, and it got me thinking." She sighed again and squirmed deeper into the cushions. "I'm not happy in Seattle anymore. I think Susan figured out a way for me to reconnect with…well, me. By pushing me to stay with you, she opened my eyes." She looked out toward the water before her gaze roamed the expanse of my living room. "For the past few days, I've been here alone." She raised her hand and stopped me from speaking. "No...wait, you don't understand. I'm not blaming you. I dropped a bomb on you. I get you needed time."

I acknowledged her and considered ways I could make it up to her.

"I've done a bit of snooping," she said, and where I expected guilt, I got eyes alight with excitement. "I started with the pictures on the walls, but when I found your albums, I couldn't stop myself. God, your designs are beautiful."

Her words of praise warmed me over. Unfamiliar emotions I didn't want or seek. With effort, I shoved them down.

"I'm inspired. Seeing the passion you keep shuttered come out on paper. Your art has a voice of its own. It got me excited."

I shifted to the cusp of the couch cushion. My leg shook, but I stopped the involuntary motion with my hand and hoped she didn't notice. I shared my work with people. Completed pieces. I was damn proud of my final designs. The drawings in my books were not for public viewing. They were a part of me I didn't share.

"I started drawing again," she said, pulling me from my internal worries.

I focused on her, the present. She bit her bottom lip. Her eyebrows scrunched as she studied me, and I latched onto the unexpected information she presented before she saw my apprehension.

"That's great. Can I see?" I rested my hands on my

knees and angled my body toward her.

Her fingers tapped a scattered rhythm against her thigh. "Don't be mad."

"Okay?" My inflection rose at the end, turning my statement into an unintended question.

"During the course of my snooping, I found your movie collection, underwear drawer, and your work orders," she said. The slight hesitation at the end piqued my curiosity and amusement.

"You think going through my undies is better than going through my paperwork?"

She nodded. "Well, yeah. We all wear underwear, but your business is private."

"And what I wear under my jeans isn't?"

She didn't answer, but her eyes sparkled.

"Never mind, that," she said and waved her hand in the air. "I used your notes and…well, here." She reached behind a pillow, pulled out one of my sketch pads, and held it out to me.

I obliged and took it from her. I kept my gaze on her face and the fingernails she bit. For the first time I sensed an insecurity below her constant composure. I opened the book, studied each drawing, and admired her abilities.

"You did all this in three days?"

"I did more with less time at Hustle and Heart. Give me three more days and I'll have every design finalized. To answer your question, I'm the happiest I've been in a really long time."

Her voice carried a hint of wistfulness, and a slight blush colored her cheeks. I loved it and contemplated other ways I could make her flush.

I put the book down on the coffee table and pulled

her fingers from between her teeth.

"These designs are how I envisioned them." Her smile reached her eyes, and I forged ahead. "Hear me out," I said. Waited for a nod and continued. "Stay here. Work with me. Design with me."

Her breath hitched, and I wondered if I had gone too far.

"Are you serious?"

"Yeah. I'm swamped. I love building the bikes. Don't get me wrong, I love the process, but getting my hands dirty is what I enjoy. I can teach you the basic structures of a bike. Knowing the parts of the vessel will help you make your designs fit."

"I don't know."

My heart pulsed steadier against my chest the longer I spoke. Words didn't come easy to me, but I was never more honest than I was in that moment.

"You said you're feeling lost, yet you're happy here. The water has always been a calming place for me. I think it is for you too. Stay. Take time and regroup. Design, keep doing yoga down at the dock, sleep, eat, take care of yourself. The baby." I reached for her belly but stopped.

"You know I do yoga?"

I nodded. A lump formed in my throat, and my body reacted to visions of her fluid movements as she went through the poses.

"Okay. I'll stay, but I have conditions."

I wanted to leap from the couch and pull her into my arms but didn't.

"Of course. I'd expect nothing less."

She lifted her hand and raised her fingers. "One, I make dinner every night, I'd appreciate some company."

"Okay."

"Two, I want you to speak at least five words to me each day."

With each condition she curled a finger down, and I found it difficult not to smile. "Any particular words?"

She rolled her eyes, and I held back a chuckle.

"Sorry, please continue."

"Attach my name to each design. I don't often give my work away, but I don't want payment for them either." She lifted her hand. "I want to draw and create for the pleasure of it, not for the money."

"I can't accept. Your talent shouldn't be free."

"For now, pay me in hospitality. We can renegotiate if either of us finds the agreement insufficient."

I thought for a moment before I held out my hand. She grasped it in a firm shake.

"Why did Susan send you a dildo?" I asked and hoped the off-topic question yielded an involuntary answer.

"Susan's trying to help me with my sexual tension."

I was pleased with the outcome yet confused with the statement. I studied her with a cocked head. "Sexual tension?" I asked, with a voice deeper than intended.

"Yes."

"Care to elaborate?"

She huffed out a breath, stood, and paced the living room. Although I wanted to pull her to me, the evidence of my hardened dick kept me seated.

"I have this insatiable need to orgasm. Pregnancy hormones are fucking with me, and I'm horny all the time. All I have are my hands and they're no longer enough. I'm frustrated and unfulfilled."

I gulped and shifted and adjusted the erection threatening to burst through my zipper. Imagining her masturbating was hotter than fuck. The more she paced and talked, the more vivid the images in my head became.

"If I knew staying with you would make things worse, I would have brought toys. I haven't had sex…I don't know…you were my last. I'm not cut out for a celibate life. I like sex. Fuck, I love it."

She stopped pacing and flopped down beside me with a sigh.

I said nothing, not sure what to say. Another idea formed and seeped through the crevices of my brain before taking a stronghold.

She picked up the toy and wrapped her hand around it.

If I wasn't rock hard before, I was then. She rubbed it up and down and smiled. Whether she intuited my discomfort or had her own visuals running through her mind, I wasn't sure.

"This thing is enormous."

I hid the desire vibrating through my veins as she fondled the fake penis. My idea solidified. I rolled my shoulders and forced my head and not my heart to direct the conversation.

"Not so big."

She faced me, a mix of amusement and curiosity in her gaze. "True. You are bigger."

I gulped and focused.

"If it's orgasms you seek, I can help you with your problem."

****

Ann Marie

"I'm sorry. What?"

"You heard me." He sat stoic, not giving any indication of his inner thoughts.

"I did, but I'm not sure I understood."

He tilted his head and presented me with a slight upturn of one side of his mouth and crinkled eyes.

"You have needs, and I can satisfy them. Let's make a second deal."

I focused on keeping my ass on the couch and not on his wet inviting lips. I didn't notice the stubble coating his chiseled jaw, and I for sure did not consider how it would feel against my bare thighs. I even avoided looking at his messy hair. Nor did I contemplate sinking my fingers through it. No, I didn't do any of that. What I did was sit and play my lies over and over in my head.

Sex, over the past nine years, was a necessary, need satisfying action. Feelings and emotions shoved behind the wall I erected around my heart. I couldn't ignore the threat Morgan posed. Yet I also couldn't deny his offer had my interest.

"I do have needs. But now I have this large, rock-hard penis in my hands. I'm sure it can do the job my fingers can't."

His miniscule squirming reinforced my fortitude. Desire, want, lust, we both had it in spades. As long as we kept our involvement surface deep, I would remain unscathed when we ended our agreement.

"Yet a body craves human touch. The weight of your partner pushing you into a mattress. A shared release," I said.

He nodded and studied me with quiet amusement. "I'm listening. Tell me more."

"If we do this, it's for physical release. We sleep in separate bedrooms. Sex does not make us a couple. Neither of us can develop feelings for the other." I stopped and recentered myself. Just thinking of him touching me, bringing me to completion, and then holding me as we slept was an insurmountable temptation.

"I can live with that," he said, and I was disappointed, yet relieved with his quick answer.

"I have one more condition," he said. "No sharing."

I ran his words through my mind. "As in, no one else as a partner, or no one knows?"

He took a minute before replying. "Both. No one needs to see things that aren't there. Especially Susan."

I nodded. "We do this, no strings. This is about sex. Nothing more."

I struggled with my affirmation. My heart wanted a say, but I denied it a voice. With determination and strength learned from facing a room of executives, I continued. "I end our arrangement when I want."

"Add the same clause for me, and I'll sign on the dotted line."

I raised my hand for a deal-closing shake. He advanced but hesitated before clasping our palms.

"Don't stop. We've made progress. Speak now or forever hold your peace."

He gulped, and it took me a second to note my phrasing.

"What else do you want to talk about?"

"I have questions…and requests about the baby."

I stiffened in my seat but schooled my features. "Okay, I'm an open book." He tilted his head. "Okay, fine. Maybe not so open, but I'll be as honest as I can."

"Tell me about the other guy."

"What do you want to know?"

"Who is he? Are you in love with him? Does he want to be a part of the baby's life? Anything."

I nodded, swallowed, and faced him. "His name is Scott. No, I'm not in love with him. Never was. He doesn't want to be involved until I have a paternity test. We were never in a relationship because I don't do them. But it doesn't mean I sleep around. I stopped sleeping with him a week before I was here in the fall."

Morgan's shoulders relaxed, and the move raised my hackles.

"Were you worried I was sleeping around? Why would it matter? You and I weren't in a relationship. I'm a single woman. I make my own choices."

He lifted his hands in supplication. "I don't care about before. The past is over. What matters is the future." He shifted, took my hand in his, turned them this way and that, and studied our connection. "For the past few days, I've thought a lot. Although, I never saw myself as a father. Didn't want it. But…" He stopped and rubbed his free hand against the back of his neck, "The idea's grown on me, and in some ways, I look forward to it."

"Okay?"

"I should be involved. Go to the baby appointments with you. I will be a part of this kid's life, at least from here on out. Whether or not I'm the father is irrelevant. There's a fifty percent chance I am. I will do what is right."

I failed to hide my reaction. My surprise and fear of his oath clear in my gasp. "You don't have to." His declaration went against the very thing I fought to preserve. All those years ago, all I needed was for my ex to support me. I spent time since then growing stronger. Independent. Self-reliant. I vowed never to be a burden.

"What if this baby isn't yours?"

"Like I said. For now, it doesn't matter. I will be a part of his life, and I will provide for him."

"I don't know if it's a boy." I didn't know what else to say. His passion spoke for the type of man he was underneath the tough exterior, and a little crack appeared around my bruised heart.

He rolled his eyes and grinned. "When she is born, I will be her dad," he said in a huff.

I smiled, and my uterus somersaulted as I imagined him holding a baby encased in pink against his hard and unyielding tattooed chest. The intensity set me off balance, and I was glad I was already seated.

"When's your next appointment?"

"In two weeks. It's in Seattle, but since I'm staying here, I'll ask my doctor for recommendations."

"I would like to go with you. I can drive. After, we can swing by your place and grab whatever items you need for the extended stay."

"I have to call Lian."

"Lian?"

"My business partner."

"I'll give you some privacy."

He stood and headed to the garage when a thought filtered through my mind.

"Morgan?"

"Yeah?"

"We have to tell your parents, don't we?"

He crossed the room and sat beside me.

"My parents. My brothers and cousins too. Not something we can hide, since family brunch is in four days and Ma already knows you're staying with me."

"How would she know?" I asked and groaned at the same time. "Susan told her, didn't she?"

"Yep. She doesn't know about the baby. Susan left that to us."

I stood and paced, stopping at the windows and faced the lake. I hoped the water's slow and melodic flow would help center me and raised my face to the warming mid-day sun. I cringed at the thought of telling his family. Not that I was ashamed. I kept my secrets close to my chest. I didn't see the need for people to be all up in my business.

I didn't feel his approach until his fingers cupped my chin. He tilted my face and my gaze shifted to his. "We'll worry about my family tomorrow. Right now, if you're not making that phone call, I believe I have a deal to deliver on."

His nearness scrambled my brain, and his ensuing grin advertised his joy of my current state.

"Huh?"

"You're insatiable need to orgasm. I'm good at providing relief. Want a demonstration?" he said, his voice low in timbre.

I closed my eyes against the onslaught of the pleasure humming through my body triggered by his words.

Did I want a demonstration? Hell, yes.

"I like the way you think. Phone call can wait. Please note that although I appreciate your eagerness to impress me, your performance and the resulting outcome will be under review. If you feel you are up for the task, then yes. Please commence with said proposal."

His eyes crinkled in amusement and his gaze darted to my lips. I licked them, wetting the sudden dryness.

"Such a polite request."

"There's nothing polite about me." I hoped I sounded genuine. I needed to keep my wits about me when his thumb caressed the skin at my jaw.

"I assure you, when I have you under me, you will not only be begging but you will be doing so nicely," he said, before his mouth descended on mine.

Chapter Twelve

Ann Marie

With every swipe of Morgan's tongue against mine, I lost a bit more of my tenacious hold on my sanity. My blood pounded in my veins and my panties flooded with wetness. His lips soft in contrast to the stubble of his chin. The dueling sensations churned the butterflies in my stomach and the nerves at the apex of my thighs.

Quick, sure moves. He had my back propped up against the window, nudged my feet apart, and wedged one leg in between mine. His exploring hands added to the mix sent me into sensory overload. His fingers traced the skin along my shoulders, then my arms. He drew patterns I didn't have the wherewithal to decipher. I flexed my hips, looking for the friction I needed to reach fulfillment.

"No rush, sweetheart. We have all night," Morgan said. His breath caressed my ear.

I moaned. Forming coherent sentences proved difficult. "Don't…need…stop, don't…so close."

"Wasn't planning on it."

He licked the groove where my neck met my shoulder while his fingers rubbed a path across my ribs. They traveled to the hem of my top and pushed it up.

I stopped the glide of the shirt. Morgan lifted his

face and his gaze penetrated my soul. I hated my sudden insecurity. He ran his thumb against my jaw and waited.

I took a deep breath, enjoying his mixed scent of musk and oil, and used it to center me. "My body's changed."

His eyes narrowed in confusion and studied me until his features softened in understanding.

"You are beautiful, and you're sexy as fuck."

His fingers skated against my breast, teasing out a whine. "God, that feels so good."

He chuckled in my ear, and his breath cooled my heated skin. "Can I take this off?" he asked, tugging my top once again.

After a brief hesitation, I nodded. He lifted my clothes up and over my stomach and exposed my virginal white cotton bra. He ran his fingers over the material as his eyes closed, and my breathing quickened.

"I'm surprised this isn't purple, and I love lace, but this," he continued caressing the fabric, "this is doing all kinds of things to me. Fuck, you're sexy."

Amused with the effects my garment had on him, I licked my lips in anticipation. "Wait until you see my underwear."

"Hmm, I can hardly wait. First, though, I need these nipples in my mouth." He punctuated his want with a pinch. I arched into his touch and dug my fingers into his shoulders, using him to stabilize my weakened knees.

He pulled me in by my waist, not leaving an inch between our bodies. His erection pushed into my stomach, and I rubbed against him.

"Couch, now," he said. His hoarse voice reached deep within me.

He squeezed my thigh. I took the hint and wrapped my leg around him. He yanked my other leg and rested it on his hip. He supported me with his hand on my ass and walked us deeper into the living room, never breaking our kiss.

He lowered us onto the cushions and kneeled between my wide-open legs. I pointed my toes and dug them into the rug beneath them, giving my pelvis a tilt to line his cock with my covered opening. His weight a welcome constriction.

His masculine scent seeped through on my next inhale, and I moaned as he licked up the column of my neck. He unsnapped the front clasp of my bra and with slow deliberate moves, slipped the straps down my arms. Instead of removing it, he bound my wrists with the fabric loops. With a gleam, he lifted my tied hands and placed them over the top of the couch.

"Don't move."

His grasp firm but not painful. I tested his resolve, and he reprimanded me with a gentle bite to my shoulder. I gasped. The sting of his teeth against my flesh followed with his tongue eased the pain and hauled me into the heavens.

I undulated beneath him, my blood on fire, and my core clenched with need. His hardness against me euphoric, and I groaned when he took it away, stepping back.

"What the fuck?" I said, from between clenched teeth, bereft without his touch.

"Like I said before, we have all night."

"Ugh."

"What was that? I didn't quite understand the grunt."

"Too much talking, not enough doing."

He bent at the waist and nudged my chin, none too gentle with his finger and thumb. "You're hot when you're angry," he said, leaning closer. "Don't move."

"Or what?" I arched a single eyebrow and licked my lips, turned on by his commands.

I planted the balls of my feet on the rug and lowered my arms. In an instant, he pushed me into the cushions, straddled me, and weighed down my chest with his. He clasped the makeshift tie and held my hands behind me. The unnatural position forced my tits out.

It had been six months since I relinquished control to a man, and before that it had been nine years. Morgan's command of my body turned me on and freed me. I succumbed to the sensations he evoked, without my usual encumbering thoughts or worries.

No matter our non-existent past, and our uncertain future, I trusted Morgan.

His breath fanned over my face, our noses touching and our lips a whisper apart. I closed the distance and drew his bottom lip between my teeth. He growled and sealed his lips over mine. Held me captive with his body and one hand. Explored me with the other. Goosebumps broke out across my skin in the wake of his trailing fingers as they traveled down my ribs. He rested his thumb on the underside of my breast. Rubbed. Pinched. Drew circles on my sensitive nipple.

He brought me to the cusp then pulled me back. A process he repeated three more times, before my body buzzed, and I was delirious with a violent need. Our tongues tangled, hips flexed, groans echoed off the walls, and skin sweated.

He lifted away, smiled, and flicked his tongue against my jaw. He set a maddening pace and took his time exploring my neck and collarbone. He stopped at the swell of my breasts and buried his nose in my cleavage.

Sniffed.

Licked.

Nipped.

"Morgan, let go of my hands," I said and tugged against his hold. "I want to touch you."

"You smell so good." He inhaled again and released me.

My bindings hindered my movements. I formed a circle with my arms and draped them over his head. I burrowed my fingers into his hair and scratched his scalp with my nails. His grunts grew louder, emboldening my need for him.

He rocked his hips and the friction ignited a blaze in my core.

"I wonder if you taste just as good," he said, his hot breath blowing on my chest.

I hummed, lost to the sensations he incited. "Only one way to find out."

He lifted his lips from the swell of my breast. "In a minute. I'm not done with these yet. God, I love your tits."

He covered my nipple and sucked hard before biting me, then soothing the sting with languid licks.

"I can play with these all night," he said then moved his mouth to my other breast and gave it equal attention.

"I…I think you can make me come just from that alone." I hummed, reveling in the warm wetness of his tongue.

"Wrap your legs around me." He took my thighs and helped me adjust and ground harder against me. He increased the pressure against my core and whispered, "Come for me."

I dropped my head back and used the couch for support while I cataloged every sensation. The fabric of my panties intensified the friction on my clit. His murmured dirty words fanned against the shell of my ear. My nipples tightened and rubbed against his muscular chest. The pulsating of my inner walls readied me for release. The blood rushed through my body, heating me from the depth of my being, and stars imposed on the inside of my closed eyelids.

A convulsing tightness I could no longer control prepared me for the mother of all orgasms.

"That's it, Gorgeous. Take what you need."

His husky voice compelled me forward, and I came, screaming and thrashing, my legs shaking. My body vibrated. Sated, yet eager for more. He rocked against me, dragging out my orgasm. Intractable endless shivers ricocheted through me, and I held onto him with noodle arms. The binding the sole reason they didn't slip.

As the white lights ebbed, and the quivering eased, Morgan rested his forehead on mine. I peeled my eyes open and stared into his bewitching stone-gray ones, darkened with desire. Finding his gaze too intense, I pushed away and giggled at the new sight before me. His cat sat beside me, watching us with a cocked head.

"Oh my God. Your feline friend's a dirty voyeur."

"How'd he get in here?"

"I let him in."

"Huh."

He turned his attention back to me with a shrug. His eyes grew darker and hooded. "I know a more private place."

I tightened my hold on him. The anticipation of having him buried deep inside me gave me the boost of energy I needed. "Then what are you waiting for?"

He grabbed my ass in his powerful hands, lifted me with ease, and walked us to his bedroom.

****

Morgan

Her clothed orgasm rocked a few stones loose around my heart. Her climax sent me back to my teenage years, and I feared I too would come in my pants. I held it together by a thread, thought of anything but the beauty beneath me. My cock was so hard it hurt. I wanted inside her. My self-imposed denial blown away in my hurricane of need.

Holding her close, I walked us to my room and placed her on the bed. I undid the bra around her wrists, and she shifted her weight onto her elbows. Her hooded eyes coated with sexual arousal. I took a step back and pulled my shirt over my head. Her eyes widened. Her gaze darted across my skin. She studied each of my tattoos as I exposed them.

The clink of my belt buckle drew her attention away from my ink. With sure fingers, I opened the clasp and yanked the leather strap through the loops. Her hitched breath and rubbing thighs threatened permanent damage to my dick.

"Up for some more bondage?" I asked, my focus on the flush reddening her skin.

She swallowed and nodded.

"Not tonight, Gorgeous. Tonight, I'm taking you slow, and I want your hands on me when I'm inside you."

Her dilated pupils told me all I needed to know. With a flick, I undid the button on my jeans and left my shaft open to her perusal. She licked her lips. With a growl, I palmed my rock-hard length and tugged it twice. She tracked my movement.

"God, that's hot," Ann Marie said, her voice husky with need.

I chucked off my boots and jeans, crawled on the bed, and straddled her legs. I stopped her from unbuttoning her pants, grasped her wrists and raised her arms above her head.

"We've done this already," Ann Marie said.

"Good. For now, hold on to the headboard." I kissed my way down her jaw. Her neck. I lingered on her breast and sucked one distended nipple and fondled the other. I lifted my mouth long enough to speak, "I want to taste you first," and continued my explorations.

She writhed under me. Her moans filled the silence of the room. I took my time and trailed my tongue along her skin from chest to belly button, pausing at the indent. Her skin clammy beneath my fingers, and a new aroma wafted through the air. I inhaled the scent of her arousal, burrowing it deep into my lungs.

Feelings. Emotions. Ones I didn't want crept to the surface of my mind. I shoved them back and concentrated on the tangible. The silkiness of her skin. The softness of her body against the hardness of mine.

The moans escaping her kiss-swollen lips. The sweat dotting her forehead.

"Morgan," she said and shifted, her tone pleading. "Please."

My hard as granite cock pushed at the fabric covering her inner thigh. Painful. And I fought for control. After six months of fantasies, having her under me tested my restraint. A steadying breath later, I grabbed the waist of her jeans and underwear and removed them with one swift move. I threw the clothes over my shoulder and knocked something to the floor.

I ignored it. My attention riveted on the pink skin I exposed. With a firm grip on her ankles, I opened her legs wide.

"Are you going to touch me or just look at me all day?"

My gaze lifted to hers. Her chestnut eyes now the color of dark chocolate. Lids half-closed. Cheeks flushed.

A sight I craved more than I realized.

Without warning, I descended and licked up her center with one long swipe. She whimpered and slapped at my shoulder. I lifted away and blew a breath across her lips, enjoying her shudders.

"Don't stop."

"Keep your hands on the headboard."

Her arms flung back.

"Move them, I stop."

She nodded and took a deep breath. "Got it, Adam," she said, her eyes shining with mischief.

I tightened my grip, careful not to hurt her. "My name is Morgan. Yell it, whisper it, revere it. I may look like him, but I assure you, I fuck a whole heck of a lot better than he does."

Her pupils dilated, and she giggled. "Sounds promising."

I hummed my agreement and closed my mouth on her center.

Sucked. Licked. Bit.

Her hips jack-knifed off the bed. I grabbed her hips and repositioned her. I opened her lower lips with my thumbs, creating space for my hungry tongue. I ignored her clit and focused on finding every one of her sensitive spots.

She chanted my name. Her voice grew louder with each rendition. I urged her on, gave her clit the attention it needed. Her hips rocked. Her knuckles whitened against the headboard. Her head thrashed on the pillow as the scent of her arousal filled my nose.

I held her hips steady, desperate for her orgasm. To taste her release in my mouth. To hear her scream my name. I became relentless in my pursuits. With each swipe and dip of my tongue, I built her need higher, each time retreating before she came.

"Morgan…"

Lifting away, a primal growl escaped at the sight before me. Flushed skin. Eyes shut tight. Bite-swollen lips. Hair fanned across the pillow. Her chest rose and fell in quick succession, fighting for oxygen.

"Ready?"

Her body tightened beneath me.

"Yes. Yes. God, yes."

I lowered my mouth to her again and swiped my tongue against her folds. Her legs shook. Vibrated against my shoulders. I pushed one finger into her hot pussy, followed with another. Scissored then curved them as I found her g-spot.

Her body jerked. Her control obliterated. Her screams filled the room, and I didn't relent until the waves shaking her body subsided. She lay limp on my bed, hairline soaked with sweat, and hands no longer holding the headboard. She wasn't unconscious, but damn near close.

"Open your eyes, Gorgeous."

She did, her gaze unfocused.

"Ready for more?"

She licked her lips, and I leaned over her for a condom from my nightstand. I crawled up her body and fitted my covered cock against her center. She opened her legs wider and dug her heels into my ass and pushed me forward with determination.

"Got your energy back, huh?"

"Shut up and get in there."

I enjoyed our banter and messed with her although my body screamed for my own release. I knew the moment I entered her warm, tight channel I would lose the battle. I wasn't ready for the night to end.

Leveraging her feet on the mattress, she pushed and sucked the first couple of inches into her. There was no fight left in me. With my hands bracing most of my weight, I thrust my hips forward, giving her all of me.

We groaned, our foreheads rested together, our breath intermingling. I held steady, gave her a minute to adjust, and the tingles in my spine to abate.

"God, I'm so sensitive. I fucking love pregnancy hormones," Ann Marie said to the ceiling,

I stilled, my thoughts becoming lucid. Although I was hard inside of her, my lust vanished.

"Fuck. I can't do this."

Ann Marie raised herself on her elbows, her confusion clear. "Do what? Fuck me?"

I shook my head and pulled back. I groaned at the loss of her, but I kept my wits about me. "You're pregnant."

Shock, or maybe sarcasm, colored her face. "Thank you, Captain Obvious, for telling me what I already know."

"No…I…no. I forgot for a minute. I've been rough on you. I could hurt the baby."

I stood from the bed. Paced the floor. Ran my hands through my hair. She tracked me but remained silent. The tension thick.

"What if he can see my dick? What if every time I fuck you…push in, I'm harming him?"

Ann Marie sat on her knees and pulled the sheets around her body, and I hated her sudden modesty. More the fact I caused her withdrawal.

"Morgan, the baby's fine. It's not like you're going to knock on his door."

Funny, yet I didn't laugh. "How do you know? Did you ask the doctor?"

She shook her head. "No. But if it wasn't safe, she would have told me at the last visit."

"No. No, we can't do this. I can't hurt y…the baby." I stopped pacing, grabbed my boxer-briefs from a drawer, and dressed. "I'm sorry. I…just can't."

I strode out of the room, silencing further argument and avoided her. Avoided her disappointment and pain. Leaving near about killed me.

I leaned against the wall in the hallway and took big gulps of air. My heart thundered against my ribs and my vision wavered. White spots swirled, and I closed my eyes against the wave of lightheadedness. I didn't know which was worse. Fucking her and hurting the baby or abandoning ship.

I cursed and scrubbed my face. I couldn't stay away. Succumbing, I took two more deep breaths and walked back into the bedroom. I laid down behind her, pulled her to me, and spooned her in silence. I rested my hand on her belly, thumbs caressing the tightened skin, and nuzzled her hair.

"What are you doing?"

I pulled her closer, but I didn't have an answer.

She didn't push.

Forcing air into my lungs, I held her tighter against me. Her body softened, molded to mine. Her breathing evened out and soft snores filled the quiet room.

I wrapped my leg over hers and tucked her cold feet between my calves. Surprised by the unexpected comfort of having her in my arms, I sighed and drifted off. We were sharing a bed and although it was against our rules, I didn't have the energy or mindset to care.

Chapter Thirteen

Ann Marie

I woke up with a kink in my neck and Morgan's hard body beneath me. I lay still. My head rose and fell with the beat of his breathing and recalled the previous four days. We hadn't had sex yet, but he took care of my needs each day. Sometimes, more than once, since I admitted my nausea subsided, and I slept better after having an orgasm. He made it his personal mission to keep my sickness at bay.

His concern surprised me. It shouldn't have. He loved his family and was protective of them. He opened his circle of protection and included the baby, but his actions opened a void I usually ignored.

Morgan's breath danced across my hair, but I didn't shift away. Earlier, tiredness tugged at me, and Morgan applied his creative talents and encouraged me to nap. Conflicting emotions ran between my heart and brain when I awoke and discovered—not for the first time—he slept beside me. Although I shouldn't, I liked the feel of his body pressed against mine.

With a weary sigh, I stowed my inner struggles and enjoyed the serenity of the moment. Dust particles floated in the air, visible through the shaft of the early afternoon sunlight streaming through the windows.

A knock on the door disturbed our peace. Morgan

stirred from his slumber. It wasn't until he tightened the arm around me, I realized my hand's placements. One beneath my cheek and the other on his very impressive and hard erection. I lingered longer than I should and fought the temptation to wrap my fingers around him, slide down, and wake him in the most delicious way.

He tugged the strands of my hair. I lifted my head and stared into eyes lit with lust and amusement.

"Enjoying yourself?"

His scratchy, gravel-like waking voice dove straight to my core, and I clamped my legs together. A sad attempt at staving off the rising heat between them. After a final squeeze, I removed my hand.

"He's impressive. Couldn't help myself."

His fingers played against my scalp, and moans escaped untethered.

The doorbell rang again, and Morgan stiffened. I pushed off his chest, and he moved so we sat side by side. I shivered at the immediate loss of his body heat. His gaze roamed over my minimal clothing and skewed tank top. He rubbed his hands down his face and inhaled before pinning me with a heated stare.

My body responded, and I leaned toward him.

Instead of pulling me closer, he reached behind us for the blanket off the back of the couch and wrapped it around my shoulders.

Repeated knocks pounded at the door.

"Expecting someone?" he asked and retrieved his phone from the floor.

"Nope."

"Everyone knows the code to the garage."

He shook his head, stood, and adjusted the bulge in his pants. My rapt attention was met with a smug smile.

With a wink, he held out his hand and steadied me to my feet.

His laugh warmed me, and without thinking I stood on my tiptoes and kissed his jaw. His sharp intake delightful to me. I dropped the blanket and headed to the kitchen with an extra swagger in my step.

"Want some coffee?" I asked over my shoulder.

He grunted his answer, and I giggled.

"For every action there is a consequence," he said as he stepped to the front door.

Away from his knowing eyes, my smile grew, and I made my drink. Muffled voices carried through the air, incoherent because of the distance. I listened for a minute and when no one approached, I daydreamed, looking out the window at the peaceful lake. I held the steaming mug close to my chest and inhaled the rich aroma.

"Ann Marie," Morgan yelled, startling me out of my reverie.

I headed for him, cautious of the hot drink in my grip. I couldn't see past Morgan's broad shoulders. He rested his arm against the open wood and kept the guest outside and hidden from view. His tense neck and back muscles a loud warning sign.

At my approach, Morgan shifted, and I glimpsed the man standing at the threshold. Shocked, I stumbled and dropped the mug. It shattered on the entry-way slate tile. Pieces of ceramic ricocheted off the floor and lodged into my shins. I didn't know which was worse. The pain from the hot liquid, the pain in my pierced skin, or seeing the asshole at Morgan's door.

Morgan was by my side before I blinked and lifted me into his arms. He raced me to the kitchen, turned on the faucet and set me on the countertop. With a gentleness I found surprising, he took the hand I braced against my stomach and placed it under the running lukewarm water.

"Don't move," he said and knelt but kept one hand on my thigh. He grabbed a clean rag, a first aid kit, and tweezers from the cabinet beneath the sink.

His fingers skimmed my leg and traced the trickling blood. With steady hands, he pulled fragments of the mug out of my skin, and with a tenderness I didn't expect, he tended to my wounds.

My heart stuttered at his quick, focused and loving attention. Tears I failed to keep at bay welled in my eyes. He noticed, stood, and swiped the drops, cupping my cheeks in his large palms.

"Does it hurt? You can take acetaminophen. I have some in the bathroom," he said and stepped away.

I grabbed his wrist before he moved too far. The concern on his face when he turned to me didn't help my ever-increasing heart rate. I pulled his arm. He came closer and stepped in between my legs. I rested my hand on his jaw and to my surprise, he leaned into my touch.

"I'm okay."

Lost in the moment, I forgot about our visitor until he cleared this throat. I jumped back, and Morgan planted his hands on my hips, steadying me. I peered around Morgan's broad shoulders and narrowed my eyes as tension rose in my body.

"What the fuck are you doing here?"

Scott stepped forward, and Morgan moved out from between my legs to stand by my side. He kept his body angled so he could see Scott and me at the same time.

"I'm here for you," Scott said, undeterred by my scowl. "I went by your apartment yesterday. Your neighbor told me you were out of town."

"So you tracked me down? How the fuck did you know where I was?" I shifted, wanting to stand and confront him, but Morgan squeezed my thigh and held me in place.

Scott waved his hand, dismissing my question. "You're carrying my baby, and I've decided you need to be with me."

I almost fell off the counter, and if it wasn't for Morgan's fingers digging into my leg, I would have.

****

Morgan

"Be with you? Not happening. How the hell did you find me?" Ann Marie shouted at him.

He didn't answer her question. Violence, other than goofing with my brothers, never had a place in my life. I could remember one other time I had the urge to deck another person, but a six-year-old Susan beat me to the punch. The asshole in my kitchen would not be so lucky. I clenched my fist by my side and fought the impulse.

Ann Marie squirmed under my hand. "Sorry," I whispered, and loosened my hold. I helped her off the counter and secured her behind me with an arm braced around her front.

Scott widened his stance, legs bent as if readying for an attack. Despite my best efforts not to, I chuckled. Dressed in a pastel green polo and khakis, he was the least intimidating twat I ever encountered. Ann Marie could have toppled him with a single puff.

I was fed up with his display and mirrored his posture, reaching for a deep, growling baritone. "She asked you twice now. If she has to ask you a third time, things will get ugly."

Scott's glare swung between Ann Marie and me. His leering rubbed against my already frayed nerves. I disliked him on sight, but his remarks and the continued stand-off pushed me toward hatred. An emotion I never experienced before.

I shoved down my repulsion and stepped closer to Scott. He backed up a step for every one of mine until his back hit a wall. He raised his hands in surrender but didn't have enough smarts to keep his mouth shut.

"I came to collect Ann Marie. Her friend told me where she was."

Ann Marie shifted behind me. With a hand on my arm, she stepped to my side and shook her head. "No one knows I'm here. Not even Lian."

He let out a nervous laugh and swayed on his feet. His shoes took his attention as he mumbled. Ann Marie pushed at my back, and I canted closer to him.

"Say again?"

His gaze flickered, never on either one of us for long. With pinked cheeks, he said, "I tracked you."

Without thought, I charged. I slammed into him with my hand around his throat. My reaction unusual for me. My need to protect, not.

Ann Marie moved behind me. The heat from her palm on my bicep calmed the burning flames running through my veins.

I leaned close so Scott could see the anger in my eyes. "How did you track her?"

He gulped and looked at Ann Marie. I shifted and used my body to force her out of his line of sight.

"How. Did. You. Track. Her?"

His Adam's apple bopped underneath my palm, and I loosened my grip. Gave him the air he needed to speak.

"Through her phone," he said around his coughing fit and lifted his hands to mine against his throat.

I tired of his evasive answers and tightened my hold. My reaction better than the violent one I was inclined to commit.

"How?"

"There's an app…" he said.

His stuttering grated on my nerves.

"What are you talking about? I have nothing that allows you to find me. I have never given you access to my location," Ann Marie said and stepped closer.

His gaze swung between us, sweat beading on his forehead.

"I installed one on your phone."

In an instant, I dropped Scott and wrapped my arms around Ann Marie. I pinned her to my front as she leaped at his crumbling body.

Her chest heaved, and I dared a tighter hold without compromising her belly and the baby. I ignored the wheezing coming from Scott and gave Ann Marie my entire focus.

"Breathe," I said and lowered my mouth to her ear. I regulated my breath for her to match. She synced hers with mine, and I loosened my grip. She sagged against me, using my strength to stay upright. I worried for her, but first I had to deal with the now rising Scott.

"Uninstall the app on your phone. Then show us

the app on hers and she'll do the same," I said with a growl.

Scott used the door frame to regain his footing, and I shifted, so Ann Marie was once again behind me. With a snarl, I stormed forward and smiled when he backed into the wall.

He pulled out his phone, and with shaking hands, he clicked at the screen. He showed me the display and waited for my nod before pocketing it then extended his arm to Ann Marie. She didn't move, and I dipped my fingers into her back pocket. I plucked out her phone, held it to her to unlock.

Moving so I could watch, I handed him the phone. "Show me what you're doing."

He maneuvered through each step and passed the phone back to me after he deleted the app. I handed it over to Ann Marie and spoke to her without taking my eyes off Scott.

"Change your password."

Ann Marie's gaze flickered back and forth between me and the phone. With a huff that made me smile, she relented.

She pocketed her device, glared at Scott, and stepped into his space. Her bare toes butted against the edge of his shoes. The full foot in their height difference didn't deter her malice.

"Leave. Don't come back. Don't call. You are not welcome to any of the appointments. I will let you know when I'm in labor, but I'm not allowing you in the room. After the baby's born, I'll get the paternity test. If the baby is yours, then and only then will I talk to you. 'Til then, you are out of my life. Are we clear?"

I wasn't going to lie. I grew hard at her vehemence.

Her strength and self-assuredness arousing. The fire burning in her eyes, thrilling. I wanted to throw her over my shoulder and do wicked things to her.

Tearing my gaze away, I slanted it toward Scott and arched an eyebrow. I almost laughed at his hasty retreat. The house door slammed, and I chuckled low.

Ann Marie's heated gaze wavered for a second, before her focus lasered on me. I fought my instincts. The desire to slam my lips against hers too tempting.

"Thank you for taking care of my cuts and this situation, but if you ever decide for me again, you better protect your balls," she said and wagged her finger in my face.

I snatched her wrist and met her hard stare with one of my own. "What the hell are you talking about?"

She yanked her hand from my hold, and if I was a lesser man, I would have cowered. Leveling me with a fiery gaze and pinched lips, she angled closer. Her breath brushed across my face.

"You don't get to tell me how to handle him, nor what to do. Ever."

She stepped back, and I followed. Bent at the waist, I leaned in her space. Our mouth a whisper apart.

"As long as you are in my house, you are mine to look after."

The words escaped before I thought about it, but I didn't care to retract them. They were the truth coming from deep in my gut.

She huffed, but behind the irritation lay lust. With a narrowed stare and a smile that had me protecting my crotch, she said, "The only thing that owns me is my new pink slice of dildo heaven."

She startled a chuckle out of me. Her anger

diffused replaced with a smile that stole my breath away. For the first time since she delivered her news, a weight lifted off my shoulders.

"We're leaving for my parents in one hour. Go get ready, Princess."

Ann Marie poked a finger at my chest. She shook her head and lowered her hand after tapping it against my hard pecs, which I flexed—of course.

"Cut that shit out," she said. Her giggle music to my ears. "I'm going to go, not because you demanded it, but because I'm starving, and your mom's cooking is amazing."

She turned on her heels with a hair flick and hip flair.

I tracked her wiggling, heart-shaped ass as she walked out of the kitchen. At the foot of the steps, she stopped and looked at me from over her shoulder, with a fist on her cocked hip.

"By the way, never mistake me for a Princess. I am a Queen."

I held in my laugh until her door clicked shut.

Chapter Fourteen

Ann Marie

"Are you kidding me right now? It's a five-minute walk."

"Just get in the truck, Ann Marie. You're pregnant."

To say Morgan's unpredictable behavior confused me was an understatement. Between the one-eighty in his actions the previous few days and the new non-walking mandate, I was about ready to wring his neck. Fighting for the better half of the past hour had exhausted me, and a ride was what I wanted, but my stubbornness kept me from admitting it.

"I'm pregnant, not an invalid."

"Walking can put a strain on your back."

I stopped my factitious stomp, with one foot raised inches above the floor. I stared at him, and attempted comprehension. "Where did you get that idea from?"

I stood in shock as Morgan's face colored a deep red beneath his two-day-old stubble. He rubbed his hand along his nape and avoided eye contact. His demeanor sheepish, but I knew better. There was no way his answer would embarrass this cocky, laissez-faire man.

"It's not important. Get in the truck. We're going to be last ones to arrive."

He held the passenger door open. If our volatile relationship hinted at our future, I anticipated more arguments. Better to give in to this one and stand my ground on others. With a straight back and an air of indifference, I sauntered—yes, sauntered—to the truck, and grabbed the 'Oh Shit' handle. I hoisted up onto the bench and almost lost my footing when he helped guide me in with a palm to my butt. I reached for the seatbelt to find Morgan pulling it across my belly and clicking it in place.

"Gee, Morgan. It bears repeating. I'm pregnant, not an invalid."

He removed his hand but didn't step away. His lips close to mine as he turned, his eyes darkened. My breath hitched. My desire mirrored in the dark pools of his irises.

With a shake of his head, he stepped back, and the lust infused air dissipated. I took a deep inhale as he crossed the front of the truck to the driver's side. He slipped in with ease and filled the small space with his scent. I wondered if I could hold my breath without dying from lack of oxygen for the two-minute drive.

"Looking a little red there. Need water?"

I shook, then nodded my head. My mouth grew parched, and I struggled to swallow. "Water would be great."

I groaned when he reached in front of me and took a bottle out of the dashboard compartment. I hoped he would have left the truck and gave me time to gather my wits about me. He twisted the top off and handed it to me. I concentrated on taking slow sips. I didn't want water dribbling down my chin, although my dry throat demanded I guzzle.

I capped the bottle and placed it in the cup holder in the middle console. I didn't realize Morgan's hand rested in the same place and my hand brushed against his skin. A zing traveled up my arm, and I flung away and hit my face in the process.

"Ouch," I yelped, holding my nose.

Big, calloused fingers wrapped around my wrists, and Morgan pulled my hands aside. My watery vision blurred his features, but his breath fanned across my skin. Blinking, I cleared the tears. Morgan shifted in his seat, leaned over the center, and brought his face close enough our mouths hovered. Any movement would result in our lips touching.

"Twice in one day, Miss Damsel."

I pushed at his chest. My fingers itched to play with the pebbled nipples under his shirt. "I am no damsel, and I don't need a hero. Not my fault you like playing the role."

With a single raised eyebrow, he plopped back in his seat. "Would you rather I be the villain? Besides, they have all the fun."

I laughed and winced at the twinge of pain in my nose. "I've been known to break a rule or two," I said and smacked his chest—again, because hello, pecs.

He rubbed his hands together, and the look of childish glee on his face made me laugh again.

"Stop. It hurts."

"Want some ice?" he asked, unbuckling his seat belt.

I stayed him with a hand to his forearm. "No. I'm fine. Just don't make me laugh for a few minutes."

"I'm not a funny guy."

I stared at him in disbelief. "Seriously? I would

have never guessed. Would you say you're more the broody, quiet, pain-in-the-ass kind of guy?"

"Ha ha. Sarcasm noted."

"Just shut up and get us to your parents. I'm hungry."

"I could say something here, but I value my balls."

"That's the least of your worries. If you make any pregnancy jokes, I swear I will strangle you."

He chuckled and started the truck. "I'd like to see you try."

I faced him and studied his profile. The light streaming in the window shadowed his angular face. He pulled off serious, but his twitching lips gave him away.

"You better watch out. I know where you sleep, and I can be as quiet as a mouse."

"Considering you are the size of a mouse, I don't find that hard to believe. However, if you are in my bed, I guarantee you, you won't be quiet. In fact, you just might wake the neighbors."

My pussy tingled at the innuendo, and I fought the urge to rub my thighs together.

"No sex. No screaming," I said under my breath, frustrated with his continued hold-out.

He braced his hand on the back of my seat and backed out onto the road. Instead of removing it once we were on the street, he caressed my neck, sending a shiver down my spine.

"I heard that."

"Is that so?"

"Yep." He pulled into his parents' driveway and parked. He turned my way and placed his hand on my thigh.

I stared at his fingers, and I swear I felt the heat

from each individual digit. His other hand cupped my chin, drawing my attention to his face. He leaned close, his cheek against mine, and whispered in my ear.

"Tonight, I will prove to you what I can do between the sheets. I have all the time in the world to bring you to the brink over and over again until you're begging for release. And when you're sweating and begging, I will grant you mercy. Let you come. I won't do this once, but I will do it until your body's sated and your mind's devoid of thought. There is nothing more amazing than a woman letting go, and you Ann Marie will let go. You will give me complete control."

I straightened my spine, counteracting my need to melt into the seat. His words heated me from the inside out. No other man had ever done that. Yet with Morgan, I allowed him the control to give me my pleasure. I almost pleaded he took it, and that scared the crap out of me.

I turned so my lips brushed his cheek. It was my turn to whisper. "Don't forget, two can play this game, and I hate to lose."

I pulled back, opened my door, and jumped down. I waited for him at the front of the truck. He approached with his swagger and smirk in place.

"I'm still angry with you. This little banter we had going means nothing."

He put his hand to his heart and leaned down with an innocent look. "Are you trying to convince me or yourself?"

"You. I already know all I need to know."

"Oh, yeah?"

I stood on my tiptoes, and he closed the distance until our noses touched. "You don't do love or relationships. The reason you're putting up with me is the possibility of you having fathered my child. This banter, friendliness, sex, and hospitality are all just for show. Lucky for you, I'm not the type to delude myself into thinking otherwise, and I am right there with you. I don't want a relationship or love or forever." I tapped his cheek, turned on my feet, and walked away.

What I told him was the truth, and if I kept repeating it, then maybe I could convince my heart to fall in line.

****

Morgan

I stayed back, simmering in my anger as she walked up the steps. I didn't know what possessed me to say what I did in the truck. I was on a razor's edge since we started our deal. I refused her offers to return the favor, and I had the worst case of blue balls in history of mankind. Her ex showing up at my front door triggered a new level of possessiveness I never felt before.

Her reminder should have cooled my jets. Instead, it fueled the fires. Her words pissed me off, and I wanted to prove her wrong. It wasn't all about sex.

I shook my head and dislodged the nonsense formulating in my brain. I focused on the sway of her hips. The ass hugging jeans. The hair I wanted to gather and hold as I took her from behind.

I growled. Glad I was far enough she couldn't hear me. I didn't know which was worse. Fighting my unorthodox thoughts or the growing problem in my pants.

"Hey, are you going to stand there and check out

my ass all day or are you coming?" she said as she stepped onto the porch.

I grunted and concentrated on putting one foot in front of the other. With a calming breath, I pulled ahead and reached the door. I opened it without knocking and waited for her to enter.

She flicked her hair back and a hint of her fruity scent wafted around me. I closed my eyes in appreciation. My house already smelled like her. At first it irritated me. The lingering scent reminded me of her presence, but the longer she stayed, the more pressed I was to find reasons to dislike it. Or her.

Ma's shrieks and open arms greeted us as we stepped in. She wrapped them around me and squeezed my waist. Although she was a foot shorter than me, her hold was bone crushing. I kissed the top of her head and gave in to the embrace.

After a moment, she pulled away, squeezed my cheeks—the sole person I allowed the concession—and turned to Ann Marie.

"I'm so glad you came. Susan wasn't sure you would. Tell me, how are you?"

"I'm good, Mrs. Anderson. Thank you for having me."

She took Ann Marie's hand in hers and tugged her to the couch. Their heads canted toward each other, and they spoke like long-lost reunited friends. My mom's enthusiasm brought a smile to my face.

I loved my parents. They welcomed everyone into their home. Throughout the years they invited our friends. They welcomed them into our fold. Often Ma fed over sixteen people with an unwavering warmth.

With their attention diverted, my mind wandered.

Conflicting emotions played on repeat. Ann Marie's words from earlier rang true, but I hated the hollowness they created in my chest.

I rubbed the heel of my hand against my sternum and attributed my unease to the task before me. I stepped closer and sat on the coffee table in front of them.

"Actually, Ma. There's something I'd like to talk to you and Dad about before everyone else gets here."

Ann Marie glared, Ma smiled, and Dad scowled from his recliner to my right.

I groaned at Ma's smile. Although not a meddler, she hated my lifestyle. She wanted to see all of us settled with families of our own.

Without preamble and time ticking away before my siblings arrived, I faced my mom.

"Ann Marie's pregnant."

Ann Marie stiffened, her frown grew deeper, and skin flushed red—either with anger or embarrassment. I couldn't tell.

Ma's ear-piercing squeal punched through the air, and I cringed.

"I might be the dad."

"Might be?" Ma quieted, and confusion marred her face.

Ann Marie's skin turned ashen—a look I wasn't used to seeing on her—before she squared her shoulders and glared at me.

"Mrs. Anderson, what Morgan's trying to say is that I'm not sure who the daddy is."

Ma wrapped her arm around Ann Marie's shoulder and pulled her closer. "Oh, sweetie. Whatever the circumstances, I'm certain you and Morgan will figure this out."

Ma tilted her head, her gaze unwavering. Questioning. Yet she held back. Her control impressed me. Dad, though, surprised me.

"This might be none of our business, but if Morgan's not the father, then who is?"

"Ted," my mother said with admonishment.

"It's okay." Ann Marie side-eyed me and placated my mother with a hand on her leg. "Mr. Anderson, Mrs. Anderson, I'm sorry I'm putting you through this. The other man is someone I saw for a while. We ended things before…before I was with Morgan."

"Is it rude of me to say, I hope the baby is Morgan's?" Ma leaned into Ann Marie with a gleam in her eyes.

"If you make her a grandma, it will elevate you to the top of her favorites." My dad chuckled, lifted his newspaper, and settled back, but kept his gaze on Ann Marie. "You're family now. We're here for you both."

For him, any further discussion was fruitless. Without the facts, my dad and I didn't dwell on an issue.

The front door opened. Pax and Susan walked into the house. Susan approached with trepidation, and at Ann Marie's smile, Susan's shoulders dropped. Without a word, she closed the distance between us. She hugged me from behind and rested her cheek on my shoulder.

"I'm so happy for you."

I tapped her arm, but before I could respond Pax pulled her away. "You have your own woman now, hands off of mine."

"I'm no one's woman," Ann Marie said as she tugged Susan's elbow. Together, along with my mother, they headed out of the living room.

I stared at their retreating backs, dumbfounded with the renewed twinge in my chest I refused to acknowledge. I hated not being able to claim her as mine. I should have felt relief, yet I wanted to race after her, pull her into my arms, and kiss her until she took her words back. I didn't realize I growled until Pax laughed and smacked my shoulder.

"Welcome to the club, man."

I shoved his hand off and fought the urge to hit him back. "It's not what you think. I'm looking out for her and the baby."

Pax's eyes wrinkled in the corners, and he patted my shoulder, again. "Sure thing, brother. Whatever gets you through the day," he said, and followed the ladies into the kitchen.

My responding huff made my father laugh, and the empty feeling returned to the pit of my stomach.

Chapter Fifteen

Ann Marie

"Ann Marie is taking some time off from work. She's staying with me while we decide on parenting arrangements."

Morgan's answer to his mother's question about our immediate future infuriated me. I moved my leg, dislodging his hand from my thigh. His family sitting around the large dining table kept me from decking him.

"Shit, man. For a second there I thought you would say you were moving to Seattle," Dustin said from beside me.

"That wouldn't work," Morgan answered with a shrug of his shoulders.

"Why not?" I asked, and anger rose in my veins.

"Don't be ridiculous. We already discussed this. Besides, my house is bigger than your apartment. My family's here. My business…"

"Man, shut up. You're digging a hole you'll never climb out of," Pax warned Morgan.

"Ridiculous? You think I'm being ridiculous? I didn't create my company and make it into a success by being ridiculous." I wished my fiery gaze scorched him into silence, but either he was too stupid or too cocky to notice.

"It's probably the hormones then."

My chin dropped as a collective groan echoed around the table.

"Typical." I raised my arms and sat back in my chair. "Why is it men use hormones as an excuse for women's behaviors? Come up with a better argument. I dare you."

"You dare me? That's childish…"

"Oh my God, he didn't. Did he just say that?" Foster whispered, yet loud enough others nodded their heads.

"So now, I'm not only being ridiculous, but I'm also hormonal and childish. Do you have any more insults you want to lob my way?"

"I don't see what you're all worked up about. Stress is not good for you or the baby."

A hand tapped me on the shoulder, and I turned to Mrs. Anderson's smiling face. I hadn't noticed her advance.

"You two have either been hostile or fighting since you walked into this house. In our family we deal with an argument in one way."

"Ma. You've got to be kidding me," Morgan said while everyone snickered.

Bewildered, my gaze narrowed as not a single person looked me in the eye. Mrs. Anderson held up what appeared to be an old, well-worn, tattered shirt.

"You know what this means? Time for The Get Along Shirt. We're waiting," she said, and handed it to Morgan. He took it with hesitation before he stood and pulled my chair back.

I stood, confusion slowing my movement.

"When we were kids, lots of arguments broke out.

Ma got sick of it and to teach us to work out our differences, she devised this T-shirt of torture." Morgan shook the clothing in his hand.

"Not before she tried a couple of other things first, but this one worked best," Dustin said.

"We all hated it so damn much we did what we needed to do to get out of it," Parker added.

Still lost, the unsolicited remarks didn't help.

"This is going to be fun," Pax said, as Susan smacked him in the arm and then agreed with him.

"Ignore them," Morgan said, and slipped his finger along my jaw and urged my focus back to him. "She came up with this idea, and since none of us dared fight her on it, it became a thing. Whenever we argued with no end in sight, Ma made us wear this shirt." He held it up for me to see.

I ran my fingers along the fabric, stretched and faded, from use and too many wash cycles.

"Whoever was arguing had to wear the shirt and work out their differences if they wanted to get out of it," Morgan continued.

"It was horrible when more than two of us were fighting," Pax said around a contained laugh. "Especially in the summer when boys, hormones, heat, and sweat mingled. We agreed really fast when that happened."

"Hey, remember the time Parker and I wanted to go jet skiing and you, Caden, and Morgan wanted to go for a hike, but Mom wouldn't let the older boys go without us young ones? You were supposed to be watching us. Oh my God, and then Parker needed to pee, and we had to work as one to get to the woods so he could, and then he peed all over Morgan's leg.

Morgan's scream was so high-pitched, and none of us could cover our ears. Then…then…" Dustin said as he held onto his stomach. "Then we fell, and everyone was so grossed out, we kept rolling over each other in the puddle of pee."

I couldn't help but smile at his sheer love for the memory.

"Or how about Kate's first date, when Pax and Caden hated the idea, and started an argument so when her date showed up, they were huddled in the shirt? They refused to agree because they wanted to go on the date with her because a friend told them the guy liked to dine and dash," Parker said, and Kate rose and hit Pax.

"I didn't know that. I thought you were trying to keep him from kissing me."

"There was that," Pax said with a shrug.

Morgan huffed, and all eyes focused on him.

"Are there any more stories involving Morgan," I asked.

His family looked at each other, a few heads tilted. "No. Morgan hardly wore the shirt, come to think of it," Jesse answered.

"If you guys are done, I'd like to get this over with." Morgan waited for the head nods, then brought his gaze back to me. "We stayed in it until we came up with a solution. Ma is now saying you and I have to wear it."

My jaw dropped open. "Are you kidding me?"

" 'Fraid not. It's tradition. It's the shirt or agreement," Mrs. Anderson said. "Wear it and find a way to get along."

With a resigned sigh, Morgan pulled the shirt over

his head, tugged me into his side and rolled it over mine. I slipped my right arm through the hole, but with our height difference, my face didn't reach the neck.

"We're going to have to sit down for this," Morgan said. He hoisted me up, sat down in his chair, and dragged mine closer to his. I plopped down, but the pulled-tight shirt gave us little room to move.

"There is no way we can eat in this," Morgan said under his breath.

"I'm hungry. Just say you're wrong in bossing me, and we can get out of it."

"Hell, no. You agree I'm looking out for you and the baby."

"Looking out for us doesn't give you the right to rule my every move."

"I'm not. You're in hysterics…"

Irritated and not wanting to hear any more of his bullshit, I bit his neck. I chuckled when he fought me off with a little wiggle.

"Shit, woman. Why're you biting me?"

"I told you I was hungry…and you insulted me again."

He sighed deep, and our gazes locked.

From across the table, Susan giggled into Pax's shoulder. He buried his face in her hair, but his laughter rang loud and clear through his shaking chest. I shot them my meanest glare, but that sent them into a deeper fit of laughter. If I wasn't so uncomfortable and wasn't the one in the T-shirt, I would've laughed along with them.

****

Morgan

"Stop fidgeting," I hissed and dug my fingers into her waist. "Straddle me."

"I'm not straddling you."

"Why not?"

"Your entire family is right here."

"You forget my mother is the one that put us in this T-shirt to begin with."

I ignored everyone at the table. I hated being the center of attention and the sooner Ann Marie cooperated, the faster our release from hell.

"I'm hungry."

"So eat already. What's that got to do with me sitting on your lap?"

"I can't with one hand." I shifted in my seat and didn't give Ann Marie a choice. I hauled her across me and spread her legs on either side of mine.

She struggled and with her tits smashed against my chest, her spread thighs positioned her pussy over my cock, I grew hard in an instant. I ignored my growing problem, but the more she moved, the tighter my pants became. I knew the moment she felt my erection. Her breath hitched on the next inhale. I tightened my arms around her, one inside and the other outside of the T-shirt.

Under the cover of the material, I slipped my fingers in the back waistband of her jeans and caressed the skin. "Having you on my lap is turning me the fuck on. Stop moving," I whispered in her ear and couldn't resist nipping the lobe. She did as I asked with another snag in her breath. "Pull your arm in."

"Why?"

I pinched my lips against the forming involuntary smile. "Because I want to eat."

Ann Marie's huff held little heat and with a bit of help she pulled her arm through the hole.

"Baby bump is in the way. I have nowhere for my arms."

"Wrap them around my waist."

With a gleam that had me regretting my directive, she inched her small hands under my shirt and rubbed her fingers against my skin. I fought a groan and swatted her butt with my still hidden hand. She giggled in my ear, and I forgot about the food, my family, the baby.

"Morgan," Pax said.

I looked his way and nodded in thanks. If it had been one more minute, I feared I would have gone too far. He laughed and took a bite of his dinner.

With my composure somewhat reset, I maneuvered my arm through the second hole and picked up a fork. I speared a piece of chicken and lifted it to her mouth.

Her eyes narrowed, and she shifted back on my lap, separating us before she wrapped her lips around the food. Her gaze never left mine as she licked off the remnants of the sauce off the side of her mouth. Skin I wanted to run my tongue over.

"They're cheating," Dustin said.

My mom's amused stare studied us. "They're not. They're already working together."

"No, they're not, and my innocent eyes can't take much more of this."

Ma guffawed. "Innocent eyes my-you-know-what."

"Whatever. I still say they're cheating and canoodling at the table. You've never let Parker or me get away with that."

Ann Marie snickered and whispered, "Canoodle? Did he just say canoodle? How old is he?"

"Unfortunately for the world, he's a grown man stuck in a teenager's body."

"I heard that," Dustin yelled.

"Good."

"I'll have you know I am no teenager. I've had years of honing my skills." Dustin blew a breath on his fingers, shined them on his shirt, and earned himself a smack on the head from my dad. "Sorry," Dustin grumbled and hung his head as if in shame, but his smirk said otherwise.

For ten minutes I fed us, alternating bites between us. It was intimate and although my family surrounded us, my need for her grew under the cover of her butt.

"When I suggested the shirt, it was for you to talk, not make kissy faces at each other. I hate to admit it, but Dustin's right," Ma said, and Dustin cheered while the others laughed. "It might be best for you two to go out on the deck and clear the air."

Arguing with Ma was pointless. I stood, arms wrapped around Ann Marie, and gripped her ass. She circled her legs around me, and I walked us out. I sat on a chaise lounge and straddled the sides.

Neither of us spoke for several minutes.

"Morgan?"

"Yes?"

"How did you know what kind of pain relief I could take?" At my hesitation, she elaborated. "You said I could take acetaminophen when I broke the mug earlier. How did you know?"

I turned to her and swallowed. "I downloaded some books."

"What books? Pregnancy ones?"

"Yes."

Her smile almost blinded me. "Why, Morgan Anderson, color me surprised."

"It was no big deal. Just thought I better catch my brain up to my reality."

"What else did you learn?" she asked, and I battled to contain my developing grin. "Please. I want to know."

"I found the chapters on sex."

"Yeah? Anything useful?"

I shrugged. "Sex is safe during pregnancy. Heightened heart rate because of an enthusiastic fuck isn't harmful to mother or baby. In fact, an orgasm can calm hormones and increase the cardiovascular flow in the woman. The author recommended more foreplay to help you relax as you may be more sensitive and tighten up. Several positions aren't comfortable in the final trimester. The best are the ones where you aren't on your back or belly. Spanking, flogging, tying you up are all okay, as long as you trust me and stop me if you experience discomfort. And despite popular belief, a dick, no matter its length, will not knock on the baby's head. Was that enough, or would you like more?"

She shook her head. "I got it, thanks."

I reached for her face and cupped her cheeks. "I'm not apologizing for who I am."

"I don't want you to. I like control too, but we have to find a middle ground. Talk to me. Don't boss me around, and I'm willing to listen. You have to do the same."

"Okay. I can do that. At least, I'll try."

She leaned in and kissed my cheek, surprising me,

and laughed when I shifted underneath her. She ground her hips against me, and my self-control wore thin. By the twinkle in her eye, she enjoyed the effect she had on me.

"Ma won't come out for another ten minutes. Be careful what you do. I can have you yelling my name in under two." I lifted the shirt over our heads and tented us within the fabric.

Her eyes glazed over in lust.

"That's a no-brainer," she said through her licked, wet lips.

"Do you have a thing for doing it in my parent's house?" I rubbed my hands along her side, over her shoulders to her nape.

"Damn, this shirt's making me hot."

"I guarantee you it isn't the shirt." I tugged her closer. Her chest vibrated against mine. Her eyes flashed with desire, and I lowered my mouth to hers.

I kissed her with urgency. I wanted so much more. My movements frantic. I licked the seam of her lips. Sought her tongue. With a groan, she opened up and welcomed me. Her hands rubbed my back and slid down to the waistband of my jeans. With my fingers digging into her hips, I held her steady and ground my cock against her center.

I was close to losing it in my pants, and I slowed down. I needed to savor her taste. I pulled away. Our groans of discontent mixed in the air at my withdrawal. I licked along her jaw to her neck and nipped the skin of her clavicle. Her gasps added fuel to the fire.

In desperate need for her, I moved us lower on the chaise. I lay flat, opened my legs, and planted my feet on the ground. She fit between my thighs with her upper body sprawled atop of mine. The offending shirt rode up my back. With the fabric no longer constricting her movement, she lifted my T-shirt over my chest and pinched my nipple. Hard. I bit the inside of my cheek to keep from yelling.

"Wicked woman."

"You have no idea."

Sweat pooled on my upper lip, not from the heat but from self-constraint. Her tongue licking my neck did not help.

"You taste so good," she whispered and rested her forehead on mine. "Kiss me."

I couldn't deny her if I wanted and sucked her bottom lip into my mouth. With a giggle, she locked her arms around me as she splayed her hands across the skin at my lower back. Her fingernails scraped, and I welcomed the touch of pain.

"I see you've come to an agreement" Dustin spoke, his voice too close for comfort.

Ann Marie yelped and jerked out of my hold. The shirt bunched around our heads personified a noose.

I popped my head out of the neck hole and glared at my cousin. He gripped the arms of the chair he had pulled closer and laughed. Tears ran down his cheek.

"You're an ass," Ann Marie said to Dustin as she pulled the fabric over her head.

"You got that right, baby," he responded as he opened his flannel and revealed the shirt underneath.

As always, it had something rude, dirty, and inappropriate, yet funny on it. This one had the word SMART and a picture of a donkey wearing glasses underneath it.

"Just be glad I didn't call out for Aunt Emily.

Consider it a favor, and since I've always wanted to be Rumpelstiltskin, you now owe me your first-born child. But the next favor I'll give you for free." He pointed at Ann Marie, "You might want to fix your hair," and then me, "and your pants. No one needs to see that," before he turned to the sliding door and called out for my mother, not giving us a minute to straighten out our dishevelment.

Ann Marie laughed and smoothed her hands down her hair and accomplished nothing. With a shrug and a smile of my own, I adjusted my cock.

Chapter Sixteen

Morgan

Before Ma stepped out, Ann Marie stood. She swayed on her feet, and I was on mine in a flash, supporting her with an arm around her waist.

Dustin, all humor gone, ran to her other side.

"Come sit, you've turned white," I said and guided her to the lounge. Her steps shaky at best.

"I'm okay," she said, but her grip on my bicep weakened. I lifted her. Pressed her against my chest. And none too soon. She went limp and her eyes rolled to the back of her head.

"Dustin, call nine-one-one," I screamed, grabbing my family's attention.

She lay motionless in my arms as Susan ran toward us. I put her on the lounge, kneeled beside her, and rubbed her neck. My hand shook. I dropped it and took her delicate one in my larger calloused one.

Dustin recited my parent's address to someone on the phone, but I tuned out the rest, my focus on Ann Marie.

Sweat dampened my skin, and I concentrated on loosening my tensed muscles. Ma handed me a wet towel. I placed it on Ann Marie's forehead and paid close attention to her closed eyelids for any signs of stirring.

Jesse appeared beside me. His fingers pressed to her wrist, and his gaze locked on his watch.

"Mom, bring me something with a potent smell, please," he said. His calmness did nothing to alleviate the spike of adrenaline coursing through me. He sensed my unease and spoke to me without moving his attention away from Ann Marie. "If you're going to lose it, go do it somewhere else."

"I'm fine. Just focus on her."

"I am. Morgan, take a breath."

I rocked on my knees. "Where's Ma? What's taking her so long?"

"She'll be back in a minute."

True to his word, within seconds her arm extended over us, handing him a bottle of cologne. She patted my shoulder and moved away. Jesse popped the top and swiped it below her nose. Her eyes fluttered.

"Keep doing that." My voice pitched high.

"Susan, see to Morgan. Pax, take his place," Jesse said.

Small yet strong fingers gripped my biceps. "Come on, Morgan. Leave Jesse and Pax to tend to her."

Never would she have the strength to pull me away, but I relented. My heart wanted to stay by Ann Marie's side, but my mind won. I was useless to her. It wasn't a feeling I liked. It brought me back to that day in the car, as I screamed for my uncle to wake up.

"Shit." Big hands pushed my head forward and supported me at the torso. "Breathe, man. Come on, just like that," Pax said in my ear. "This is nothing like the past. Don't you dare pass out on me. Dustin and Parker will never let you live it down."

I followed his instructions, regulated my breath,

averted the queasiness and threat of faint, and straightened. Parker handed me a bottle of water, and I chugged it down. The cool liquid swirling down my throat grounded me into reality. I acknowledged Pax, and he patted my shoulder, nodded at Parker, and returned to Ann Marie.

It made sense—regardless of my feelings on the matter—when Jesse asked for Pax. My brother, a trained firefighter and paramedic was the logical choice. I stood back, concentrated on staying calm, and observed my brothers take care of the woman I…

I stopped my thought train dead in its tracks.

To my relief, Ann Marie opened her eyes and took in her surroundings. Pax moved, and I kneeled before her, pushed strands of hair off her face, and sighed in relief. "Hey. You shaved a few years off my life there," I said, and rested my forehead against hers.

Jesse stayed close and checked her pulse. "Dustin. What is the ETA on the ambulance?"

"They should be here any second now. The sirens are coming closer."

I lifted away and assessed her face. Color had returned to her cheeks, but she was still too pale for my liking.

"Hey. What happened?" Ann Marie's voice slurred.

"You fainted." I squashed the impulse to look at Jesse for more and kept my gaze on hers. I relaxed my features when her brows furrowed. "Everything's going to be okay."

Her eyes tracked the EMS crew movement behind me as they hustled to our location.

"They need to check you over," I said, and moved

away. A piece of me, one I refused to acknowledge, twisted up from being far from her.

Ma hugged my waist and witnessed the commotion before us in silence.

"Is the baby going to be okay?" I asked no one in particular. By the looks I received from Susan and Ma, I wasn't sure if I asked the correct question or not.

"We'll transport her to the hospital where she and the baby can get a full checkup," a paramedic said.

"I'm…I don't need to go. I'm fine." Ann Marie's words gained strength the longer she spoke.

I kneeled beside her once again. "You're going."

She huffed but must have seen something in my eyes because she relented without argument. They loaded her and Jesse—the bastard got to ride with them—in the ambulance.

Pax dangled keys from his finger before my face. "Come on, let's go."

"Can you use your siren?"

"He can't. I've asked him. But if it makes you feel better, he breaks speed limits now when he's given a good incentive."

He growled at Susan and reached for her. I was happy for them, but in that moment, I couldn't bother with their love nonsense. "I'm driving myself."

Pax's large hand landed on my shoulder. Stopped my forward motion. "No way. I'll drive and get you there. The baby needs his daddy alive."

"Come on, Morgan," Susan prompted and tugged me toward the truck.

"We're right behind you," Ma said as we all got into different cars.

I stared out the windshield but saw nothing.

Buildings blurred and disappeared. I noticed not one detail. Pax and Susan didn't speak to me or each other for most of the ride. I silently thanked them for leaving me be.

"She'll be okay," Susan said, breaking the stillness in the truck cab.

Her reassurance meant a lot to me, and I reached back and crammed my hand between the door and my seat. Susan clasped it in hers and squeezed.

"I know."

"Has she been feeling bad, sick? Maybe not eating?" Pax asked.

I shook my head. "I don't know."

"How can you not know? You're living together."

Pax's irritation caused a tightness in my chest. "We're not a couple. We share living space, not our lives."

"Not what it looked like on the deck."

I growled at his inference.

"Pax, cut it out," Susan said from the back seat. "Morgan, have you noticed anything off with her? She mentioned feeling restless the other day."

I looked out the side window. Our actions of the past few days, not any of my family's business.

"Morgan?"

"She eats, sleeps, works. Other than her throwing up every night, she seems fine."

"She told me about that." Susan leaned forward and braced her arms on the top of the front seat but moved back when Pax grunted his disapproval. "Anything else?"

"No."

Pax directed a side-eyed glare at me with a slight

smile. His expression smug and all-knowing. I held eye contact. Anything less, a sure sign of my feelings. And in that moment, the reality gnawing at me for the past several days made its imperious presence.

Shit—I could be a dad.

Double shit—I wanted it all.

****

Ann Marie

I laid on the bed in the emergency room and waited for the doctor. When we first arrived, Jesse went in search for his friend and promised a quick return. Morgan came in minutes after he left. His shoulders hunched like he carried the weight of the world on them.

He sat silent and vigilant on the edge of the mattress. Close without touching with his gaze on his lap and wringing hands until the doctor arrived. He stood and took my hand in his. Gave me the strength I didn't realize I needed. He glared at his brother and the doctor as they hovered in the corner as they conferred over my chart.

They broke apart and approached us.

"I'm Dr. Morris," she said, extending her palm first to me, then to Morgan. "Dr. Anderson tells me you fainted and you're in your second trimester. Although fainting is not uncommon, I want to run a few tests. I've requested your files from the listed OB for review." She looked around, noting the people in the room. "May I?" Her palm hovered over my belly, and I nodded. She adjusted the gown and sheets and shifted the hem, exposing my abdomen.

Morgan growled from beside me, and I bit back a

smile. I liked that side of him.

Dr. Morris stopped and lifted her gaze to Jesse. "I see what you mean," she said with a smile. She turned and faced Morgan. "Mr. Anderson, I assure you, the examination will not harm either Miss Tosto or the baby."

For a tense moment Morgan stared at her, but when Jesse coughed, Morgan relented with a nod.

Dr. Morris probed my belly. And true to her word, she didn't hurt me.

"Can you tell me about your pregnancy? How have you been feeling? Weight gain?"

"It's been good. No complications. I've gained a few pounds each month, even though I get my morning sickness every night."

"Are you taking any anti-nausea medications?"

"I get sick once a day and then I'm fine. My OB prescribed them, but I don't feel like I need them."

"Sleep? Exhaustion?"

"I sleep at least seven hours a night, and about an hour nap during the day. I'm tired but nothing that's worried my doctor."

"Excellent." She tapped my ankle and covered my abdomen. "I understand the pregnancy was unexpected. Can you tell me what happened?"

"My IUD failed."

"Did it expel?"

"Yes."

"Is that what you told me about the other day? Copper kind can do that, right?" Morgan asked me, to which I nodded.

"I didn't know it happened. I wasn't due for my checkup and replacement for three more months when I found out I was pregnant."

"It's not a common occurrence, but over the years I have seen a few cases where the IUD expelled prematurely. No birth control method is a hundred percent."

The doctor and I went back and forth for a few more minutes. She asked questions and I answered. Morgan and Jesse stood by, listening without interruption. A nurse knocked, entered the room, and handed the doctor a clipboard. Dr. Morris scanned through the paperwork of information and several minutes passed in tense silence.

"I see here you've had a previous fainting episode. Tell me about that, please."

"I didn't find out I was pregnant right away. I had no reason to believe the fatigue and nausea were because of a baby. One day, I fainted at work. At the hospital they ran all sorts of tests. The pregnancy one came back positive. I was two months along."

"You're due August twentieth. Your weight gain's steady, like you said. How about episodes of dizziness?

"Sometimes. If I get up too quickly."

"Vaginal bleeding?"

Morgan's hand squeezed mine.

"No."

"Pain in your abdomen?"

"No."

"Has the baby displayed stilted or decreased movement?"

"No. Active as always."

Morgan's voice hitched. "You can feel the baby move?"

Jesse chuckled, but I focused on Morgan's glowing

eyes. I pulled our intertwined hands and lay them flat on my belly with his hand beneath mine.

"I don't feel anything," he said. Sadness tinted his voice.

"Babies like the sound of their parent's voices," Jesse said.

Morgan looked back and forth between his brother and the bump. He nodded, bent down, and brought his face close to our hands.

"Hey, little lady. Can you move for me? I know you're strong. Show me what you got," he said, and I gasped at the responding kick.

Morgan's exhale told me he felt it too.

"Shit, does that hurt?"

I laughed along with the others. "No. At least not yet. In the final few months when there's not much room, it might get uncomfortable. But now I love the feeling."

Dr. Morris nodded her head. "I'm requesting an ultrasound and blood work. Like I said before, fainting is not all that uncommon." She flipped the papers back on the clipboard and hung it up at the end of the bed. "Syncope often occurs when there's a drop in blood pressure. This can be due to the hormones released during pregnancy that relax the blood vessels. It's not dangerous to the fetus or mother. The fall from fainting is the worst culprit."

She stepped back. "Since this is your second episode, I'm admitting you to the maternity ward for the night for observation. At this stage of your pregnancy, we can tell the sex of the baby during the ultrasound. Please let the tech know if you wish to keep the information undisclosed. I'll be up to check on you once you're settled."

"I'll leave you guys to talk. Press this button if you need anything," Jesse said and showed us the call button before following the doctor out of the room.

Morgan dropped to his knees on the floor beside my bed. His hand rested on my belly. He lifted the gown and stared at my skin, lost in thought.

"Do you want to know?" he whispered after a moment.

"I do. But if you don't…"

"No. I do…I don't…I do…Shit, I want to know, but a part of me doesn't. What's the right decision here?"

My heart rate sped at the unexpected show of vulnerability. "There's no right or wrong. Do you want the surprise now or in the delivery room?"

"Shit." He swayed a little. "I hadn't thought about the delivery. Fuck." His skin paled, and I worried it was his turn to faint.

"Morgan, I'm calling Dustin if you pass out on me."

That did the trick, and he pulled himself together just as the nurse came in to collect me.

"Hi, I'm Izzy. Your room is ready. Dr. Morris wants you walking, so if you're up for it we'll head up to the ultrasound, and then I'll take you to your room. Dad, if you can grab her bag, we'll be on our way." She busied herself pulling off the wires attached to me with stickers. "I have a different gown and robe for you. These paper ones don't close so well."

As soon as she popped my last tether, I swung my legs over the side of the bed. Cool air caressed the skin on my back, and I shivered.

"Hope the gown is warmer than this one," I said to Izzy.

"Sure is. I'll help you undress."

"Um," Morgan said from the corner, attracting both our attention. "I'm just…just…" He rubbed this hand across his nape.

I smiled at the hint of blush on his cheeks.

"I'm going outside and send my family home. I'll be back in five."

He bolted out of the room as if the fires of hell licked at his feet. Izzy and I laughed.

"Cute. First time dads are always so flustered. Helpless when all they want to do is fix things. His love for you brightens the entire room."

I gulped against the rising tide of tears. Damn hormones. Yet I didn't correct her mistake. A growing part of me wished her words were true, but it wasn't my reality. It would be better if I remembered my mantra. I didn't need his protection. Or love.

Chapter Seventeen

Ann Marie

Morgan came back into the room just as Izzy snapped the last button on my gown. His gaze swung elsewhere and shut the door, but not before I spotted his reddened cheeks.

"Everyone but Jesse's gone. He's outside waiting for us," he said and turned away.

"I'm dressed." I tried but couldn't keep the amusement out of my voice.

He turned and took the robe Izzy offered him. He held it open for me, and I slipped into it as he shifted to the front and tied the ribbons together.

"Dr. Anderson?" Izzy said. Her wistfulness came through loud and clear.

I laughed under my breath, understanding her fascination. Young, handsome, and successful. "Yeah, he's Morgan's brother."

Izzy's gaze snapped to Morgan, and she raised her hand to her mouth.

"See the similarities?"

She nodded, and I chuckled more.

She recovered and positioned herself to my right and behind my elbow. "Let's not keep the good doc waiting then."

Jesse pushed off the wall as we exited the room. He

joined his brother, and they followed as Izzy guided me to the elevators. At our destination, she left Morgan to help me onto the bed. Although I didn't need his aid, I liked his attentiveness.

Jesse stepped out and promised to find us once I was in my room. The minute he left Morgan's agitation filled the air as he paced the tiny space.

I reached out and wiggled my fingers. "Hey, you heard the doctor. The baby's fine."

He stopped and stared at my out-stretched arm. With a nod, he approached and took my hand. I placed them once again on my belly. His hands stopped shaking the instant he made contact.

His breath hitched at the activity below his palm, and he sank onto the available chair in the room. He rested his forehead on the bed by my hip. I believe overwhelmed by his feelings, and I itched to sink my fingers in his hair. Safeguard him as he processed his emotions. I gave into temptation and smiled at his show of vulnerability.

The door opened, and the technician walked in. Morgan came to his feet but kept our connection secure. My breath stuttered and heart hummed in content. His actions, whether purposeful or not, created havoc within me. His support gratifying yet frightening.

"Ready for your ultrasound?"

"Yes," Morgan answered without hesitation.

"Dad, you can swing to the other side of the bed. I can bring in another seat."

"No, I'm fine standing, thank you."

"Okay, so I'm Chloe. We're doing the images today with a 3D machine. I have to note down measurements for Dr. Morris, and then we can have some fun," she said with a smile.

"Will it hurt?" Morgan asked.

"No. I have warmed gel so it won't be cold either."

Morgan acted like a protective boyfriend. He asked a series of rapid-fire questions about my safety. He stunned me into silence.

"Ready?" Chloe asked. Her voice penetrated my muddled brain. She grabbed the rolling stool, which seconds before Morgan had occupied, and prepped her station. The beeps and lights further centered me, and I nodded. She squirted the gel on my skin, and with a giggle I moved Morgan's hand when he didn't.

Chloe smoothed the wand across my belly. Stopped often and typed on her keyboard. Loud, quick, and repetitive swishes breached the tiny computer speakers, and I smiled as tears formed in the corners of my eyes.

"That's the baby's heartbeat. It's strong," she said.

Morgan collapsed onto his knees and looked on in awe. "It's fast."

"That's a good sign."

Without overwhelming us, she familiarized us at each step with the ease of an experienced tech.

"Want to know the sex?"

Morgan and I stared at each other for several seconds before we both nodded.

"It's a girl."

"Holy shit. No way. We're having a girl?" Morgan's face turned white.

"Breathe daddy. A beautiful, healthy baby girl, with ten toes and ten fingers. Want pictures?"

"Yes," Morgan bellowed. Chloe and I chuckled.

She did her thing for a few more minutes, and a

printer on the cart whirled into action. She held out the images to us. Morgan took them from her with barely concealed emotions.

He didn't talk as Chloe finished up, as Izzy returned and escorted us out, or for the duration of the walk to my room. He followed. His stare fixed on the pictures in his hand.

"He's going to end up walking into a wall," Izzy said after the tenth time she turned and checked on his progress. I giggled, but deep inside I worried my return to Seattle would break his heart.

****

Dr. Morris and Jesse checked in on me during their rounds and declared both me and the baby healthy. With Morgan's superfluous help, I dressed in the clothes Susan dropped off late the previous evening. After an hour of arguing with Susan and Pax, and a promise from me to call if I didn't feel well, Morgan left with them.

He returned as soon as the sun rose, coffee in hand. His untucked shirt, hair standing on end, and bloodshot eyes all indicators he had gotten as much sleep as I had.

Throughout the night I wished Morgan was in the bed beside me, holding me as we listened to the machines monitoring my body and the baby. Self-recrimination often followed close behind. I hated I wanted more from him. I hated my weakness. In the past two weeks in his home, there were new cracks in my cultivated walls that took years to build. And if I wasn't careful, those safeguards would soon tumble.

We left the hospital and drove away in silence. I caught him looking at the sonogram photo now affixed to his visor. Each time I turned away and hid my sad smile.

"I was wondering…" Morgan started but didn't finish. His gaze darted back and forth between the picture and the road.

"Wondering what?" I asked after several moments. "How lucky you are? How sexy I am? There are so many things that could be running through your head right now. Don't leave a girl hanging."

He glanced sideways at me, his lips twitched upward, yet not a complete smile.

"I want to swing by my parents' place before going home."

"Are you asking, or stating fact? Because, I mean, each is a whole different thing. If it's permission you seek…"

"If you make me sound like a teenage girl, I swear I will kill you."

"Huh?"

He turned his full gaze my way before he shook his head and adopted a high-pitched squeak. "I feel the need for an OMG response to your rambling."

"Considering you just said it, I'm guessing you've now satisfied your urges. But if you are so inclined to say it again, give me some warning. I need to record it." I pulled my phone from my pocket and turned it to him, pretended to hit the red button, and twirled my hand.

With a tilted head, he glared at me. He reached for the phone, but I was quicker and shoved it under my thigh. "Not cool. Don't mess with my phone."

"Don't record me."

"Chill, man," I said, and infused a teenage girl pout into my voice. "I wasn't. Jeez, you're sensitive."

He growled and shifted, so one hand rested on the

back of my seat. His fingers tapped a rhythmic beat on the headrest while his jaw ticked.

I fiddled with the radio and stopped when my celebrity crush's singing crooned through the truck's speakers. I sang along to my favorite band's song. Morgan's eyes twitched, and I raised my voice. I enjoyed riling him up and found it difficult to keep my amusement at bay.

He glanced at me from the corner of his eye and smirked. I waited for him to turn the radio off but call me holy-shit-fucking-surprised when he sang with me and mimicked the artist's high-pitched tenor. I threw my head back in laughter, with my eyes closed and mouth open.

"Stop, I'm going to pee," I said between breaths.

Morgan raised his voice, and I laughed harder. He even danced with one hand in the air. I held onto my aching sides. Never had I thought Mr. Serious had a playfulness to him. A side of him I enjoyed and wondered how often I could make it come out.

When the song ended and my laughter died down, his lips turned up in a blinding smile. My panties dampened—no, not from a leaky bladder.

"Keep those teeth hidden. They're dangerous to a woman's vagina."

His eyes crinkled, and he blessed me with another smile.

"What? These teeth? I don't bite…unless you ask me to."

I fanned at the sweat breaking out across my forehead. Horny pregnant me couldn't handle flirtatious Morgan. Not when I wanted him to take us home and do wicked things to my body.

With a deep cleansing breath, I focused on the road instead of his striking angular jaw. "We can go to your parents if you want. We can even give them a picture of the baby," I said, remembering the start of our conversation.

He didn't respond at first but studied me for a minute or two. "What's wrong?"

I rubbed the creases from my forehead, pushing my thumbs into the throbbing at my temple. Trusting others wasn't easy. Over the years, I'd hardened my heart, held people at arm's length, and found solace in solitude. Yet the more time I spent with Morgan, the more I liked our newfound familiarity.

I didn't want a relationship, but for the first time in nine years I wondered if that was a lie I hid behind. Since my return to Bellevue, the idea of a family unit drew me in, but it also scared me. I didn't want him or his family forming attachments to a baby that may not be theirs.

My vacillating emotions waged an unrelenting war in my mind. An exhausting, unchartered fight.

Heat from Morgan's hand on my thigh penetrated through the worry and dislodged my thoughts. With the one touch he provided a level of comfort and assurance I hadn't felt in a long time.

"Hey, what's going on in that head of yours?"

I covered his hand with mine, and he shifted so our palms faced and twined our fingers. With a deep breath, I squeezed his hand and thought of the best way to tell him the truth.

"What if this baby isn't yours? I don't want to disappoint you or your parents."

He nodded, and I waited for him to remove his

hand, but he didn't. Instead, he circled his thumb against my skin. The slight, soothing touch sent mixed signals to my vagina and brain.

One screamed *yes*. The other screamed *no*.

****

Morgan

"My parents and their feelings shouldn't factor in your thoughts. My mom and dad will love the baby as their own whether or not she's mine," I said and slid my palm from hers. I pulled the sunglasses perched on my head over my eyes and used the mirrored lenses as a shield before I replaced my hand on her thigh.

I wanted this baby. The ultrasound solidified what I'd felt from the moment Ann Marie shared her news. It didn't prepare me for the bonus feelings though. Ann Marie's company. She eased a knot in my chest with her sass and smile. I couldn't deny the hold she had on me, but my deep-seated convictions denied my enjoyment.

I drove in silence, lost in thought and snuck glances at the sonogram photo. Ann Marie's moan pulled me from my thoughts. Her head rested against the seat and her eyes were closed.

"Ann Marie, are you hurt? Is something wrong with the baby?" I asked, and my ears picked up the panic in my voice. "I'm turning around. We're not far from the hospital."

I let go of her thigh and flipped the turn signal on and prepared to take the next right. She reached for me and yanked my focus back to her.

"I'm fine. Baby's great. She has the hiccups."

"Hiccups? How the hell can you tell?"

I pulled over and parked, too enraptured to give the road the attention I needed. Ann Marie's eyes twinkled, and I rushed to unlock my seatbelt. She moved my hand to her belly underneath her shirt. The warmth of her skin against my fingers filled me with fire and want. I grazed the tips against her. She shivered and her pupils darkened. Her breath hitched, and I grew hard in my pants. A simple touch, and I was ready to jump her right there in the cab of my truck, public be damned.

A continuous succession of soft jolts under my hand stopped my lustful notions in their tracks. I stared at her belly as if it would give me answers. I couldn't trust what I felt to be true. My baby had the hiccups. Several seconds passed before the light movement twitched under my fingers.

I didn't think. I moved, unclipped Ann Marie's belt, and hauled her across my lap with her back to my door. I wrapped my arm behind her until my hand joined the other on her abdomen. She giggled. I liked the sound and once again reacted without thinking.

"Shush."

She cackled and her body shook. The baby kicked and hiccupped again.

Ann Marie cupped my cheeks and forced my gaze from her belly to her face. Her lighter mood shone through the windows of her eyes. She licked her lips, snagging my attention to her tongue.

I stirred in my pants, and I knew she felt it as her smile turned to a groan. I answered her siren call and slanted my mouth over hers. Her soft lips became compliant under mine, and I took my time. Explored her. I wanted to find and taste every crevice. I ran the tip of my tongue along the seam of her mouth and sucked her lower lip between my teeth. She opened for me on a gasp.

I stroked her skin and played with her breast. Used the lace to caress her taut nipple with my thumb, never breaking contact with her fiery mouth. With the other hand, I reached behind and snapped open her bra.

"God, you're good at multitasking," Ann Marie said against my mouth. Her jagged breath wafted across my face. She ran her fingers in the back of my hair. Tugged the strands when I pinched her nipple. I growled, loving her uninhibited reactions.

She shifted on my lap and spread her thighs on either side of me. Her small baby belly hindered us for a fraction of a second, but soon she ground her heated core against my stone-like hardness. I pulled my lips from her glorious mouth and moved along her jaw. Nipped and licked as I went. I buried my nose in the crook of her neck. Took in her delicious scent, and open mouth kissed the skin at her clavicle.

Her movements turned erratic. Mindless in my lust, I pushed my hand through the back of her jeans and cupped her erotic rounded ass cheek. The tightness of her pants hindered my pursuits, but I managed. My finger span so much larger than her butt, I slid my pinky through her soaked channel and swallowed the escaped groans from her lips with my own.

"I'm going to come. Yes…Morgan…shit…yes!" Ann Marie screamed my name as her body undulated against mine, her head resting on the steering wheel. Uncontrolled tremors traveled across her body. She closed her eyes against the onslaught. Her channel pulsating against my fingers near broke my restraint.

"That's the most beautiful sight." Her flushed

cheeks, sweaty forehead, and open mouth an image forever burned on my retinas.

I couldn't look away. Her complete and utter trust in me to protect and guide her through her moment of defenselessness a humbling experience.

As her breathing normalized, she leaned her forehead against mine, and I took a minute to fix her bra and shirt. And none too soon. A rap on the driver side window jostled her limp body from my arms, and I reinforced my hold. Without moving her off my lap, I lowered the barrier and prayed for a lenient officer.

"Well, I'll be damned. Morgan Anderson," Justin said.

I closed my eyes in thanks for whoever answered my prayer.

"J., good to see you."

"Nah uh. That's Officer Hoyt to you. Mind explaining what's going on here?"

Ann Marie stiffened in my arms, and I rubbed up and down her back. I wanted her to enjoy her post-orgasm bliss for a while longer.

"Just two people enjoying each other's company."

Justin laughed and curled an eyebrow. He reached in and held out his hand out for Ann Marie. "Can't say we've had the pleasure."

I slapped him away and helped Ann Marie climb off my lap and back to her seat. "Are you writing me a ticket?"

Justin's gaze danced from me to Ann Marie and landed on her exposed belly. He looked at me once more and shook his head. "When Rachel was pregnant, she…you know…all the time. I get it, but don't make it a habit. Consider this a warning." He tapped the open windowsill and backed away. "Say hi to Pax and be sure to tell him I let you off," he said as he walked backward down the sidewalk.

I stuck my hand out the window and flipped him off. He laughed all the way back to his patrol car. With a wiggle of his fingers and a shake of his head, he drove away.

Chapter Eighteen

Morgan

I drove us to my parent's house with a smile on my face. Try as I might, I couldn't wipe it away. Ann Marie fell asleep seconds after I pulled onto the road, and I felt a certain level of satisfaction. I stopped in their driveway and took a minute to admire her.

Her temple lay against the window. Her face serene and angelic in the late morning sunlight filtering through the trees lining the path. Ma stood at the front door, having come out as soon as I parked. Cars lined along the lawn. Even on a workday, my entire family awaited our arrival and news.

I pushed at the ache in my chest. I loved them all and with one gesture I felt their unspoken yet unwavering support. I choked up and cleared my throat. The noise woke Ann Marie, and she looked around with sleep-filled eyes.

"We can go home if you prefer," I said, surprised my words rang true.

My house was our home. I wanted her with me. I could admit that, but I could also admit the idea scared the shit out of me. Sharing my heart with another person who wasn't family induced hives.

She's already a part of your family, my inner self taunted.

"No. I'm okay. Guess my body needed a little rest after you made me come." Her voice rasped and pumped my ever-present—around her—libido to life.

I shifted in my seat and looked at the cars, letting my dick calm down.

"Yeah, let's not talk about that."

Ann Marie went rigid beside me. I swerved my gaze to her. Her face scrunched up, and I smacked my forehead.

"Shit. That's not what I meant. Well, it is...but not...I..."

A small smile graced her lips, and a soft tingle stirred within my heart.

"Didn't think you were a stuttering kind of guy," she said, and poked me in the ribs.

I snatched her hand, placed it on my cock, and her eyes grew wide. Down and out of sight of my mom, I intertwined our fingers and took in a deep breath.

"Seeing you come on my lap was one of the sexiest things I have ever witnessed. But my mother is standing on the front porch waiting for us, and my dick is out of control. Hearing you talk about your hot little body and what I did to it isn't helping. Stop talking and give me a minute to think about old ladies and their walkers."

She laughed, and I loved the sound as it vibrated within the walls of the cab.

"Again, not helping," I gritted out, and she laughed harder.

She unbuckled, left the truck, and walked away her hips swaying. When she reached the porch, she stopped, and with an exaggerated twirl, turned and looked back at me. The delight on her face evident from her beaming smile to her sassy wink.

I groaned out loud. The tightness in my pants a direct answer to her actions, and I cursed her under my breath. I cupped and adjusted what I could while sitting. Lucky for me, Pax stepped out behind Ma and the sight of him shriveled me right up. I jumped out of the truck and followed Ann Marie up the walkway, keeping my focus on my brother—and not Ann Marie's hot ass.

"Hey, Justin called. He couldn't stop laughing. Said your name a couple of times and told me to ask you what happened." Pax raised an eyebrow in question and just like that my mind—and cock—went back to the events from a half hour ago.

Ann Marie giggled and followed my mom into the house.

"You don't want to know, but until now I planned on sending that asshole a bottle of whiskey." I walked past my brother without giving him any further explanation. Understanding lit his eyes with amusement and concern.

"Were you parked?"

I nodded but did not elaborate. I didn't regret what we did, and I wanted to get her home so we could do it again. This time with no clothes between us. And my perpetual problem stirred anew.

Ann Marie sat on a stool at the kitchen island surrounded by my family. Ma placed a steaming cup of tea and a piece of pie before her.

Susan doled out more plates and handed me one. "Your mother wouldn't let anyone touch yesterday's dessert until you guys got here."

Dustin stood beside me and stuck his fork in his food. He took a generous piece and spoke with a full mouth. "We all came back, because, hello? Pie."

I pretended to wipe away his spittle. "Dude, close your fucking mouth."

Dustin's response was to open wider and show me his half-chewed bite.

I punched him in the gut, and he mimed spewing over the island.

"Boys," Ma chastised, her forehead furrowed and arms crossed against her chest.

I shrugged and elbowed Dustin when she averted her scolding glare. He laughed and rubbed his abdomen.

"Don't get me in trouble. I want a second slice."

"You do it to yourself. Go bug the other numb nut."

Dustin's gaze followed mine across the island watching the events unfold as Parker flirted with Susan. An amused Pax stood behind him. Susan spoke to Parker, who turned and paled at the sight of Pax. Parker stepped away, and Pax's large hand on his shoulder stopped him from fleeing. He leaned in and whispered in Parker's ear. He gulped and looked everywhere but at Susan. Susan and Pax laughed.

I loved my family. I loved the ease and comfort we had with each other. My gaze landed on Ann Marie and for the first time since my aunt and uncle passed away, I wondered if I could open my heart to her. Could I protect both Ann Marie and our baby? Could I be a good father to this child? Could I love Ann Marie without relinquishing control and live with the unrelenting fear of loss?

Losing them—losing Ann Marie—would destroy me. Could I open myself up for that kind of pain?

I didn't have the answers, but I had three months to

figure it out. On one hand, that was a lot of time and on the other, I already knew it wasn't long enough.

****

Ann Marie

Morgan's eyes flitted through an array of emotions. Oblivious to the noise and commotion surrounding us. Lost in thought. Yet another side to the man. He wasn't the stone-cold being he showed the world.

"Penny for your thoughts," I said in his ear.

He startled for a second. Had our arms not been touching, I would have missed it. His gaze darted around the kitchen before leaning closer. "Do you have the sonogram pictures?"

I nodded. "They're in my purse. I'll get them."

Morgan placed his hand on my thigh and shook his head. "You sit."

I laughed and his eyes crinkled. "You sound like Tarzan. You sit. I go."

Morgan chuckled at my baritone and turned me to face him, his nose almost touching mine. "I will always protect you and our baby. Don't ever doubt that."

My heart thudded against my ribcage, and I inspected the floor for the puddle my body had surely become. It was the first time in over nine years chauvinistic words didn't irritate the shit out of me. Instead they made me smile.

I returned my gaze to his and got lost in his smoldering stare, mesmerized by his darkened irises. His family, their chatter, and everything else around us faded into the background. The bubble he surrounded us in my sole focus. Morgan pushed my hair behind my shoulder, exposing my ear and neck. Heat flushed my core as his breath heated my skin. I closed my eyes and savored the feeling.

"Shh," someone said, disrupting our moment.

I felt Morgan shift away at the same time I noticed the silence. No conversations. No sounds of moving bodies. No stool legs scraping the floor. No forks hitting a plate. Absolute stillness in the air.

I peeled open one eye and scanned the room. Morgan's family regarded us with varying degrees of shock and excitement. My face heated, a blush formed at being caught in an unexpected intimate moment.

Dustin flung popcorn in his mouth and winked.

Morgan raised his middle finger and scratched his chin to a laughing Dustin and Parker. "Show's over," he said to no one in particular before he bent to my ear. "I'll be right back."

Commotion ensued around us. His brothers and cousins laughed, and his parents scattered. Susan smiled at me from across the kitchen, and I returned her optimism with an exaggerated and painful eye-roll.

She chuckled, blew me kisses, and laughed louder as I flung out my arm and pulled them from the air. Mrs. Anderson watched us with a growing smile when Morgan reappeared by my side, and his arm encircled my shoulder. I took my bag and retrieved my sketch book and pictures. I handed them to him, but he shook his head.

"You pick," he said.

"No, you should pick."

He stared at me for a moment before he took the photos and skimmed through them. He held up one to me, and I agreed with a nod.

"Hey, Ma, Dad. I…we have something we'd like to

give you." Morgan extended his arm to them.

Mrs. Anderson took the paper and looked at it in awe. She gasped and covered her mouth as tears pooled in her eyes. Morgan's dad stood behind her and placed his hand on her shoulders as he too peeked at the picture. He kissed his wife on the top of her head and his smile thawed something in my heart.

They were the perfect example of love done right. Like my parents. It was a love I wasn't sure I could attain. Between my disillusionment and work schedule, I hadn't been willing to make space in my life for someone else.

I rubbed my belly, realizing my movement when Morgan stilled my hand with his.

"You okay?"

I lifted my gaze to his, and my knees weakened at the intensity of his regard. I wobbled on the seat and Morgan tightened his hold.

Morgan's actions proclaimed an affection I had never seen from a man. It—he—sent me into a tailspin. He wasn't interested in long-term, and if I wasn't careful, he would destroy me. My life was no longer my own. I had a daughter to think about. Yet Morgan and the idea of a relationship had crept their way in, and I didn't like the hope they represented.

I shook off my confusion and reverted to the Ann Marie everyone expected me to be. I fortified my walls. It did me no good yearning for something I couldn't have—nor wanted. I pushed off the island and stood on shaky legs, using the counter-top to keep me stable. I would not show Morgan or his family how he affected me anymore. Once steady on my feet, I crossed the kitchen to Susan.

"We should get home. You're tired," Morgan said as I walked away from him.

"I'm fine. Actually, I'm in the mood for a game. Who's in?"

"I'm not sure, depends on the game," Susan answered me with her gaze fixed on Morgan.

I chuffed. I didn't need Morgan's approval, nor did I want Susan seeking it. "Why are you looking at him? Last I recall, I'm my own woman."

"Come on, it's been a long day," Morgan said, and pulled me from Susan.

I yanked my arm, angry—yet glad. I wanted to go back to the house, take a nap. I liked him watching over me. But damned if I let him know that. I knew I sent him mixed messages, but I was too tired to fix it.

"I can stand on my own," I hissed at him and the room went quiet.

I dropped my gaze to the floor and hid my reddened cheeks. Embarrassment turned my blood to ice, and I hated my hastiness.

I took in a deep breath and recentered.

"Mrs. Anderson, Mr. Anderson, I'm sorry. Please forgive me. I appreciate your welcome and didn't mean to abuse it."

Mrs. Anderson wrapped me in a hug. I closed my eyes and kept my tears at bay. "You did not offend us. Nothing to forgive. You've had a long couple of days."

I leaned back, but she kept me in her grip.

"It has. I think it best I go get some rest."

"I remember those days," she said around her smile, leaning in so the others couldn't hear. "I know this is overwhelming. Past hurts have a way of percolating and knocking us down."

My breath hitched. Sweat broke out across my forehead and upper lip. Her astuteness disarming.

"Let him be your rock. Whether or not you are aware, he needs you as much as you need him. Whatever your decision, please take care of his heart."

She ended with a kiss to my cheek and another embrace. I turned and hugged Susan. They then passed me from person to person as I walked to the island to get my bag. I rushed from the room. If I didn't get away, Morgan and his family would witness an epic meltdown. I held back my tears by a thread.

It took years to perfect my don't-give-a-shit attitude, and in a short period, the Anderson's breached my blackened heart. I didn't look as Morgan bid his goodbyes. I got as far as the bottom of the driveway and onto the sidewalk before he reached me.

He grabbed my elbow and stopped me. I didn't face him. I refused to show him any vulnerability. "Please. I just want to walk home."

He said nothing and instead tucked me against him, transferred my handbag from my shoulder to his, and supported me as we walked back to his house.

"Your truck?" I asked as we crossed the threshold.

He squeezed me and shrugged. "I'll get it later. Can I make you a hot drink?"

He directed me to the couch, lifted my feet so I lay prone, and covered me with a blanket. I wasn't cold, and I hated to admit I liked his attentiveness, but I did.

"No thanks. I'm tired, though. Mind if I turn on the TV? I like it on when I nap."

By answer, he switched it on and navigated through my favorite shows. He queued one up, turned the volume down, and sat on the other couch.

A few minutes later, an engine rumbled followed by the sound of closing doors, penetrated the air.

"Was that your truck?"

His eyes flickered with amusement before he schooled his face. "Sounds like someone had the forethought to drive it home for me."

I looked up but couldn't see out the front window. "Your family's amazing?"

He chuckled low. "Yeah. Yeah, they kinda are."

Chapter Nineteen

Ann Marie

Eleven days after finding out the gender of the baby and my fainting spell, our new normal was a source of unexpected contentment. Morgan prepared breakfast and lunch. We worked side-by-side during the day. I cooked dinner and experimented with ingredients claimed to help with nausea. We talked and shared our bodies, and his bed at night.

I set up my computer in his garage and for a few hours I suffered the uncomfortable chair, designed the graphics or paint job while he built the bikes shirtless. Always shirtless. The sight of his naked, tattooed, sweaty chest ricocheted my desires into the stratosphere, drove me out of his workspace earlier than him.

At the end of each day, my body reacted—much like Pavlov's dogs—at the silencing of the machines in the garage. I often perched on the couch, pretended to be engrossed in sketching or my computer screen. Other days, I hustled, snuggled under a quilt, and feigned sleep. Those days he stopped close to me for a few minutes. Each time, I fought my curiosity and kept my eyes closed.

As I sat scouring the internet for nursery ideas, crying filtered through the shut front door. The braying grew louder, and I stood, wrapped a blanket around my shoulders and approached the door. At first, the distorted view of Morgan's driveway appeared through the peephole. I hesitated with a hand on the knob as shadows moved in the peripheral. Dustin and Parker popped into sight. I jumped back and screamed in surprise.

Morgan rushed through the garage entryway with a crowbar raised high above him. The sight made me laugh until the crying resumed. I stepped further into the living room, not sure if I wanted to discover whatever his cousins had outside the door.

"What the fuck is that?" Morgan asked, his head tilted in question.

"Your cousins are out there." I pointed to the general vicinity of the foyer. "No idea who's crying, though."

Morgan stomped toward me; crowbar, still poised at the ready.

"You might want to put that down."

He looked up at his hand and shrugged. "Nope. God only knows what those two numb nuts are doing. I need to be prepared for anything."

He pulled the door open. Dustin screamed and I giggled.

"Shit. Are you trying to kill us?" Dustin said with a smirk and swept past Morgan without invitation.

Parker followed with a blanket wrapped object in his arms. Morgan eyed them, his shoulders rigid and elbows tight against his side as he moved to stand behind me.

"Did they wake you?" he asked and angled closer. Warmth heated my back.

"No. I was working."

His gaze flitted from couch to the TV and returned to me with a smirk. I huffed.

"Fine, yes, I was watching my favorite movie again…but I was also on my laptop."

His low chuckle vibrated through my veins, all the way down to my greedy core.

"You idiots interrupted her down time, depriving her of some hunky male in tights."

I reached back and smacked his thigh. "No foul. I shouldn't nap too much during the day, anyway. Makes it harder at night."

Parker and Dustin snickered and coughed something I couldn't decipher behind their hands.

"Are you serious? The word hard makes you giggle like a couple of middle school girls," Morgan said, clueing me in to their mumblings.

They laughed harder, and I responded in kind. It was hard not to. Then I chuckled as the word played on repeat in my head. Morgan tilted his head, eyes scrunched at the corners, and he raised his arms and crowbar in defeat.

"Don't encourage them," he said and walked to the kitchen.

He grabbed three beers and a water from the fridge, handed the alcohol and a bottle opener to Dustin, then twisted the cap off my drink before giving it to me.

"What do you morons want?" He took the opened beer from his cousin and downed a hearty swig.

"We got you something," Parker said and stepped closer to me.

"Before we give it to you, I have one thing to say. There will come a time when you look back at this moment and want to thank us for our thoughtfulness. You need to make me a promise, that when that time comes you will remember you already promised me your first born as thanks," Dustin said and stepped back, puffing out his chest.

Morgan's brows scrunched. "As usual, I have no idea what you're talking about."

I giggled as the scene played out before me. I loved how Dustin and Parker pushed Morgan's buttons with ease.

"Morgan, just agree. There's no way you'll ever be thankful for whatever these two are up to."

He shrugged and nodded. His version of acquiescence.

Parker raised his arms and offered me the bundle. "Careful," he said as he placed it in my arms.

Sounds of a crying baby rose from within the blanket, and I almost dropped it. Morgan was by me in an instant.

"What the fuck? Where the hell did you get a baby?"

"It's yours," Dustin said to Morgan, his smile beaming.

I stuttered and flopped down on the couch in confusion.

"I don't have a baby." Morgan's posture stiffened.

"You constipated, brother?"

Morgan angled his head in silent question.

"I wish I had a camera. You should see the look on your face," Dustin said.

Parker bent over, laughing. Their behaviors odd enough, I dared a peek at the baby in my arms.

"Morgan. It's not real," I said as the wailing got

louder.

"It sure as shit sounds real."

"It's one of those dolls used to teach contraception," Dustin said, laughter crinkling his eyes. "You know, the ones they use in the schools to discourage teens from having sex. It's too late for you to learn that lesson."

I unwrapped the baby and laid it on the couch. Although awestruck by the details of the doll's features, body, and weight, now I realized it was a doll, I didn't possess the urgent need to hold it.

"Make it stop crying," Morgan said. To whom, I wasn't sure.

"I don't know how," I replied and examined the doll for a shut off button.

"That's the beauty of it. You have to treat it like a baby. She won't stop crying until you feed her, change her diaper, hold her." Parker whipped out his phone and touched the screen a few times. "We downloaded the app that monitors her. We'll know everything." He held out the device and showed us the minute counter.

Jumping into action, I pulled her to my chest, stood up, and rocked back and forth in place. She quieted, and I sighed in relief.

"Take it back to wherever you got her." Morgan paced the room. His muscles bunched under his form-fitting black shirt as he ran his hands through his hair.

"No can do, brother. She's all yours for one week. Here, we even got you supplies," Dustin said and placed a bag I hadn't noticed on the coffee table.

Before either of us could react further, Dustin and Parker bolted out of the house, into their car, and drove off onto the quiet street. I stood in the living room with an ever-growing fussy baby in my arms.

"Morgan," I squeaked as the baby's eyes opened. "This thing is freaky."

He walked to me and with an arm around my waist, leaned in over my shoulder. "It looks so real. What the fuck?"

"It's getting cranky. What's in the bag? I don't want it crying again."

"Who cares, let it cry."

"We can't. It's going to annoy the fuck out of me. We have to figure this out and then tomorrow you can get back at your cousins. Hide it in the bar. When it cries and they can't find it and then who's the bitch laughing?"

He kissed my temple before moving away. "I love your devious mind. We need to teach those two idiots a lesson."

I hid my reaction to the *l* word, the kiss, or the comfort of his arm, but it all made my insides gooey.

He rummaged through the bag, removing items one at a time, and placed them on the table. "This is fucked up. Who the hell came up with the idea? They must be wrong in the head."

I didn't have a response and in no time the baby wailed, kicked her legs, and a tear ran down her cheek. I rocked her, fed her, changed her diaper, and even sang, yet she wouldn't calm. After two hours, I was ready to march down to the bar and strangle Dustin and Parker with my bare hands.

****

Morgan

Ann Marie paced the room with the baby in her

arms. She looked tired, and I wasn't happy about it. I offered several times to relieve her of the doll, but she refused. Said it was a good lesson. Whether it was or not, my urge to alleviate her tension, to take care of her, to protect her was in overdrive.

With nothing to do—because I sure as shit wasn't leaving her and working in the garage—I pulled up Dustin's name in the message app on my phone and sent him a text.

—This isn't funny.—

Dustin was quick with his response.

—Huh? Everything I do is funny.—

And several texts from Parker and Dustin followed it.

—Not sure about that.—

—Parker, are you calling me a liar?—

—If the shoe fits.—

And a surprise text from Foster.

—Woohoo! Group text.—

I closed my eyes, staving off the impending headache. The last text clued me in to my mistake. The incessant vibrations coming from the phone in my hand, already angering me. I flipped it over to read the ensuing insanity, starting with my mom.

—What's going on?—

Then Dad's response made me laugh out loud.

—Woman, why are you texting me? You're sitting right next to me.—

—Hush, Ted. I'm talking to the boys.—

Dustin, with his ever-present need to make his presence known, was quick to answer.

—Hi, Mom. Hi, Dad.—

—Hi, sweetheart. Are you getting enough to eat? I

always have something for you.—

Ma's question was the permission my family needed to be absurd, and right on cue, they began.

—Dustin, don't come over. There's no food for you here.—

Dad's shoot down ignored, Parker chimed in, with his need to top his brother.

—Don't forget about me. I'm your favorite.—

—This brings back memories. Remember, Emily? When little ears were always nearby to eavesdrop?—

—There are no favorites. We love you all, equally. Ted, remember when those little ears heard things in the middle of the night?—

I read through the rapid texts and waited for a break. Instead, more family joined in, starting with Pax.

—Mom! This isn't a private conversation. We can ALL hear you.—

—Oops! How do you say blushing with one of those pictures?—

—It's an emoji. Click on the smiling face icon. You'll find what you're looking for.—

—Thanks, Foster. You're always so helpful.—

She found it and a few others, including the eggplant, which I assumed she meant as an invitation for food. Parker followed up with the hand smacking the face emoji. And although I wanted to stay angry, my family made me smile.

—She's blushing because I have my hand on her…—

Dad never failed to throw out innuendos. What once embarrassed us as kids, now amused us as adults.

—While I find this conversation invigorating, some of us are trying to work.—

—And some of us are laughing our asses off.—

—Hi, Jesse, my brilliant doctor. Foster, cut it out.—

—Hi, Mom.—

I shook my head. My family was nuts.

—Can we get back on track please?—

—Caden! Hi, sweetheart. You're always so polite. We miss you.—

Ma always addressed each of us with an endearment and compliment, which of course no one could ignore. Parker with an eye-roll, Dustin with a gag, and Foster with a pout all displayed as action texts.

—Jealous I'm her favorite?—

Caden's quick response meant to rile up his brothers successful in its endeavor.

—Some we love more than others.—

—Ted!—

—Morgan, you started this. What's up?—

I was glad for Pax, the mitigator and voice of reason of the group. Ma replied before I could answer.

—Wait, Morgan. Kate and Susan aren't here. We should include them.—

—I'm here. I'm studying.—

—Hi, baby. I have pie for you. Come over soon.—

—There's nothing here for any of you. Your mom cooks just for me.—

—Except for you, Princess. There's always pie here for you.—

That set off a stream of protests, starting with Pax.

—Hey.—

Then Foster.

—I want pie.—

Followed seconds later with Parker and Kate's

responses.

—What kind? Doesn't matter. I'm in.—

—Thanks, Dad. Thanks, Mom. I'll come over tomorrow (winking face emoji).—

I typed a message and waited for the right moment to send it, but the conversation continued with yet another tangent from Parker.

—Caden, what the f*@$ happened to TJ?—

—Sorry to disappoint. He's out for the season.—

—Rotator cuff injuries take time and patience to heal.—

And another response from Kate.

—I just realized I can't come by tomorrow. I have a test.—

Then we were back to the baseball player Caden represented.

—Fix him.—

—Doesn't work that way, Foster.—

The number of conversations running alongside each other gave me a headache.

Ma responded to Kate.

—Good luck on your test, Princess.—

Jesse responded to Ma.

—I have a quick break before my next patient…How's Ann Marie doing?—

Jesse's question gave me the moment I waited for. I deleted my message and typed in a new one.

—Exhausted because of the numb nuts.—

Case in point numb nut number one, Dustin, replied.

—Hey, that's no way to talk about Pax and Caden.—

—I wasn't…I was referring to you and Parker.—

—Oh, that hurts dude.—

—By the way, how's Annabelle?—

—Who's Annabelle?—

At Ma's question, I lost them again. I sighed and watched the multiple texts appear on my screen.

—A doll.—

Parker answered, and I smiled after reading Kate's response.

—Why would anyone name their doll Annabelle?—

—It's a beautiful name.—

—Not for a doll, Mom…it's demonic.—

I chimed in before the topic went too far off-kilter again. Followed by several texts between Ma and me.

—You pricks need to come pick it up.—

—Why is the name demonic?—

—Ann Marie's exhausted from all the crying.—

—Who's crying?—

—The baby is, Ma.—

—I'm so confused.—

Pax responded before I could type out a reply.

—Same here, Mom. Somebody explain.—

My eyes hurt. My head throbbed, and I wanted out of the crazy. Dustin and Parker obliged and were none too eager to offer their two cents.

—Your wish is my command, Pax. She's a sweet baby. Parker and I gave Ann Marie and Morgan.—

—She cries, pees, needs food. She's awesome. We found her at the baby clinic downtown.—

I held back a growl as I typed, not wanting to clue Ann Marie in on my anger.

—Yeah, come tell me that to my face. The thing hasn't stopped crying for hours.—

—Why were you at the baby clinic? What did you

do?—

—Relax your britches, Caden. We didn't get anyone pregnant.—

Pax was quick with the question we were all thinking.

—Were you there hitting on moms?—

—Ann Marie's pacing with it now. Come get the damn thing.—

—What do you take us for, Pax? We went there to educate ourselves.—

—That's so sweet.—

—Nothing sweet about this, Ma.—

—Whatever, Dude. Let's get a doctor's opinion. It's a good learning experience for them. Am I right?—

—In some ways, yes. In others, no.—

—Care to elaborate, oh wise one?—

—Sure thing, Foster. Labor and delivery are exhausting. A pregnant woman needs all the rest she can get.—

—However, Morgan and AM are gaining valuable experience with this little experiment. I just hope it doesn't cause complications.—

If it hadn't been for the private text Jesse sent me, I would have panicked at his words. Instead, I got a chance to play along with his ruse.

—What complications?—

—What Morgan said…What complications?—

—Pax, as a first responder I'm sure you can attest to the crazy things tired people can do. The increase in blood pressure. The possibility of depression. The lack of appetite. The delusions if the person doesn't recoup with sleep. All things that can put mom and a baby in distress.—

Although I knew he was kidding, I still felt a twinge in my chest.

—*Shit, we didn't think of that. I'm coming over right now.—*

—*We didn't realize.—*

—*Relax boys. Women having been having babies for hundreds of years. I'm sure Ann Marie will be fine. But you're right Parker, go over and get the doll.—*

—*Think they've learned their lesson?—*

Jesse's question produced a couple of texts from Pax, Foster, and Kate with either a *huh* or a question mark. I enjoyed Parker and Dustin's backtracking, even if their hearts were in the right place.

—*Jesse was just kidding.—*

—*What do you mean, joking?—*

—*Dude, not cool. Parker almost peed his pants.—*

—*No, I didn't. You're the one standing here behind the bar taking shots of tequila.—*

I responded. I wanted them to feel sorry, not horrible.

—*It's okay. She's fine. Just tired.—*

To which Jesse was quick to reply.

—*To be expected, given she's in her third trimester.—*

—*When the baby arrives, we'll babysit anytime you need us.—*

—*You do that brother. Anyway, I have to go. Bye everyone.—*

Several more goodbyes followed Caden's exit, leaving Pax, Jesse, Dad, and me to close out the conversation.

—*Those twats need to think before they act.—*

—*Don't be too hard on them.—*

—I know Dad. I just hate what they put Ann Marie though.—

—Susan's planning on visiting her tonight. I'll have her pick up dinner for you guys.—

—Thanks, Pax.—

—I'm out. Patient's waiting.—

—Bye, Jesse. Pax, are you coming over to watch the game?—

—Can't. I'm at the station.—

—Okay. Be safe. Bye Morgan. Mom and I are here for you. Anything you need.—

—Thanks, Dad.—

I put my phone down and noticed the quietness in the room. Ann Marie lay on the couch holding the doll to her chest. Protective, as if she feared dropping her. I took off my boots and with care placed them on the floor before approaching on silent feet. I tugged the blanket off the back of the couch and draped it over Ann Marie and the baby and tightened the ends around them.

She moaned in her sleep but didn't wake. After several minutes of creeper-like staring, I turned and walked to the garage. I stopped at the last minute and studied her face once more. In sleep, the worry lines I hadn't noticed before smoothed out. She seemed younger. Carefree.

And one thought replayed in my head.

Beautiful.

I returned to her side, lifted her feet, and placed them in my lap as I sat down. I hit play on the remote and watched—our commonality unbeknownst to Ann Marie—one of my favorite movies.

Chapter Twenty

Morgan

One week with the demon doll and my prided patience was in question. Ann Marie handled her with a stoic steadfastness I admired. Yet the day Dustin came to collect her, we both breathed a sigh of relief.

The quiet allowed for thoughts I wasn't ready to face. I needed time alone to think and retreated to the garage, but it wasn't far enough. I needed somewhere I couldn't smell Ann Marie, hear her, or feel her presence.

I stormed through the house door. "I'm heading out to get us food," I said and snatched my sunglasses and keys from the kitchen island. I didn't extend her an invitation and hopped into my truck, revved the engine, and shot out of the driveway.

Seeing her with the baby stirred emotions deep inside I couldn't decipher. She turned me on with her endless determination, control, and kindness. I loved observing her unaware. Regardless of my feelings on love and relationships, she invaded my every waking and dreaming thought. Changed me in ways I wasn't sure I was ready for or even wanted.

I rode around the back streets of Medina and caught glimpses of Lake Washington as I went. Although a big city, Bellevue had a small-town feel. I returned waves as people strolled by with their dogs and strollers on the way to the neighborhood's private beach. I scanned my resident card through the slot at the parking lot and pulled into a spot by the access boardwalk. The early May morning sun warmed rather than overheated my skin.

I walked down the weathered wooden planks and found a people-free area facing the water. Kids played along the shoreline, while parents stood guard. Laughter drifted across the air, and I closed my eyes, turned my face toward the blazing sun.

I opened my mind to the memories I kept buried. This was the same beach my parents, uncle, and aunt used to take all of us on Saturdays when we were kids. After their death, none of my brothers or cousins wanted to come to our special place and over the years we stopped. We chose to hang at the dock behind our home instead.

My phone vibrated in my pocket, and I answered it without looking at the screen.

"Hello?"

"Hi, honey. It's Mom."

I smiled. I loved that she still announced herself, even though the caller ID—had I looked—identified her.

"Hi, Ma."

"I'm at your house, standing on the porch. I don't see your truck. Are you home?"

"Sorry, Ma. I didn't know you were coming over. I ran out to get Ann Marie and me something to eat. Are you staying? I can get extra for you and Dad."

"Oh, no. Don't do that. I'll make something. You have food in your pantry?"

"Yes, Ma." I chuckled. "You know it's full. Don't you buy nine of everything when you shop and stock all your kid's pantries?"

"Oh hush, you. I do not."

"I'll swing by the store for salad stuff and be home in twenty."

"Don't rush. Ann Marie's coming to the door. I'll call Dad and start cooking."

"Okay. See you soon."

I left the tranquility of the beach behind and rushed to the store. I zipped through the aisles, got what I needed and headed home to find Pax's truck in my driveway.

With bags in hand, I walked in through the garage door. Conversations drifted from the kitchen where Susan cut vegetables at the countertop and Ma sautéed ground beef in a skillet at the oven. Dad, Pax, and Ann Marie sat at the table by the sliding glass doors, watching the baseball game on an electronic tablet between them.

Ann Marie jumped from her seat, yelled, "Strike! You couldn't hit water if you fell out of a boat." She fist-pumped the air and did a little dance. I smiled at her unadulterated enthusiasm.

I put my bags on the counter, kissed Ma and Susan on the top of their heads then headed to the table. Dad raised his hand for a shake while Pax fist bumped me. I stopped behind Ann Marie's shimmying body and wrapped my arm around her waist and kissed her neck. Her gasp and the lack of conversations around us stopped me mid motion with my lips on her skin.

I hadn't considered my actions, my behavior second nature when Ann Marie and I shared a space. I swallowed the knot in my throat and my mind whirled with ways I could play off my impulsiveness. For a second, I gazed around the room and caught my family's various levels of bewilderment and elation.

Anne Marie shifted in my arms, and I focused on her.

"Careful there. Don't twist an ankle," I said, choosing to ignore the continued stares.

"To your untrained eye, it's called dancing," Ann Marie said with a blank expression.

My eyes narrowed. Ann Marie and I enjoyed an easy banter most days, but considering we had an audience, I couldn't pinpoint her intentions.

"If you call that dancing, don't audition for any of those talent shows," I replied, hoping I made the correct choice.

She wrapped her small fingers around my forearm, stepped to the side, forcing me to follow. "I'm a great dancer. I can teach you a couple of things."

"Yeah? Gonna show me the moves?" I asked with an internal sigh of relief and jiggled my legs.

"Dancing is all in the hips."

Pax and Dad snickered, but I ignored them.

I leaned closer and kept my voice low. "That so? Like George Shaw once said, dancing is the vertical expression of a horizontal desire legalized by music." I punctuated my words with a hip thrust.

Her eyes lit up and her tongue peeked out and licked her lips. I held in my groan and shifted, giving my pants extra room. She graced me with a bigger smile. Her white teeth almost blinded me. I leaned forward and kissed her.

"Ahem."

Clearing throats, various chuckles, and tsking penetrated through my Ann Marie curtain of lust, and I pulled away. I covered my mouth with my hand and hid the smile I could no longer hold back.

"Food's ready if you two are done making out," Susan said around her snickers.

Ann Marie turned a fierce shade of red, making my cock strain even more within the confine of my jeans. At that point, I imagined I had a distinct outline of the zipper teeth permanently embedded in my skin.

"How about we eat in the living room?" I asked no one in particular.

We served ourselves, grabbed drinks, and settled in the living room. I took Ann Marie's plate and waited for her to sit at one end of the couch. I sat at the other, handed her our food, lifted her feet, and placed them in my lap so she leaned against the arm rest. Ma and Dad sat on the opposite couch while Pax took the chair after Susan insisted she preferred the floor.

I looked around the room with a feeling of contentment I never imagined. All the uncertainties of the situation I faced slid into the recesses of my mind, and I relaxed surrounded by a safe and healthy family. I could enjoy the moment for what it was. Worry about tomorrow…well, tomorrow.

The future was there when I was ready to acknowledge it. For the first time in a long time, I focused on the now, not the past. To have room to breathe and feel. I found I enjoyed the sensation. Yet another thought saved for later.

****

Ann Marie

The weeks passed, and my body morphed. The roundness of my belly became visible through my shirts, and I succumbed to elastic waist clothes. My breasts were a full cup size bigger, and Morgan liked them, although I gathered that from his looks, not his words.

We watched movies lying together on the couch, with me cradled in his arms, my back to his front and our legs intertwined. His hands rested on my rotund bump, and we smiled at each other when the baby moved. With fourteen weeks left to go, it was time for Lamaze class.

In a room lit with diffused light, our teacher instructed us into position. I sat between his open thighs on an oversized rocking chair without legs, inches off the floor, much like we did at home. Morgan sat propped up against the back rest, me between his legs, my back against his chest, and his hands on my belly. His warmth enveloped me and the steady beat of his heart and breaths lulled me. I worried I would fall asleep as the instructor started the Conception to Birthing video.

Scratchy music played through the speakers and Morgan huffed. "Is this woman joking?"

"I don't think so."

In the darkened room, he leaned forward and whispered. "Is the music supposed to be suspenseful? It reminds me of horror movies."

His arms around me tightened when I attempted to move away. I tilted my head to the side and back so I could look at him as his focus lasered on the makeshift screen of the large white wall opposite us.

"Let's play a game," he said. His face glowed from

the projected image, softening his stern features. The smile playing at the corner of his lips made my heart leap.

"What kind of game?"

"As this shit excuse of a video plays, we take turns identifying the elements making this the worst horror flick we've ever seen. Whoever has the most observations, wins."

"Sounds like fun." And I wasn't lying. "What does the winner…win?"

"To be determined. And…go."

"The doctor visit is the girl ignoring her elder's advice. She got pregnant anyway," I said.

"And her partner is the jock."

"Which makes her the blonde ditz. Too bad she's a brunette."

Morgan chuckled. "I prefer brunettes."

Although my blood spiked at his casual remark, I pushed the sensation away.

"Look, they're telling the parents. Doesn't the dad look angry? This is when they realize that sex gets you killed."

"Ha. The doctor's office has the cryptic message on the wall," Morgan said.

My snicker came out as a snort, followed with few huffs from around the room. Our antics only amusing to us if the several glares we received were any indication.

"Forget them. I love your laugh," Morgan whispered in my ear and pulled me tighter against him.

"The couple's Lamaze class is foreshadowing," I whispered back.

"Good one. Watching a video of the horrors to come."

"Just like us. Oh my God, are we the jock and blonde versions in our own flick?"

"Ultrasound day. The wand is the creepy crawly thing."

"That wasn't creepy."

"Yes, it was. I thought they were going to stick it up your vagina. That was fucking freaky." Morgan's shudders shook me.

I lifted my hand to my mouth and stifled my laugh. "The woman just got a picture of the baby. Look, she's stumbling around just like the running woman who always falls down."

"Of course. I mean look at the heels she's wearing." I felt Morgan shake his head. "Is she in labor? Her whimpering betrayed her. No hiding from the inevitable now."

"Oh, no. They split up. Nothing good comes from splitting up."

"The jock's trying to make a phone call. Crap, no cell reception. Should have gone with a different carrier."

I laughed, drawing the other couples' attention. Morgan muffled me with his hand on my mouth, which made me laugh harder.

"Shush, you're going to get us thrown out before this suspenseful movie ends."

I grabbed his wrist and pulled him away. He turned his palm over and interlocked our fingers. His thumb circled the back of my hand, and I lost my ability to speak. He took advantage and continued noting his observations.

"No. No. Don't go in there. It's the dark, scary place," he said as the woman walked into the birthing room. "She's unaware of the disfigured monsters awaiting her entry. Run, lady. Turn around. Run."

My sides hurt from my stifled laughter. I couldn't get a word in if I wanted. "Why are they all wearing white clothes with ducks and trucks? It's a mystery."

Several shushes echoed through the room, but we were having too much fun to care.

"Ah. That man pretending to be the doctor is the horrific monster."

"Wait for it…She's screaming for help. No one can hear her. The duck-scrub-wearing zombies are smiling behind their masks, imagining their next meal."

"The heroine springs from the bed. The audience jumps in fear." I buried my face in his shoulder.

"That's right, love. Look away. Dismemberment ensues." His lips danced against the shell of my ear as he spoke. The feeling intoxicating. "Argh. Creepy children alert. It's the one-eyed purple people eater." Morgan held my head down against him. "The duck-scrub-wearing zombies have surrounded the purple being. Hands everywhere. They have probes. Watch out. No. No. Take it away. Don't give it to the unsuspecting ditz. No. It's transformed and is fooling her into offering her tit as a sacrifice. The jock looks on with a smile, but little does the ditz know he is now also the non-believer."

I bit his shirt and hoped the fabric muted my snorting. He wrapped his arms around my shoulder and held me to his chest as I sensed the lights brighten.

"She's fine. A bit emotional." Morgan's deep voice resonated through his chest against my cheek. He rubbed his hand up and down my arm. "No. She has a bottle in her bag…Thank you…I'm just going to take her outside for a minute."

He shifted his hold and stood with me in his arms. I squealed in surprise and wrapped my arms around his neck. I kept my face hidden. I was emotional, but not the kind the instructor expected.

The door clicked behind us, and I felt Morgan's hurried steps. We rounded a corner, and he leaned against a wall. I wiggled until he set me down and held me with his hands on my hips as I grew steady on my feet.

Once composed, I looked up into Morgan's dark red face. Lips flattened. Eyes scrunched closed. With one look at his constraint and the floodgates of laughter opened within me. I hunched over and held my belly as I cackled. It didn't take long for Morgan to lose his tenuous hold, and his deep boisterous laugh mixed with mine as they echoed off the walls of the empty hallway.

His eyes crinkled in joy and face flushed from his laugh and it was my undoing. I stopped laughing, and my body lit up with a sexual zest. As he quietened and straightened to his full height, our gazes locked, pulling me into his orb.

I reacted on instinct.

I closed the space between us, stood on my tiptoes, and wrapped my forearms around his neck. My belly threw me off balance, and he supported me with his hands on my hips.

"You're hot when you laugh." I didn't give him a chance to respond and crushed my mouth to his.

I kissed him with vigor, which he returned in kind. He pushed his thigh between my legs and supported most of my weight. I rubbed my core against him as our tongues clashed. My fingers tunneled through his hair, keeping his head close. A slow growl escaped his throat and the vibrations in his chest reverberated against my breasts. I pulled back and took his lower lip between my teeth.

I rested my forehead on his and waited for our breath to even out before I spoke. "Take me home. I need you inside me."

He kissed me with a couple of quick pecks and lifted me. "You don't have to tell me twice," he said, pushed off the wall, walked us outside, and to his truck with me in his arms and my face tucked in his neck.

Chapter Twenty-One

Morgan

Early light filtered around the curtains, and I woke with Ann Marie in my arms, her scent in my nose, and her breast in my hand. We spent the days after our lone Lamaze class wrapped around each other. Her sex drive was insatiable. It almost equaled my craving for her. She loved fucking in the shower. I loved it at dawn in the bed we shared every night. Beginning my day with her taste on my tongue was far better than any breakfast.

Her quiet snores and whimpers wreaked havoc with my morning erection. I grew harder the more she and the room came into focus. Her nipple peaked in my palm, and I squeezed her flesh, firing her up until her groans increased both in volume and vigor. She shimmied her ass, backed up, and nuzzled my cock between us.

I silenced the growl threatening its escape but didn't move my hips away. With an arm acting as a cushion for her head, it left one hand for exploring. I moved from her breast, over the swell of her abdomen into the elastic of her panties and cupped her heated mound.

She writhed in my hold, but I kept a light pressure against her. She shifted her leg. Opened herself to me. I took the silent invite and slipped a finger inside her.

"Uhm. That feels so good. Best alarm clock ever." Her voice slurred with her morning grogginess.

I didn't use words to answer. I let my fingers do the talking.

Her hips gyrated against my hand. I added another finger, crooked them, and stimulated her G-spot. She grabbed my wrist and stilled my movement deep inside her.

"Totally unsexy, but I need to pee before you do that."

I guffawed. "Sexy is a perception." Ann Marie personified the word.

"It kills me to say it, but if you don't move your fingers, I might commit the most heinous of crimes."

"Murder?"

"Yes. If I pee on you, I'll have to kill you."

"Wouldn't want me to live to tell the tale?"

"Something like that. Now extract yourself…or prepare to meet your consequences."

I retreated, torturing her along the way.

She moaned, gasped, and then turned and smacked me.

I grabbed her before she landed a second blow. "Hit me again and prepare to meet *your* consequences," I said, repeating her words but softened with a smile.

Her gaze darted across my face with a matching grin of her own. With a twinkle in her eye, she pulled back, and I released her wrists. The moment she was free, she straddled my lap and rubbed her core against my erection. She leaned in, licked my neck, and pinched my nipple before scrambling off and running for the bathroom.

I yowled in surprise and grabbed for her. I hadn't planned on giving chase since the baby hindered many of her movements, but I heaved off the bed. She took off as best she could and giggled all the way. I slid off my boxers and stalked across the room. I gripped the door frame above my head, widened my stance and waited.

She walked out and screamed when she hit my chest. I wrapped my arm around her, not wanting her to fall back.

It was a good excuse.

I hauled her to me and lifted her straight up, so her feet dangled off the floor and her belly rubbed against my stomach. It brought her mouth closer to mine, and I indulged. Her lips parted on a gasp. I swirled my tongue. Tangled it with her eager one. A kiss with no finesse but loaded with need and heat. My favorite kind.

Ann Marie, with my help, spread her legs, and wrapped them around my waist, using my butt cheeks as a foothold. She ground her core against my naked cock, and I felt her dampness on my skin. I walked us to the bed and twisted so I could lay her down on her back. She moaned as I extracted from her hold.

I took the elastic of her underwear, and for a moment, I rubbed their silkiness between my fingertips before I yanked and ripped them.

"If you keep doing that, I will not have any panties left," she said on a pant.

"I'll buy you more."

I covered her body with mine and took extra care not to put weight on her belly. I nuzzled her neck. Nipped at her skin. Tasted her. My feeble attempt at drawing something of her into me. My desperation for this woman grew with each tango. I thought of her when she wasn't with me. I wanted her when she was. My lust for her overwhelmed me.

"Morgan," she whispered. "I want you inside me."

I pushed off her. "Not yet. I have other things in mind." I scooted down and dragged my lips across every inch of her skin, stopping at her breasts. Her luscious growing breasts. I latched around one nipple and licked her into a peak in my mouth. Not wanting to deprive her other tit, I lavished it with attention. I went back and forth until she squirmed beneath me, and her breath grew labored.

"Am I hurting you?"

"No… More…I want more."

I squeezed her tits, conscious of her heightened sensitivity, until her moans and gasps filled the air. I licked her skin down to her belly button. I spent a few minutes soaking her in before venturing further south. I nudged her thighs open with my shoulders and settled between them, kissing the inside of her legs.

I shuffled and laid on my stomach. Her anticipatory shivering encouraged my slow exploration. I buried my nose in her core and inhaled.

"You smell so fucking incredible."

The fingers in my hair yanked at the strands. I welcomed the sting of pain and used it to prevent me from exploding too soon. Without warning, I sucked her clit into my mouth, held her between my teeth and flicked my tongue over the bundle of nerves.

"Shit…Morgan…Shit…Oh my God." Her voice rang through the room like music to my ears. I wished I could record it.

I wrapped my hands around her legs and held her hips steady as I licked and touched every part, inside and out, of her I could reach.

"Close…so close."

I hummed deep in my throat. The vibrations traveled into her through my tongue. Her hands flew to her knees, holding herself wide.

My gaze drifted up. The sight of her open lips, closed eyes, flushed chest and face, and beaded sweat along her forehead fanned the flames rushing through my veins.

"Come for me. I want to taste your climax."

I blew on her heated pussy before wrapping my lips around her again. Relentless in my pursuit of her orgasm. Her legs shook, and she grasped the sheets. Her gasps echoed across the room, and her back arched off the bed. Within minutes her personal flavor, tangy yet sweet, flooded my mouth.

I didn't let up and pushed her past her limits. Prolonging the waves ricocheting through her body. Her energy depleted, she dropped her legs, unclenched her fists, and lay limp on the bed. I climbed up her body, licking as I went, unable to resist.

"Is it me or does it get better each time?"

I chuckled and pulled her with me so she lay with her back to my chest and her head rested on my forearm. We spooned, and I rubbed my fingers across her hip, and enjoyed the erupted goosebumps on her skin. She wiggled and burrowed further into my hold.

"Not just you."

She sighed, and her breath brushed the hair of my arm, and I flattened my palm against her chest. Her heart thumped and slowed as she relaxed, and I tuned my rhythms to hers. Satiated and happy, I closed my eyes and postponed the inevitable outcome of my actions.

Post-coital cuddling had become one of my favorite parts of being with Ann Marie. Not because I got to hold her. Because with her back to me, in the stillness of the aftermath of our passion, my burdens evaporated. I could block out the world and revel in the simple feeling of contentment. For a moment, I didn't have to control every aspect of my life. I could let my mind relax.

Ann Marie shifted and turned so we faced each other. I sucked in a breath as her fingers walked along my rib cage and over my hip, then danced over my abdomen. She continued lower to trail through the line of hair leading to my cock.

She rubbed me with the back of her hand, and my hips thrust toward her. Her touch much too gentle and my body begged for more.

"Stop teasing."

She let go of my dick, and I suppressed my disappointed moan. She lifted herself onto her elbow, pushing at my shoulder with her other hand. I took the hint and lay on my back and watched her with hooded eyes. She was so damn sexy when she demanded control. I didn't relinquish it often, but her ragged breath and flushed skin would coax any man into relenting.

"Put your hands behind your head."

My cock jumped at her command, and I lifted my arms. Gave her a slow show. I laced my fingers and supported my head with my cupped palms.

"Don't move them."

She wedged her knee between my legs, like I had done to her moments ago. Heat flooded my veins. I complied and opened wide enough to accommodate her. Her hands ran up and down my thighs. They came close but didn't touch my cock. A yearning like I never knew overtook my every sense, and I reached for her.

She moved away and shook her head. "Nuh uh. Hands behind your head."

Her dark as night wavy hair flowed over her tits, and I found I didn't much like this game of peek-a-boo. With an arched brow, she waited. Eager to see the results of her playfulness, I returned my hands to the requested position and used them to raise my eye level. I didn't want to miss a minute of the show.

****

Ann Marie

The head of his cock leaked. An erotic visual of the effect I had on him. Desperate to give him the same pleasure he gave me, I wrapped my hand around his hardened shaft. He swelled in my hands. Pulsed against my skin and a groan came from deep within his chest. It was all I needed to push him for more.

With my gaze glued to his, I leaned forward, and used the tip of my tongue to lap at the drop of moisture. His head fell back, but he otherwise didn't move.

"Jesus."

I smiled and used his moment of bliss to open my mouth wide and wrap my lips around the head. His hips leaped off the bed, pushing himself deeper. I hummed and flattened my tongue against the vein on the underside.

He held my head still, defying my command with a

gentle but unrelenting hold. He didn't pump, and I continued exploring him with my tongue. After a moment he relaxed his grip. I bobbed my head and took him as deep as I could. He hit the back of my throat, and I fought my gag reflex. Buoyed by the exuberance of his grunts, I alternated between moving my hand along his shaft in unison with my mouth and then in the opposing direction.

"I can't…Fuck."

My core heated. I anticipated more, regardless of the climax I had already experienced. I liked sex, but with Morgan, my pussy was tenacious in its wants.

I inched up his cock and squeezed my lips at the end then released him with a pop. "Someday I want to finish you with my mouth, but I need you now."

I straddled his hips, took him in hand, and aligned him at my opening. Putting just the head inside me, I ran my hands along his chest and stilled, fascinated as his eyes darkened with want and constraint. His need to impale me vibrated through every muscle of his body. I teased us a moment longer until I couldn't bear the empty feeling anymore.

With a nod, I gave him my silent permission. One quick push and he drove his cock deep within me. He stretched my walls and filled me to the brim. His hands flew to my hips and held me steady. My head fell back, eyes closed in ecstasy. Our bodies made for each other. A perfect fit.

"I love the gasp you make at my first thrust. I love your whimpers, your moans, your tongue peeking out, wetting your lips. I especially love the face you make when you come."

My hips rocked against him of their own volition. I

was so lost to the sensations I didn't notice his migrating hand until he pinched my nipple, creating a flood at the point of our connection.

"Ahh, so good."

It was all the acknowledgment he needed. He moved, and with a hand under my butt, he held me several inches above him. He planted his feet on the mattress and used them as leverage as he took over and pounded into me. My arms flung back, and I rested my hands on his thighs, giving him better access.

"I love looking at you," he said, low and deep.

I opened my eyes to find his gaze fixated on where he disappeared into me. He reached for my exposed clit and rubbed it until I could do nothing but pant.

"Ride me, baby. I want to see your tits bounce."

I pushed off, shifted my weight, and rested my hands on his chest. Morgan dropped his arms to either side of him, and his fingers grazed my calves. I rocked and ground against his pelvic bones, but soon I needed more. I lifted my hips halfway up his length before dropping again. I set a frantic pace, chased my euphoria, and lost myself to my single-minded pursuit.

"That's it. Use my cock. Take what you want."

I closed my eyes, and with each dirty thing he uttered, I inched closer to my climax.

"Morgan...I need..."

He didn't wait for me to finish, and his grip tightened once again on my hips. "I'm going to bury myself so deep inside you, you will forever feel empty when I'm not there."

"Yes...Fuck me like you do in your dirtiest dreams."

Morgan sat up and enveloped me in his arms. He

moved us until he was on his knees with me still straddling him. He nuzzled his mouth in my collar over my erratic pulse and licked, then traced his lip across my flesh.

"I want to feel you come all over my cock," he said in my ear. "I want to own your taste, your scent, the feel of your skin."

I wrapped my arms around his neck, my elbows meeting in the middle. My orgasm loomed closer, and I feared losing my hold on reality when it came for me.

Heaven awaited me as Morgan's pumping grew relentless. He took as much as he gave. His harsh breaths against my ear a welcome and coveted sound. His loss of control fed my own.

"Let go, Morgan." His breaths quickened at my words. "Let go. Take me with you."

He tightened his arms around me. Sweat made our bodies slippery. I buried my face in his neck and screamed into his shoulder. White light exploded behind my eyelids as my body spasmed with a shattering intensity. Morgan shuddered under me. His body's vibrations prolonged my orgasm for what felt like a blissful eternity.

In the stillness, resembling the inconceivable quiet after an earthquake, Morgan stretched his legs, lay back, and pulled me down with him. I rested next to him, my head nestled against his chest, my muscles too liquid to do anything else. I closed my eyes and concentrated on the feel of his warm skin beneath my cheek. My head rose and fell with each breath he took, and as his breathing slowed, mine matched his.

He pulled me closer. I wrapped my leg around his and entwined our bodies from head to toe. Tranquil and lethargic, I lost all concept of time. What could have been a minute or several hours later, Morgan raised my face to his with a finger under my chin.

He cocked his head and slanted his mouth against mine. It was a sweet kiss. My nose tingled with an emotion I wasn't yet ready to acknowledge. I bit his bottom lip, then licked at the sting of my bite.

I drew away from him. My gaze ran along the length of his body, and I traced the outlines of his ink.

"Will you tell me the stories behind your tattoos?"

His fingers tunneled through my hair and sifted the strands apart as he went from root to tip.

"Someday."

I wasn't sure if his answer made me happy or sad. In one version he promised me a future, in another he kept me tucked outside.

Chapter Twenty-Two

Morgan

I had a plan.

I set it in motion and enlisted my mother's and Susan's help. I parked my bike in the rear parking lot of my cousins' bar and entered through the Employees Only door. I arranged the meeting before the afternoon rush so Parker and Dustin could join us.

The bar's vibe differed depending on the time. At night, the low lights and loud music attracted the young crowd of Bellevue, during the day the downtown workforce flocked for a quick lunch.

I joined Ma and Susan at one of the many booths along the windowed front wall.

Kate rounded the bar for a hug. "Burger and a beer?" she asked.

I nodded.

"Baby daddy in the house," Dustin yelled as he pushed through the swinging doors separating the bar from the kitchen, his arms laden with a crate of liquor bottles. He put it on the floor, pulled the towel draped across his shoulder, and wiped his hands before he raised his fist for a bump.

Parker emerged through the same doors, grabbed a couple of beers, and popped the tops. He greeted me, sat at the table, and placed one in front of me. I took a long sip and enjoyed the cold liquid running down my throat, easing my unexpected nerves.

"Tell us why we're here," Susan demanded with a gleeful smile and wringing hands.

"Excited?"

"You bet your patootie I am."

I chuckled at her enthusiasm.

"Hate to disappoint, but you're not here to help me pick out a ring." Her crestfallen pout made me laugh. "But…"

"Morgan, cut it out. You have us all on pins and needles," Kate said as she plunked down plates of food.

"That was quick."

She nodded. "Mom and Susan came a few minutes early. They ordered, and I decided for you. We didn't want you to have any excuses to stall." She sat beside me, sandwiching me in the middle with Susan to my right.

I gave an exaggerated huff, reached in my jacket, and retrieved my wallet. Kate shifted. Her body vibrated against me. I took out a credit card and held it between two fingers. I tapped my chin as I eyed each of the women at the table. Susan and Kate lunged.

I extended my arm high above my head and laughed. Kate stood on the bench and jumped for it. Before she succeeded, I handed it to my mom.

"I trust you. These two don't understand the meaning of reasonable spending."

Susan and Kate guffawed and attacked my sides. A few minutes of scuffling and their heartwarming giggles, I had them both pinned.

"Kids. I swear you're all still kids," Ma said with a smile.

"Let us go," Kate said and squirmed in my hold.

"If you promise to behave."

"Behave? Are you serious? Where's the fun in that?" Susan asked, and Kate agreed with a vigorous nod.

"My food's getting cold."

"Oh, boo-hoo. Fine, let us go, and you can tell us your grand plan," Susan said as she raised her fingers as high as she could in my hold in mock quotes, "and we'll…"

"Unhand my fiancée," Pax's booming voice bounced off the walls of the bar. We turned to find him silhouetted in the door frame.

Kate pulled free, ran for Pax, and jumped into his open arms.

"Hey, munchkin," he said and rubbed his hands down her back.

"When are you going to stop calling me that?" Her angry words belied by her beaming smile.

"As soon as you're bigger than any one of us."

She giggled and pushed out of his hug. "No, thank you. I like my size. All seven of you are behemoths," she said and took a seat on the inside of the booth since Susan had taken her place in Pax's arms. "But the way this semester is going, I'm sure to gain fifty pounds with my horrible eating habits."

"Which professor do I need to kill?" Dustin asked.

"No one, you idiot."

"Just say the word. We'll deliver justice AJ style."

"The Anderson-Jackson team now fights crime?" Kate asked.

"Yep," Dustin said with pride. "Family first. Always."

"Pax, dear," Ma said, hugged him next, and cut off whatever ridiculous conversation was about to take place. "Grabbing a quick lunch for the crew?"

"No. Just dessert," he said, looking at Susan. She walked to another table, lifted three huge containers, and handed them to Pax. He peeked in the top one and scowled.

"Who ate the cookies?" He deepened his voice and looked through his lashes at our cousins. They didn't have the wherewithal to look sheepish.

Parker went as far as rubbing his belly. "Don't be like that, man. They were good."

Pax turned away, pulled Susan in front of him, and planted an X-rated kiss on her—hidden from Ma's view.

But from my angle their display of tonsil hockey visible. "Get a room," I said and smacked my brother on the arm.

He pulled back and by the dazed look in Susan's eyes, I worried she would fall over once he let her go. As if reading my mind, Pax directed her to the booth and helped her sit beside Kate.

"Fill me in later," he demanded. "Got to go." He waved and walked out, jumped into his new decked out Second-in-Command property of the fire department red pickup truck.

I slid in next to Susan, and Dustin sat on the opposite side with Ma. Parker grabbed a chair from another table, turned it around, and straddled it, with his arms resting on the high back.

"Okay, sweetheart. We're all here and I have your credit card. What's going on?" Ma asked.

My gaze roamed across the table, drifting from

person to person. I took a bite of my burger, swallowed, and used the extra time to shove down my nerves.

"I need help. Shopping and renovating."

"Shopping? What for? You're giving us access to your black Am Ex?" Kate said, clapping her hands together. "I love shopping."

Dustin rolled his eyes. "We know."

She reached across the table and poked Dustin in the chest with a fork. "If it wasn't for me, none of you would have furniture. You would sleep on a blow-up mattress on the floor of your bedroom surrounded with your gaming console, bags of chips, and empty takeout containers."

"True story," Parker agreed. "You'd be living in squalor if it wasn't for our little sis."

"Oh, shut up. You needed her help as much as I did."

"Boys," Ma chastised, quieting them. She nodded for me to continue.

I took in a deep breath. "Ma, Susan, Kate, I would like you to outfit the nursery."

Susan jumped in her seat, but Ma looked concerned. She didn't make me wait for her opinion. "Usually, the new mother enjoys doing that."

I nodded and pulled out my phone. I clicked through a few buttons. "I sent Susan the file Ann Marie has on her laptop. It has pictures of the furniture she likes and the decals she's designed for the walls." I held up my hand. "Before you say anything, yes, I snuck into her computer. Yes, I know I shouldn't have, and no, I'm not sorry. I want to surprise her. She's been exhausted and Jesse said she needed to rest."

Susan smiled with her hand held against her chest.

I ignored the hopeful twinkle in her eyes.

"Parker, Dustin, I'm going to need your help putting the room together. If Susan can get her out of the house the day the furniture arrives, I will have a small window to get it all done."

Parker tapped my shoulder. "Of course, man. Just tell us when."

"I'm sure Pax will help if he's not working," Susan added.

Ma's pinched brows concerned me. I reached across the table and took her hand in mine. "You have that look, Ma."

She waved her free hand. "Don't mind me. I just wish the others could be a part of this."

"I know, but Foster can't lift and besides, he's going to Hawaii for the surfing competition. I'll talk to him. I'll make sure he doesn't feel left out," I said. "Caden's changing his travel plans so he's here for the birth. He'll be home soon. And Jesse's got a lot going on at the hospital. I already spoke with him."

Ma stood, rounded the booth and took my face in her hands. She kissed my forehead. "You are a sweet boy. I'm so happy for you." She turned and wiped a lone tear from her cheek. "What about your father?" she asked and sat down.

"Figured you'd tell him when you got home. Your help is most welcomed."

She nodded. "Okay. Thank you for trusting us with this task. Kate, when is your shift over?"

"Whenever Shannon gets back from her doctor's appointment. Probably within the hour."

"Is she the new server?" Ma asked.

"Yep. She's the sister of one of Pax's firefighter

friends," Dustin answered.

"If we're going shopping for nursery stuff, what are you doing?" Susan asked me.

I shrugged my shoulders, not wanting to give away the second part of my plan. My family understood my silence, and although they weren't happy with it, they didn't push. We ate and chatted until I grew antsy.

"I'm heading out. Dustin, I'm leaving my bike in the back."

"No problem."

I kissed each of the women goodbye, tapped Dustin's shoulder and waved to Parker who was back behind the bar serving customers. Once outside, I walked quickly, checking over my shoulder as I did.

With no one following, I headed for the jewelry store.

A bell jingled as I pulled the door open, alerting the man at the counter of my arrival. Gems lay on a black velvet mat before him, which he examined with a loupe attached to the front of one lens of his glasses.

"Morgan. It's good to see you."

I reached him with big steps and shook his offered hand.

"Charley. How's the bike running?"

"Perfectly. Best decision I've ever made. I love the custom build."

Charley looked more like a biker than a jeweler with his leather clothing, bald head, and a beard that ended at his belt buckle, tied at one-inch intervals.

"Good to hear."

He smiled and pointed to a picture behind him. "I display her like she's my baby. Hell, my wife is jealous, I promised her one of her own."

I chuckled. "Anytime, man."

He nodded and placed his palms on the glass top. "Dropping by for a hello, or is there something I can do for you?"

"I'm looking for a ring."

He straightened and offered me his hand again. "Congratulations. The missus will be so excited when I tell her."

I grunted. "She hasn't said yes yet."

"She will. Let's get started."

****

Ann Marie

I woke up disoriented. The light from outside filtered through the sliding glass door. I didn't remember laying down or pulling a blanket over me. My laptop sat dormant on the coffee table. Last, I recalled, I was in the middle of working on a design for Morgan. I snuggled into the cushions of the couch and closed my eyes. Trepidation pulsated through my veins.

A few days ago, Morgan surprised me with a lumbar support pillow and footrest. He stocked the cabinets with my favorite snacks, loaded up the player with my favorite superhero movies, and found me the fuzziest blanket. His attentiveness, although appreciated, confused me. But scared me even more.

We were alike, and because of that likeness, his behaviors stumped me. We coveted control. Me with my surroundings, him with his emotions. But his actions spoke of—dare I say it—love. He tended to my comfort. Saw to my needs before I realized what I needed.

Questions loomed; one's I couldn't answer with

any clarity.

Was he mindful of me, the baby, or both? Whatever happened to my promise to never rely on another man? Yet I allowed his interference, and often with open arms, I appreciated the attention he gave me, and that in itself angered me. Not at him. At myself.

My new reality either made me giddy, an unusual emotion for me, or ambivalent. I enjoyed time we spent together. His company comforted and relaxed me. I liked the effect I had on him as well. He was quicker to smile. He laughed without hesitation and our banter a sublime form of foreplay. Arguments always landed us in bed, the shower, the couch, the counter—didn't matter if the surface was horizontal or vertical—our sexual rendezvous were off the charts.

A seamless intertwining of our lives. His room became mine. We shared the closet, bathroom, and I claimed the right side of the bed. I rearranged the kitchen cabinets and bought small accent pieces for the living room.

Instead of denying me the integration, he shrugged with each new development. He understood my nesting needs and went as far as enabling them. We tore apart what once was my bedroom and prepared it for the nursery. I spent hours online as Morgan looked over my shoulder. Although he deferred to my decisions, never once did we discuss our long-term plans.

It was just another thing I wasn't sure how I felt about. I blamed my pregnancy hormones for my new indecisiveness and used work as a distraction from my forever internal looping questions. I loved designing, using skills long-ago put on the back burner to run my company. Exhilarated to create again, I worked for hours on the bike designs. I also took an indefinite leave from my company after I told Lian about my pregnancy.

I shook my head to dislodge my wandering thoughts, reached for my laptop, and reviewed my pre-nap progress. Happy with the images, I looked forward to sharing them with Morgan. Another confusing matter—yearning for another's approval, and a particular one at that.

My gaze roamed the living room and noted the quiet and utter stillness of my surroundings.

"Morgan?" I received no reply and raised my voice. "Morgan? Are you home?"

The grumblings from my stomach my only answer. The further along in my pregnancy, the hungrier I got. I positioned my arms on either side of my hips on the cushions and shimmied off the couch.

I swear I had doubled in size over the past week. My belly now as big as a basketball. At thirty-one weeks pregnant, I no longer walked. I waddled.

The growl coming from my stomach echoed off the walls of the house and competed with the muted sounds from outside. Birds chirped and the distant hum of the boat motors on Lake Washington floated through the air. Living close to the water had its perks. My favorite was the quiet.

City life, with its multitude of background noises, encouraged constant motion. I thrived off the energy of Seattle, but the serenity of Morgan's home fed my malnourished soul.

I walked to the kitchen, seeking food and found a wrapped plate of apple wedges, a jar of peanut butter, a knife, and a handwritten folded note. I slathered an apple slice with peanut butter and bit, sighing with satisfaction at the snap of the fruit. Four wedges later, I read the note.

Had to step out for errands. Back by four.
Eat. Relax. I'll bring pizza home.
Morgan

With a smile, I settled on a stool, and reread his scribble until my phone vibrated across the kitchen island with an incoming call from my mom.

"Hello?"

"Hi, sweetheart. How are you? Haven't heard from you in a while," she said.

I took my snack and note in one hand and retreated to the living room.

"How's the cruise going?"

"One month down, two to go."

"Mom. Everything all right? You sound sad?"

"Sorry, honey. I love all the places we're seeing, but I miss you. I want to be with you?"

"I miss you too, but I'm glad you went. I'm happy." It wasn't until I uttered the words out loud, could I admit they were true. "Morgan isn't the alphahole I thought he'd be."

"Told you. Susan's a superb judge of character. She would never be friends with an asshole, alpha or not. Tell me, how are you?"

"I'm good, Mom. Tired."

"The last trimester is a doozy. I remember I slept all the time when I carried you. Are you getting enough fluids?"

"Yep. Just saw the doctor. She's pleased with the baby's health."

"And what did she have to say about *my* baby?"

"I'm doing okay too, Mom," I said, laughing at her insistent need to call me her baby. Ever since I got pregnant, I didn't much mind the endearment. "I'm gaining weight, I eat well, I sleep."

She hummed, her voice at first muffled, then clear once again. "Sorry, it seems I have ten more minutes to speak, baby girl. Between the time difference and our port stops, it's difficult finding the right time to call you."

"It's okay. Are you and Daddy having fun?"

"Oh my goodness, are we having fun? The sun, the sea, the sights, just wow. Your father has a pep in his step if you know what I mean."

"Mom," I groaned. "I don't need to hear about that."

"You shut it." She giggled. "I also remember when I was pregnant with you, I was…how do I say this? Amorous? Voracious? in the seventh month, right before my belly grew to the size of a watermelon. It was fun finding different pos…."

"Seriously, Mom. Stop."

"Oh, I'm sorry," she said without a hint of remorse in her voice. I imagined her putting her hand on her breast, batting her eyelashes. "Am I offending your demure ears?"

"Ha, ha. You're funny. Now stop hinting at all the sex you're having and tell me about the places you've been."

We spoke for another few minutes before we switched to the video calling app we had on our phones so I could show her my growing baby bump. She oohed and ahhed like a happy soon-to-be-grandma before her tone turned serious.

"Thanks for showing me, baby girl. How is Morgan treating you?"

I shut my eyes and concentrated on keeping my voice even. "He's very attentive. Comes to every appointment. Doesn't let me lift a damn thing. I swear if he could brush my teeth for me, he would."

She scoffed and waved her hand, dismissing my complaint. "Your dad did the same thing. It used to drive me crazy."

"I thought it would, but he's so subtle. By the time I realize he's manipulated me, I'm thankful he took matters in his own hands."

"Be still my beating heart. Did you just say you're okay with him taking control?"

"Seriously, Mom," I said, sounding like my tween self when she embarrassed me. "Cut it out. It's kinda nice letting someone else take care of things for a bit."

"Uh huh. Is he as controlling in the bedroom?" She covered her mouth and muffled her amusement.

"We are not discussing his prowess."

"By the blush on your face, I'd say he's good in the sack," she said and waggled her eyebrows.

I glanced at my wrist, where no watch rested. "Oh, would you look at that? Our ten minutes are up. You better get back on that boat before they leave without you. Love you, bye."

I waited for her laugh and wink before I hung up.

Chapter Twenty-Three

Ann Marie

"Let me help grab those," Susan said, and rounded her car to meet me at the trunk.

The larger my belly grew, the harder time I had bending. She grabbed most of my shopping totes and followed me up the walkway to the front door, where I reached for the knob.

The door flew open. Morgan greeted us. His flushed skin stirred my curiosity.

"Here, let me take those," he said, and wrapped his fingers around the handles of my bags.

The moment his skin touched mine, an erratic pulse beat in my core, and I crossed my legs, staving off the sensations.

"How was shopping? Leave anything for other people to buy?"

"Har har. This is nothing. You should see the stuff Susan bought."

"Yeah? Never knew you to be a big shopper," he said to Susan.

"Oh, she isn't. But she got sexy lingerie."

Susan swatted my arm and her face reddened. "Don't pick on me. I believe you purchased a few items for yourself."

"Of course, I did. I love carrying this little one, but

damn, am I ready to feel sexy again. Hell, I'll take seeing my feet as a win." I walked to the kitchen, my stomach demanding food. "It smells so good in here." I turned and faced Morgan. "Did you bake something?" My gaze skidded across the room, looking for whatever caused the delicious scent.

Morgan tugged a large plastic container filled with chocolate chip cookies from its hiding place above the fridge.

"Give me, give me." I reached for the box with grabby hands. "Are these your mother's cookies? God, I love them."

He laughed as I shuffle-ran to him and clutched my waist when I stumbled. "Careful."

With a guiding nudge, he walked me to the island, placed the container on the counter, and handed me a napkin. I bit into a cookie and closed my eyes as the sugary flavors exploded on my tongue.

"Sweet baby Jesus. Your mother's amazing."

"She is," he said and picked up a cookie, aiming it toward his lips.

I gripped his wrist and stopped him. "Mine. Go find your own mom to bake for you."

He chuckled, distracted me with a kiss, and shoved the treat into his mouth. "Ma made them for everyone. I saved them from the hoards for you. You should be thanking me and sharing."

"Hoards? Who was here? Did your mom bake these here? If she brought them over, it wouldn't smell so good in here."

"Aaand, that's my cue to leave." Susan hustled out of the kitchen and house.

Morgan took my hand in his and urged me to my

feet. When I hesitated, he chuckled again.

"I have something to show you."

I looked from the cookies to him, and he rolled his eyes at me.

"Take some with you."

I didn't argue, grabbed a handful, and contorted my arm to take a bite since he wouldn't let go of my other hand. He led me down the hall and stopped at the third bedroom. He turned the knob and swung the door wide.

"Go on."

I took a tentative step. I entered the room as my lungs constricted and released a gasp. My now cookie-free hand flew to my mouth as I studied the changes and circled in place. My gaze never landed on one place for too long.

"When did you do this? How...?" I said after several deep breaths.

"I enlisted help."

Too surprised to understand, I took slow steps around the nursery. I dragged my fingers across all the surfaces. The cherry wood crib, changing table, and rocker I wanted were in what now was a nursery. I pointed at the walls. "You printed my decals."

He nodded and stood beside me as I surveyed the room.

"I don't know what to say."

"Do you like it?"

"I love it. It's beautiful. It's how I envisioned it."

"I had Ma, Susan, and Kate buy the stuff you bookmarked. Dustin and Parker helped me get all the furniture built while Ma and Kate decorated."

"It surprised me Susan wanted to go shopping. She kept me going for hours, even though her eyes were glued to her phone. Every time I asked her about it, she said she was checking on the status of things. I was so confused, but I get it now. That sneaky little shit." I went to him and poked him in the chest. "You did this. Why?"

He took my finger and brought my hand down to my side, not letting go. "I'd apologize, but I'm not going to. You have six weeks left, and I didn't want you exhausting yourself."

Then he shocked me when he dropped to one knee.

"What are you doing? Get up." I took a step back, not getting far before he tightened his grip.

He reached into his pocket. My knees shook. He raised a box and snapped it open.

"Marry me?"

My tongue felt swollen in my cotton-dry mouth.

"Why?"

He staggered on his bended knee, and his eyes narrowed. It was too late for me to take my question back. What I hoped to hear remained undetermined, but his response important, nonetheless.

"Because it's the right thing to do."

I pulled my hand from his and shuffled back to the rocking chair. I sat and looked at him with my mouth agape.

"I know you can take care of this baby alone. But why should you have to? Over the past eight weeks we've lived in harmony, we've proven we can work together. We're compatible in bed. I believe this is the best course of action."

I opened and closed my mouth like a fish out of water. What he said made sense. The CEO in me agreed with him. But my heart didn't. And without warning, the truth hit me. No matter how much I changed, left my past behind me, grew into a strong independent woman, Morgan shoved me right back to that girl from nine years ago.

I may have believed I didn't want a relationship, but deep down I craved it. I wanted someone to hold me, cherish me, put me before all things, share their life with me, desire me, love me. Where my high school boyfriend broke my heart when he abandoned me, Morgan shattered my heart by sticking beside me.

I stood, ensured the stability of my legs beneath me, and walked out of the room. Morgan followed.

I grabbed my bag and keys from the table by the front door.

"What are you doing?"

I denied hearing the anguish in his voice.

"I have to go."

"I'll go with you."

I turned to face him and the fear in his eyes almost broke me. The look wasn't real. It was a delusion my crumbling ego wanted to see.

"No." I placed my hand on his chest. "I need to think."

"Where are you going? How long?"

"Morgan, please. Let me go. I need time."

He reached for me. I stepped further away and took in a deep breath. I plastered a forced impassiveness on my face, I turned and left before my anger—or my tears—appeared.

****

Morgan

She walked out the door, and I didn't stop her.

I should have felt relieved she turned down my proposal, but I didn't. Her rejection punched me in the gut. I rubbed at the ache in my chest. Underneath my palm, my hearts' walls ricocheted against my ribs. I blamed my erratic pulse for the sudden nausea and dizziness.

I forced my feet forward and closed the door she'd left open. I shuffled to the couch and plopped down onto the cushion. I analyzed the events of the past hour as I ran my fingers through my hair. I knew I needed help. I needed my brothers. For once, I needed to talk and get out of my head. My emotions too overwhelming to keep inside me anymore.

I grabbed my phone from the coffee table with trembling hands, and three tries later I clicked the icon to connect with Pax.

"Brother," he said as he answered. "Morgan? Morgan? What the…where are you?" His voice laced with concern.

I held the phone to my ear. Words escaped me. Somehow, I managed grunts and gasps.

"Morgan. Man, you have me on video chat. All I see is your cheek."

It took a minute for his words to register. I pulled the device away, but my trembling hand failed me.

"Dude? What's going on? Look, I can't see you very well. Are you sick? Why are you shaking?"

"I…I…"

"Morgan, prop the phone on something, man. I'm giving you one more minute before I call Mom and have her come over to check on you."

I followed his instructions and rested my phone against the helmet I bought for Ann Marie but hadn't given her yet. I took in deep gulps. I heeded his threat and focused on regulating my thoughts, my heart, my racing pulse. I did not need my mother seeing me in my current state.

"Shit. Caden's calling me. Mind if I connect him to our chat?"

I nodded and in the next second the screen's display split into two pictures.

"Hey, brother. Did I interrupt?"

I stayed silent.

Caden's brows furrowed. "What's happened? Mom…Dad…is someone hurt?" Caden's voice frantic as he leaned closer to his camera as if it would help him see us better.

"I asked her to marry me."

Two astonished and quiet siblings greeted my outburst.

"Come again?" Caden asked.

"I asked Ann Marie to marry me."

Pax sat back, and Caden squinted at the screen.

"You're not kidding, are you?" Caden asked after several silent seconds.

"No."

"Jesus, I don't know what to say. I didn't expect…"

"Expect you to jump in with both feet," Pax finished for Caden.

"She's carrying my baby."

Pax rubbed his hand across his military short hair.

"Go on, say it," I said.

He shook his head. "Not sure I should."

"Fine, if you won't then I will," Caden said. "Dude, you don't even know if this baby's yours."

His words angered me. I should have stopped and examined the reason behind my emotions, but denial ran unchecked through my veins.

"Does it matter?"

"Yes," they both yelled.

"I'm doing the right thing."

Pax stood, and his image bounced as he paced with the phone in his hand.

He stopped and stared at the screen. "Doing the right thing? What is this? The Middle Ages?" With each question, Pax's volume rose. "Doing the right thing? What the hell, Morgan?"

Caden raised his hands. "Okay, Pax. Take a breath. Go get a beer. Morgan, do the same. I'm grabbing one as well."

We didn't argue with him, retrieved our drinks, and returned to our phones. We took a few sips, each of us needing a minute to let the alcohol calm our heightened feelings. At least I did.

"I'm shocked you're considering marriage. But what is blowing my mind right now is your reasoning. People should marry out of love, but it sounds like you're asking her out of what…obligation?" Pax said.

"I don't want to gang up on you, but I agree with Pax."

"Morgan? Why do you feel like it's your duty to marry her?"

Because I want this baby.

Because I want Ann Marie.

I ran my hand through my hair, frustrated the answers playing in my head didn't jibe with my uncomplicated life. I couldn't tell my brothers what I felt deep down, because saying it out loud made it real.

"She said no."

Caden smiled around the rim of his beer bottle.

"Well, shit. She didn't fall for your bullshit excuse either, huh?" Pax said what seemed on both their minds.

"Pax, stop being a smug bastard. What you and Susan have…It's not what I want. I'm not built that way."

"What? You're not built to love? Are you fucking kidding me? Out of all of us, you love the most fiercely."

Caden nodded his head, and for a moment Pax stunned me silent.

"Why do you look like he's just slapped you? Pax is right. You've perfected this unflappable attitude, but we see through your bullshit."

"There's nothing to see through. I don't love. I don't want forever. I don't want…"

"What? The support of a good woman? The undying affection of a child?"

I opened my mouth to tell Caden no. No, I didn't want any of that, but Pax raised his hand and for a minute he looked at me like he did when I came home from the accident. Pity, angry, curious. It was an expression I never gave him or anyone else a reason to show me again.

He lifted his beer to his lips, took a long pull, and eyed me over the bottle's length. "You know, love isn't a bad thing. It's warmth on a cold winter's night. It's a laugh on the darkest of days. It's eternity in our short-lived lives. It's anything and everything."

"Shit, man. That's deep," I said, wiping fake tears from my eyes. "Still not for me."

"Stop pretending you're not affected by Ann Marie. I've seen you with her." Pax's voice rose in tempo, and if not for the bad lighting, I swore his cheeks reddened.

"Pax, stop. You know Morgan doesn't listen to reason. He's…"

"Neither do either of you. It wasn't that long ago we tried getting Pax to see reason and go after Susan."

"True. I was stupid. I could have saved both of us a lot of heartache."

"Morgan, you may not want to admit it, and that's fine, but you love. We all see the way you protect Mom, Kate, and Susan. Even though Pax is almost double your size, we know if he ever hurt Susan, you would down him."

I growled, and Caden laughed.

"See? Just thinking about it makes you angry. You love, whether or not you want to admit it. You love with your whole heart, you're just picky with whom you give it to."

I didn't give him either a verbal or non-verbal response.

"Let me ask you something," Caden continued. "When she turned you down, how'd you feel?" He raised his hand. "No bullshit. Be honest with us, and yourself."

I closed my eyes and took a minute to think. A swallow of beer and a fortifying breath later, I opened them.

"Like shit."

"Why?"

"I don't know."

I had an inclination.

"Yes, you do. Dig deeper."

Pax stayed silent as Caden pushed me, just like he did when we were kids.

"I'm not one of your clients, Caden. I don't need your help finding my inner strength."

"Stop stalling. Caden won't let up and you know it."

"I need another beer for this crap." I went to my kitchen and with a fresh drink in hand, I propped the phone up on the island and sat on a stool.

"Better?"

I grunted at Caden, and Pax chuckled.

"How did her saying no make you feel?"

My eyebrows, reflected on my phone screen, narrowed.

It made me feel like shit. Like I wasn't someone she could love. It made me angry.

"Angry."

"Why?"

Exasperated with his questions, I kept the part of my body in view motionless, but my leg jiggled on the rung of the stool.

"I offered her help, and she didn't want it."

"I'm no chick here, but I'm guessing most women don't want help. They want to be desired. Loved. Adored. Cherished."

"Are you looking at a thesaurus, Pax? Those are a lot of words."

He smiled into the screen. "Go ahead, brother. Distract yourself away from the truth. It's what you do best."

"Pax."

"Come on, Caden. You know as well as I do,

Morgan shuts down rather than feel anything real. He never draws attention to himself. But the idiot doesn't realize his broody, bike riding, leather wearing, tattoo decorated ass brings him tons of it."

"No, it doesn't." Both of them scoffed, and for the first time I pictured the version of me I'd cultivated over the years. "Fine, I concede the point. But it was never my intention."

"Of course, it wasn't. Susan calls it your leave-me-the-fuck-alone look."

Caden laughed, and Pax joined him.

"Morgan, if you want this woman in your life, you need to find the reasons you keep buried deep within you," Caden said.

"I don't want her in my life."

Caden tilted his head and raised an eyebrow but remained silent.

The longer they stayed quiet, the more my mind raced. What did I want? Why did her rejection hurt? Did it hurt, or was I a selfish asshole?

"I can see you're thinking. I'm going to add another question to the list I know isn't running through your head. When tomorrow comes, will you be okay if Ann Marie is not in your life?"

"Why wouldn't she be? We're having a baby."

Pax shook his head. "No, I don't think Caden is asking about the baby. Take her out of the equation. How would you feel if Ann Marie, and just Ann Marie, was no longer in your life?"

I was about to answer something stupid, something superficial, but when I went to voice it, a lump formed in my throat.

Pax scooted closer to the screen. "You've already

given your heart to this baby, not knowing if she's yours or not. I know you'll protect her with your last breath. The question is, would you do the same for her mother? If not, then you can't marry her. Spending your life with someone isn't about the physical, it's about the emotional. It's about sharing. Sharing your responsibilities, dreams, desires, and most important of all, your heart."

Sharing my heart?

The concept resonated. The ache in my chest subsided. My heart slowed, then sped.

She already had it.

I already gave it to her.

I gasped and almost fell off the stool.

"Morgan? Morgan? Shit, say something. You've gone white as a sheet."

I grasped the edge of the counter and followed Pax's breathing instructions. After several intakes, a calmer yet exhilarated feeling pulsed through my body. A smile played across my face, and I knew.

I knew.

I looked at the screen and found my brothers smiling.

"I think he's figured it out," Pax said.

"Think you're right. Our work here is done."

They were right. I loved Ann Marie. The realization hit me like a Mack truck, but I didn't stagger. I held onto the feeling and allowed it to envelop me. It didn't feel right sharing those words with my family before I said them to her.

"Brother, we know. Congratulations." Caden smiled and waved. "Call me when she says yes."

"I won't say anything to Susan. But I can bet if you

don't fix this, Susan will hear all about it from her cousin. Later."

My screen went black before I grunted a goodbye. Left alone in my kitchen with my thoughts, it was my heart that pushed me into action.

Chapter Twenty-Four

Ann Marie

I seethed, yet I jostled into my car. I needed distance between me and Morgan. My swollen feet hurt in the flip-flops, but at this point of the pregnancy it was all I could put on without help. Shoelaces were my enemy.

"Ugh, that man's infuriating." I hit the wheel with the palm of my hand and took out my aggression on the innocent vinyl. "What the hell were you thinking? Asking me to marry you so the baby had a daddy?" He couldn't hear me, but I voiced the questions anyway.

I pushed the start button and lifted a one-fingered salute at his house before driving away. As I passed his parents' home, spasms radiated across my abdomen. Little—some longer than others—throbbing jolts had plagued me throughout the day. By the time Morgan proposed, I was at my wits' end. I hid my pain from him. I didn't want to clue him into my discomfort. But alone in the car, I couldn't ignore the sensations taking over. Sobs of pain intermixed with the sobs of sadness.

Tears blurred my vision. The expunging cathartic. Almost like my emotional state needed a release. I cried as I drove without a destination in mind and used the sleeve of my shirt to wipe the trails of the never-ending snot. During one of those swipes a cramp fanned across my lower back to the front of my abdomen.

I let go of the steering wheel to clutch my belly and realized my mistake too late. The car swerved, and I grabbed the wheel, and in my haste, overcorrected. I lost control. My grip tightened. I slammed my foot on the brake, ended in a tailspin, and the back end of my car skidded along the guardrail. Metal ground against metal. Sparks flew, and the screeching grew in volume, threatening the well-being of my eardrums.

The world slowed but at the same time, everything happened in a flash. The rear bumper ripped off the rail and tumbled end over end, landing in the middle of the opposite lane. The car came to a deafening halt, throwing me back into my seat. My breath became labored. I forced oxygen into my lungs as my heart pumped in overdrive.

Pain speared my abdomen. I shrieked in fear. Dampness filled my panties. Terror dug its nasty talons into my chest. I couldn't see past the baby bump, at least not enough to determine if it was blood or pee. With one hand I held my belly as if I could hold in the contraction and with the other, I checked inside my leggings.

I dipped my fingers in the wetness. My door flung open, and the head of a concerned citizen poked in the car. His gaze traveled from my face to my stomach to my hand buried in my underwear.

"Are you okay?" he asked, his soft tone matched his eyes.

I pulled my shaking hand out of my pants and lifted it to my face. I dreaded every second yet needed to know the truth. I gulped as my non-bloodied hand came into view. Tears flowed. Overwhelming relief took hold.

"Shit. It's just pee. I peed my pants," I said through fits of giggles and pain. "Oh my God, this fucking hurts."

The man's bulging eyes and speechlessness did not deter me. I went back and forth between hysterics and breathing heavy.

"Carl, she's in labor. Get out of my way," a woman said from behind him. "Call nine-one-one and get the flares out." I couldn't see what they did. I shut my eyes in an effort to combat the spasms. I sensed movement. A soft hand gripped my wrist, my sullied one, and dug two fingers at my pulse point.

"Don't touch…my…hand…Pee…I…" I said through the contraction pains.

"Oh, hush, child. I was a trauma nurse for twenty-five years. A little urine doesn't scare me. Besides, I don't believe that's pee. I think your water just broke."

Her revelation increased my panic. "It can't be. I'm not far along yet. No, please. It's too early."

"Just breathe, honey. We'll have you on your way to the hospital in no time."

"I'm thirty-two weeks. It's too early. I've killed my baby." I hyperventilated, and combined with my snot-clogged nose, I couldn't get enough air into my lungs.

"Hey, hey, you listen to me now. You've done nothing of the sort, but you need to calm down so it can stay that way. Look at me." When I didn't, she took my chin in her hands and turned me to face her. "Breathe with me."

With effort, I evened out my breaths to match hers.

"You're doing great, honey. I'm so proud of you. What's your name?"

Her soothing voice kept my anxiety at bay. "Ann Marie Tosto." I breathed out as another contraction tore through my body.

"Remember your Lamaze exercises, honey." She placed her hand in mine and told me to squeeze. I had enough sense about me to pull my strength. Her bones felt fragile in my grip.

"You did good," she said, and I loosened my hold as the pain subsided. "Now, does anything else hurt?"

I took stock of my body during the temporary reprieve. "No, no. Just my uterus screaming at me."

The woman laughed and ran her palm along my arm. "Sit tight. I'm not strong enough to pull you out of the car by myself." She leaned out and yelled to who I assumed was her husband. "Carl, what's the ETA on EMS?"

They spoke, but their words became background noise as the next spasm took ahold of my abdomen, and I wished for Morgan's strength.

Realization dawned. I needed to contact him.

"Morgan."

The woman's head popped back in through the open door. "The ambulance is two minutes out. Who's Morgan?"

"My phone…console…Morgan…contacts…please call him," I gritted out.

She leaned across me and took my phone and aimed it at my face to unlock it. I was thankful she was familiar with technology and laughed at my absurd random thought.

She pushed and swiped the screen until her face broke out in a smile. She held up the phone to her ear, her gaze on me soft as she waited for him to answer.

"Hello?" she said.

"This isn't Ann Marie, I'm Greta."

She paused, and I wished I could hear his end of the conversation.

"No, no. Everything's fine. She's right here beside me. There's been an accident and…" Her gaze found mine and she gave me a reassuring smile.

"Yes, hold on a second, darling. I'll put you on speaker." She held the phone away from her ear and tapped the screen.

"Here she…"

"Ann Marie," Morgan's voice boomed from the speaker. "Where are you? What happened?"

Another contraction spread through me, and I breathed as best I could through it. A growing crowd gathered around the car, and all I wanted was Morgan by my side. The thought filtered through a second time, and I gasped.

I wanted Morgan holding my hand, reassuring me. I wanted Morgan in the birthing room, holding our baby girl as soon as she made her appearance. I wanted Morgan in my life, standing beside me as a lover, father, partner.

My vision grew hazy, black dots in the periphery, and I tried breathing through the fog.

"Please…" I squeaked out the one word before darkness overwhelmed me.

****

Morgan

"Hello, hello?" I screamed into the phone. My heart pounded in my chest. "Ann Marie? Please what?" When she didn't respond my legs threatened to give out, and I took a seat on my front steps where I had run to at the mention of the accident. Keys in hand, I was ready to get to her as soon as the Greta woman on the other end told me where they were.

"Morgan, darling, I have to hang up. Your girl and your baby need me right now."

"No!" My voice bounced off the trees in the front yard, startling a man walking his dog. I didn't give a shit and returned his scowl. "No, please. Tell me where you are. I'll be there in minutes." I begged, torn between needing to keep Greta on the phone and giving her back to Ann Marie. Greta, my single connection to Ann Marie. My gut told me if I let her go, I would lose the tenuous hold I had on my fear.

"They're loading her into the ambulance right now."

"What?" Again, my volume louder than necessary. "I thought you said she was okay. What the hell is going on?"

"Meet her at Bylake Med."

"I'm on my way." I hung up and raced to my bike. I swung my leg over the top but stopped before putting the key into the ignition. Although I could zip through traffic faster, in my frazzled mindset, driving a bike would have been dangerous. I dismounted and climbed into the cab of my truck instead. I peeled out of my driveway. The tires squealed along the black top. I flew down the street in front of my parents' home past my mom and dad as they exited their car.

I paid them no further attention and continued. My phone rang through the Bluetooth. Without looking at the display I answered my mom's call.

"Morgan Noah Anderson, what on God's green

earth makes it okay for you to drive like a lunatic?" Ma yelled across the phone line.

"I have to get to the hospital. Ann Marie's been in an accident. I have to get to Bylake," I said, the last words choked out.

"Morgan, sweetheart. Slow down. You'll be no good to her dead. Dad and I will be right behind you." Her calm mothering quieted my panic, and I took in a lungful of air. I concentrated on removing my lead foot and drove with caution yet determination.

"I have to go, Ma."

"Okay, sweetheart. I'll call Jesse and Pax. We'll see you there. Be careful."

I hung up and focused my energy on keeping my shit together. If anything happened to Ann Marie, I didn't know if I could survive. In the short time she'd been in my house, she made it a home. I didn't hate the changes. I didn't hate us working together. And I didn't hate the idea of having her as a permanent fixture in my life. In fact, I needed her to my core.

My mind replayed moments from the past seven months. With each new picture my smile widened. The first time we were together at Thanksgiving. The look on her face when she moved in two months ago. The times I took care of her after she'd been sick. Her smile after I gave her what she said were the best orgasms of her life. The belly that grew each day. The way she snuggled into me on the couch after having fallen asleep.

Images popped in and out, and before I knew it, I was at the hospital. I pulled into the first available spot and slammed the gear into park. I bolted from the truck and ran for the ER doors. Jesse met me just inside, took my elbow in his hand, and directed me to the elevators.

"Where are we going? Ann Marie…"

"She's not here. They moved her to Maternity. We need to get you up there."

My feet thudded to a stop. "It's too soon. The doctor said she needed to be thirty-six weeks. She's at thirty-two. She can't have the baby." I ran my fingers through my hair and hoped my brother would tell me she wasn't in labor.

"Traumatic events can sometimes speed up the timeline," was all he said.

My mind whirled with this bit of information.

"This is my fault," I whispered as I realized the accident would never have happened had I not proposed.

Jesse stepped in front of me and placed his hands on my shoulders. He matched me in height and coloring. Regardless of his younger brother status, he commanded respect from those around him and he had mine. "It was an accident," he said with conviction, understanding my unspoken guilt.

Bile rose in my throat, hurling almost an inevitable outcome.

He squeezed my shoulders to the point of pain and pulled me from the impending tailspin. "I know what you're thinking. Neither accident was your fault. Do not take this on your shoulders."

I shook my head.

"No," he said with force. "Aunt Karen and Uncle Dustin's accident was eighteen years ago. You survived, and it wasn't your fault. You and Parker were just kids goofing off in the back seat. That's it. Ann Marie lost control of the car. You didn't grab the wheel and turn it on her. Accidents happen."

Too lost in self-hatred, I registered his words, but their meaning didn't penetrate. Until I confirmed Ann Marie's well-being with my own eyes, I wouldn't see past my role in her accident. I worried for the baby and Ann Marie. Although I couldn't fathom losing the baby, I feared what the loss would do to Ann Marie.

For the first time in eighteen years, I loved someone outside of my family. My revelation that started mere hours ago, solidified and beat in my chest. Gained a stronghold. I wanted to stop traffic and declare my love for Ann Marie to anyone listening. Hell, even to those who weren't.

I staggered, my back hitting the elevator walls. I was in love with Ann Marie. I couldn't envision my life without her. Sweat broke out across my lip and forehead, and I clenched my shaking hands, digging my knuckles into my thighs.

I asked her to marry me, but I asked her for the wrong reasons. Pax's words hit home, and I groaned at my idiocy.

Ann Marie was right. She didn't need my help. She didn't need me holding her hand. And she didn't need me in her and the baby's life.

What Ann Marie needed was a man to love her, hold her through the light and the dark times, a partner in life. A man, who respected her, treated her as an equal. A man not threatened by her beauty or success. A man she could trust. I was that man, and I would prove it to her, starting with being there for her as she brought our daughter into this world.

But first I needed to get to her.

A ding bounced off the walls in the small space. I

followed Jesse off the elevator and to the locked entryway. He pulled his key card attached to his pants with a retractable elastic string and held it to the reader. Another beep and the doors swished open.

I squeezed through the sliver of open doors and made it to the nurse's station before him.

"Ann Marie? What room is she in?" I bellowed and leaned over. My hands rested on the chest-high platform of the desk.

The seated nurse looked me up and down, lips curled in a sneer. I raised a hand, ready to slam it on the desktop. Jesse clasped my shoulder. His touch grounded me. I dug my palms into my eyes and prayed for patience. And Ann Marie. And my baby.

"Dorothy, this is my brother. Don't mind him, he's freaking out. Ann Marie Tosto was just brought in. Car accident inducing labor."

Recognition lit up Dori's face, or was it Darla? I didn't much care.

"The doctor's in with her right now. No visitors allowed. Take a seat and someone will be out to give you an update."

"I'm the baby's father. That's my…" What was Ann Marie to me? Lover, partner, baby mama? Regardless, she was soon going to be my fiancée and wife within a couple of days if I had my way. "My girlfriend's in there."

For the first time, the word girlfriend didn't leave a bitter taste in my mouth.

Dori/Darla smiled. "Congratulations." She held up her hand as I opened my mouth to speak again. "She's being looked over. I can't let you in, but as soon as I can, I assure you, I'll allow you in to see her and be a part of the birthing."

Jesse's gentle tug pulled me away from the desk. "Come on. Take a seat and I'll check in with the doctor." I hesitated and Jesse urged me toward the seats. "Two minutes. I'll be back with answers."

I nodded but didn't sit. Instead, I paced the small area.

Before he left, he turned to the nurse's station. "Dorothy, fair warning. My family is about to descend upon us. The waiting room is going to get busy."

"No problem, Dr. Anderson. I'll make sure the coffee is on."

I somehow noted Dorothy's batting her eyelashes and Jesse gave her the smile he used on his patients. Their interaction distracted me for a moment. I shook my head and resumed pacing. Jesse turned away from the flirting nurse, smiled at me with a hint of an eye-roll, and headed down the hall. Too restless to commit to one action I sat, rubbed my hand down my face, then stood and paced, sat and looked out the window, stood and paced, sat and fidgeted in my seat, stood and paced.

During one of my staring-out-the-window sessions arms enveloped me. My family had arrived.

"Any word?" Mom asked.

"No."

"Where's Jesse? He was supposed to be with you?"

My muddled brain didn't comprehend her question at first. "He was. He went to talk to the doctor. Said he'd be back in two minutes. What's taking him so long?"

"I'm sure he'll be back soon," Susan said as she came and hugged me.

Pax stood behind her with his hand on her lower

back. Dad did the same with Ma. Foster and Dustin stood in the door's archway with wrinkled eyebrows and tensed shoulders.

"Canceled my trip as soon as I heard. Hadn't boarded the flight yet," Foster said, reminding me of his travel plans. He raised a hand. "There'll be other competitions. Family first."

Lost for words, I pulled my brother into a two-armed hug and ignored the surrounding gasps.

"Parker and Kate are on their way," Dustin said, interrupting our embrace and shifted on his feet.

"What's with the green face?" I asked him, trying to keep my mind occupied.

"Dude, there are women here pushing watermelons out of their vajajays."

My parents, brothers, and Susan erupted in laughter.

"If you're giving out comfort, man, I think I need some," Dustin said, scrunching his eyebrows.

Without hesitation, I pulled him into my arms, and he held the back of my head into his shoulder.

"It's okay, brother, we'll hold you up," he whispered. "Let go."

With my face hidden and my cousin lending me his strength, I shuddered and allowed the tears to escape.

Chapter Twenty-Five

Morgan

A few more minutes ticked by in silence. I
continued pacing while Pax sat with Susan on his lap,
Ma and Dad shared an uncomfortable-looking loveseat
holding hands. Dustin and Foster made a coffee run to
the machine by the nurse's station, flirting with any
nurse looking their way.

I was about to march down the hall and demand
entry into the delivery room when Jesse came back with
a pair of scrubs in hand.

"She's awake and almost ready. Put these on," he
said as he held them out to me.

I didn't take them. "Awake? What do you mean
awake? When was she asleep?" I asked.

"She lost consciousness at the scene."

"What the fuck?"

"Morgan?" An older woman asked from behind
Jesse. She stepped to his side with Ann Marie's phone.
"I'm Greta. We spoke on the phone. Ann Marie's water
broke during the accident and she's in labor. Now is not
the time for questions. Ann Marie needs you by her
side. Be her strength, not her crutch," she said with a
no-nonsense air and handed me the phone.

I nodded, took both the scrubs and device. "Come
on. I'll take you back," Jesse said.

My family shouted words of wisdom and love. With a distracted wave, I walked away, my mind and heart too focused on getting to the woman I loved.

I entered a room thrumming in controlled chaos. Wires ran back and forth between Ann Marie and several machines. I recognized the baby's heartbeat. Its speed worrisome.

"It's too fast," I mumbled.

"It's normal," Jesse said, surprising me. I'd forgotten his presence.

I wrung my hands, unsure of my place as nurses fussed around Ann Marie and the doctor who sat on a rolling stool at the foot of the bed.

Ann Marie's wide, open legs rested in stirrups. I wanted to cover her up from all the eyes in the room. Ever observant, Jesse noticed my discomfort, chuckled, and laid a hand on my shoulder.

"As any doctor would tell you, the important thing in this room right now is the beautiful woman having your baby, not what she's exposing. It's just another organ."

"Still, stop looking." My voice reverberated against the room's walls and the doctor turned. Ann Marie peered around the nurse beside her.

"Mr. Anderson. Come in and greet your daughter."

I stumbled back. "She's born?"

Dr. Morris shook her head. "No, but any minute now. The baby's lungs are developed, and Ann Marie isn't experiencing complications."

I sighed in relief and hurried to Ann Marie's side. Her eyes were red rimmed and skin pale. I took her hand in mine.

"What do I do?" I asked no one in particular.

"Hold her through her contractions," Jesse replied as Dr. Morris said, "She's at ten centimeters. Next contraction, she pushes. Encourage her."

I leaned down and kissed Ann Marie's forehead. With our noses touching, I spoke to her as her gaze fixed on mine. Exhaustion lined her eyes, and I squeezed her hand. "I've got you, baby. Use me. You're so beautiful. You're amazing. So strong."

Her eyes shut and the machines went crazy. I panicked at the new commotion and my stomach revolted. No one yelled for me to move, but with the increased movement around me, I feared I was in the way. I focused on Ann Marie and grew restless the more her face contorted.

"Push now, Ann Marie," the doctor said from behind me.

I placed my hand on the back of Ann Marie's head, leaned closer, and kept her hand in mine. "Push, baby. Addyson wants to meet her mommy."

Her eyes sparkled. "You remembered," she said through her labored breathing.

I bent down and kissed her temple. "Of course. You told me you loved the name. I love it too."

Ann Marie grunted and tears tracked down her cheeks. I kissed them away. As her grip on my hand relaxed, someone tapped my shoulder. I turned. Jesse held a cup of ice chips and nodded toward Ann Marie. He tapped his mouth. Understanding dawned, and I took the cup from him. Placed it to her lips and tipped so she could wrap her tongue around a few pieces. She sighed as the cool liquid did its thing.

She dropped her head back onto the pillow and closed her eyes.

"Is this normal?" I asked.

"What?" Jesse asked back.

"She's being so quiet. Don't women scream through this?"

The people in the room chuckled, including Ann Marie, and the smile on her face calmed my nerves.

"Everyone's different during labor. Ann Marie's hunkering down and doing it silently. Nothing to worry about," Dr. Morris said. "Ann Marie, get ready to push. Another contraction is on the way."

The beeping machines grew hyperactive. Ann Marie's hand-squeezing began. Movement around the room resumed. Ann Marie's curled spine brought her shoulders off the bed. I wrapped an arm behind her back and helped hold her position. She inhaled through her mouth, and I breathed along with her. Her gaze drifted to me and locked on mine as we breathed together.

"Match your rhythm to mine, baby. Focus on me."

"You guys are doing great," Dr. Morris said as the contraction eased, and Ann Marie laid back on the bed.

"Do you want to change positions?" I asked as my reading came back to me.

She shook her head.

I took a presented cold wet towel and draped it across her forehead. Her eyes fluttered shut, and I rubbed an ice chip to her lip.

"Thank you."

"Gorgeous, please don't thank me. You're having my baby. Our baby. I should be the one thanking you."

Sighs rang out through the room and Dr. Morris chuckled.

Ann Marie smiled and her eyes sparkled. "You're

right. I'm all ears."

I laughed, shook my head and leaned close to her ear. "Thank you for being you. For gifting me this and so much more. For the best sex I've ever had." She giggled, and I felt lighter for bringing her some relief and a smile, when pain was in the forefront. I kissed her. Soft and sensual. Her fingers played in the hair at my neck until they tightened.

"Another one?" I asked, shocked her contractions weren't further apart. She nodded. I repeated my actions and held her up as she bore down.

"Baby's head is crowning. Keep it up. Push through the contraction. Mr. Anderson, this is the moment. You want to see?"

"I'm good right here, Doc." I stared into Ann Marie's eyes and kept her focused on me hoping to assuage the pain of delivery. "You've got this baby. Fuck, you're amazing."

And moments after it started, the contraction ended. We repeated the cycle several more times. On the last round, Ann Marie's eyes widened as she pushed. A grunt, a growl, and a few tears later she shuddered, before she melted into the bed. Seconds later, her grip on me tightened as another wave engulfed her exhausted body.

"Let's get the rest of this baby out, one more push," Dr. Morris directed.

Ann Marie didn't look as pained as before, but still in discomfort. Too busy studying her every expression, I almost missed the whoops in the room.

"Welcome to the world, baby Addyson," Dr. Morris said as a gurgle and then a cry pierced the surrounding air. "Congratulations, Mommy and Daddy.

You have a beautiful and healthy baby girl."

I lifted my gaze from Ann Marie and tears ran down my cheeks as a nurse bundled my slimy, purple daughter in an open blanket and placed her skin side against Ann Marie's bare chest.

"Dad? Want to cut the cord?"

I couldn't take my eyes off my two beautiful girls.

"Morgan. Cut the cord. You'll regret it if you don't," Jesse said. "I'll stand watch over them."

In awe of the two ladies I loved, I did as the doctor directed and was back by their side, holding them close in my arms. Far too soon, they whisked Addyson away. I took the moment to wipe Ann Marie's face, give her ice chips, and kiss her. Pulling back, I kept our mouths close and whispered words I never thought I would say to anyone outside of my family.

"I love you."

****

Ann Marie

A new set of tears filled my eyes. Morgan's eyes shone with a love I never expected. I reached out and looped my arms around his neck. I brought his ear to my mouth and said what was in my heart.

"I love you, too."

I felt his tears against my cheek and welcomed his weight against me. We held each other, the world around us forgotten for a second or two. We let go of the past and grabbed on to our future, one that was clear and filled with family.

A throat cleared nearby, and we pulled apart. I groaned at the loss until the nurse held our baby, wrapped in a pink blanket, out to me.

"She's healthy and doing wonderful. Hold her hat as you feed her, it's a little big for her now, but she'll grow into it quick," the nurse said as she laid Addyson across my chest, helped me situate her for her first feeding.

Morgan watched in awe: his tears mixed in with laughter. We didn't speak, beholden to our daughter as she suckled at my breast with her eyes closed. In my heart, I knew she was Morgan's.

They were so alike in appearance. A full head of dark hair, bluish-gray eyes that twinkled just like his did when he laughed, a long chin and the most beautiful long fingers. Like I said, just like him.

He didn't stop touching me throughout the feeding. Both lips and hands caressed my face, my hair, my collarbone. Addyson dozed off, and with a nudge I offered her to him. He paled at first, but with a few quiet words of encouragement, he took her in his arms and held the pink bundle close to his chest. I melted in my bed when he leaned down and kissed her forehead.

I didn't pay attention to the nurses cleaning the room around him. My focus captivated by him with our daughter. Their forms silhouetted by the light coming in through the window and his husky voiced words bounced around in my brain. For the first time in years, I was at peace.

Morgan's tattooed arms cocooned Addyson with care. She fit in the palm of his hand. His fingers cradled the back of her head. I strained to hear him speaking to her.

After what felt like the hundredth kiss to her forehead, he whispered, "No kissing near your nose and mouth. Don't want you getting sick. At least that's what the books say. But I want to kiss this cute little nose of yours. I could just eat it up. You have your mother's beauty, you know, and I just want to eat her up. Wait, that didn't sound right." He bounced on his feet and supported her head in his palm. "What do you think of keeping what I said to ourselves for now? I'll never live it down if your uncles heard me. Look at us. We've already got this bond. I can tell you'll keep my secret."

I giggled, and then grunted when I attempted to sit up, drawing his gaze away from her. He rushed to my side and sat on the side of the bed.

"What's wrong? Hey, why are you laughing?"

"You're adorable with her and nothing's wrong. Just shifting hurts a bit."

"I can help, hold on, let me get Ma."

I reached out and grabbed his arms before he moved. "No. I want to talk to you first." He stilled. "Dr. Morris said she took a swab sample from Addyson. Are you still willing to go through with the paternity test? Before they can release her, you need to sign…what was it again? Oh, yeah, an Acknowledgment of Paternity. We have fourteen days after her birth to change the records if…if…"

"I'll sign whatever they need me to sign. I'll do whatever tests they need to prove I'm her dad because I am. I can feel it in my bones. Besides, I don't care what the results say. She's mine, and I'll fight Scott for her if he comes sniffing around."

"I don't think that's how it works."

"Don't care." He looked at the bundle in his arms and leaned forward to kiss her again. "She's my precious princess. I can't help myself. She's already got me wrapped around her little finger. I will kill to protect both of you, my queen and my princess. I love you both."

Tears pooled in the corner of my eyes, and I fought to keep them from falling. He loved her. He loved me. I loved him. He laid down beside me, put Addyson on my chest, and snaked a protective arm around both of us. He kissed the side of my head, and I snuggled in until I remembered the state of my body. I tried pulling away, but he wouldn't let me.

"I stink. I've been sweating. I'm gross."

"Don't care, you gave me this beautiful little human. You could be covered in ten-day-old sweat, vomit, or shit and I wouldn't care. You'll still smell like roses to me."

"Ew! That's disgusting." I laughed at his ridiculousness. This side of Morgan was one he kept from the world, and it was the part I loved most. I smacked him on his chest, jostling Addyson who smacked her lips a few times before settling. "Don't swear in front of the baby."

"Huh? Shit, that's going to be difficult. Worse when my brothers and cousins are around."

"Morgan," I chastised. "Quit fucking swearing."

We laughed as soon as the words left my mouth.

"Looks like we both have something to work on."

We fell silent, and I almost drifted off when the room door opened, and Mrs. Anderson peeked around it. Her hand went to her heart as tears rolled down her cheeks. Morgan's chuckles vibrating through his chest filled me with comfort and a yearning for a future surrounded by his family.

"I can send them away. Tell me what you want."

"No, it's okay. They're happy for you. Let's

introduce Addyson to her family."

Morgan lifted off the bed and picked up Addyson from my chest so they could see her face. His mom, dad, Susan, and Pax came through the door. Pax had a pink bear and Susan had flowers, which they set on the side table before coming to me.

"Ma, Dad, come meet your granddaughter, Addyson."

Mrs. Anderson cried, and her husband held her by the shoulders as they looked between Addyson and Morgan.

"Let me give the beautiful mommy a hug, and then I'd love to hold her if you're okay with it," she said and came to my bedside. She pulled me into a tight hug. Her mothering brought on fresh tears, and I wished my own was here with us. "My boy loves you, you know. He's stubborn and in denial, but one look at him in that waiting room, and there's no denying how he feels for you," she whispered in my ear.

"I know. I love him too."

Mrs. Anderson patted my cheeks as her gaze scanned my face. "Addyson's as beautiful as her mother. I'm so happy for you. Thank you for making me a grandma. I will always have my secret recipe chocolate chip cookies waiting for you at my house."

I giggled and winked at her. "Just don't tell Morgan. He'll eat them all."

She laughed, went to Morgan, and held out her arms. "Morgan Noah Anderson, hand over my grandbaby." He passed Addyson over, with reluctance, not because he didn't trust his mother, but because he didn't want to relinquish her.

Mrs. Anderson settled in a chair and Mr. Anderson,

Susan, and Pax hovered close to her. I didn't notice the others entering the room until several sets of arms wrapped around me.

"Get off her, you idiots. You'll smother her," Morgan said as I laughed and gripped my aching belly.

Parker, Dustin, and Foster stood at either side of me, not looking chastised at all. In fact, they looked like they were ready to come in for another tackle. I held my hand up and warded them off.

"Hugs later, boys. I need to call my mom and take a shower. Okay?"

"Then it's open season on the hugs," Dustin said.

"Foster made us watch delivery videos while we waited. Jesus, woman, whatever you want, if Morgan doesn't get it for you, one of us will," Parker said and waved his hand indicating the three of them.

"I cried actual tears of pain for you. I can't even…" Dustin shuddered and let his statement drift off.

"You can go get her favorite foods from the restaurant across the street," Morgan argued.

"We can do that," Foster said.

"Want to come?" Parker asked Morgan.

He shook his head. "Nope, going to help her shower."

The three boys cracked up and whooped. "You horn dog, you," Dustin said. "Give the woman some time. She just pushed a small human out of her loins."

"Did you just say loins?" Morgan asked.

"Duh. Of course, I did. She's a mommy now. Can't very well call her vagina a vagina anymore. Innocent ears are in the room."

"So loins is better than vagina for the baby to hear?"

"Of course. If it's good enough for those romance books Mom reads, then it's okay to say in her presence. We all know how Mom and Dad enjoy those novels in the bed…"

Morgan grabbed the closest item within reach and smacked the diaper across his cousin's chest. "Don't finish that sentence. God." He rubbed his palms against his eyes, "I don't need a visual."

Dustin wiggled his eyebrows, making Parker and Foster laugh. "For sure. The more traumatizing the visual, the less likely you'll put our girl through that again." He peered around Morgan's growling chest and focused on me. "I got your back, Ann Marie." I giggled, but in reality, I wanted to smack him too.

I loved sex with Morgan. I wanted nothing dissuading the man. For when I was healed, of course.

His brother and cousins exited, laughing, hitting each other, and betting on who would make the best food choices for me. Their mother shook her head at their antics, but her eyes told a different story.

"Sorry. I have a feeling they're bringing back a feast for you," Morgan said.

"It's okay. We can all eat then."

"You get first choice."

"Sounds good. But you know what sounds even better?" Morgan shook his head. "A shower. Does your offer still stand?"

His eyes glazed over with lust, but he gained control and nodded, then offered me his hand. "It's a freaking hardship, but someone's got to do it."

He helped me out of bed and with his arm around my waist he led me to the private bathroom. His parents watched us with smiles the size of Montana.

In the bathroom, he turned away at my request, and I took off the hospital's awful version of underwear. I unsnapped the top button of my gown, triggering Morgan's attention. He nudged my fingers away from the buttons and took over the last steps of stripping me bare. He started the water, adjusted the temperature, and then helped me into the stall. Without a word, he undressed and stepped in behind me. His hands on my hips, he guided me to sit on the ledge and with a soft and loving touch he washed me from head to toe.

Chapter Twenty-Six

Ann Marie

The rest of the day passed by in a blur. Dinner was a chaotic event, but Morgan showed off his daughter, which kept a perpetual smile on my face. After a while, I dozed off, and he sent everyone home. He perched on the edge of the bed beside me and held Addyson. He wouldn't put her down unless she needed feeding. Then he sat in the chair and watched with his unfaltering look of awe.

When she finished, he stood, bent over, kissed Addyson, planted several kisses on my face, and straightened.

"You taste so good." His breath fanned across my mouth, and I grew cross eyed trying to see his eyes. "You're so damn sexy."

I sighed at his words. "Sexy? I look awful. My hair is a matted mess. I have no makeup on, and my skin is flabby. No way am I my sexiest self right now."

"You are the most beautiful woman, and it bears repeating. You are damn sexy."

He tugged off his boots and scooted onto the bed with us. Lying on his side, he pulled me close and wrapped a protective arm over Addyson and around my waist.

"I love you," I said and snuggled into his hold.

He brushed a few of my fly-away hair strands behind my ear, and his gaze roamed across the features of my face.

"You are sexy first thing in the morning and the last thing at night. You are sexy when you're crying at something on the television," he said and placed a finger on my lips when I opened my mouth to argue. "I love it when you try to hide it. You're sexy when you're wearing nothing but my shirt, and when you're in the shop pretending to work when I know you can't keep your eyes off me."

The fabric of his clothes muffled my giggles.

"Why do you think I go shirtless all the time?"

"You're such a tease."

I placed my hand on his chest, feeling mischievous, and pinched his nipples. A growl emanated from deep within his throat and then his mouth was on mine. Wet, open-mouthed kisses trailed down my neck to the button of my hospital gown, until his cheek brushed against the top of Addyson's head. He stopped, kissed me once more, and shifted so we faced. Our noses a millimeter apart.

"Everything about you turns me on. You make me crazy. Sorry, I lost my head for a minute."

I pulled back and grinned. "You're right. I worried you'd get a mouthful of breast milk." His grimace made me laugh. "So predictable."

"Are you sure you still want to head to your place when you're sprung from this joint?"

"Yeah. I need to let go. I have a new life now. I can find an apartment here if you've changed your mind. We can wait until the paternity test comes back. It should be a few days."

He cupped my cheek and pulled me closer, so we were eye to eye and our foreheads rested against each other's. "I want you and Addyson with me in my house. Our house. If you asked me a year ago, hell, a month ago, I would've said you were crazy. I fought my feelings for you, but I can't anymore. Actually, there's something you should know. Something I've been struggling with."

My heart plummeted. My gaze shot around the room, not wanting him to guess at my inner turmoil. His fingers squeezed my chin and drew my attention back to him.

"Do you mind if I put our little princess in the crib thing?"

I nodded, and he took her from me, kissed her forehead, and placed her in the bassinet. His clenched chiseled jaw concerned me. His gaze scanned the room and landed on the window. Although wistful in appearance, I knew better. Morgan took his time to gather his thoughts. He wasn't one to speak without purpose.

I waited but wished he had returned to me. He belonged in my arms, where comfort and love abound. I rubbed my chest as I realized his pain was now my pain, and my heart broke for him.

Without looking at me, he began.

"Eighteen years ago, I made a vow." His Adam's apple bopped, and I wanted to stop him. Vulnerability oozed off him as he dredged up the memories plaguing him. My inked, tough, sweet man with glassy eyes made me hurt for him. I hated whatever caused his distress.

"My Aunt Karen and Uncle Dustin died in a car

accident. Parker and I were in the back seat. We were arguing. Uncle Dustin was telling me to be the better man. Be an example for the younger Parker. I was so mad at him for telling me to reign in my anger. I mean, we are just a few months apart in age. I said things…" he choked, and a tear fell from the corner of his eye.

"Morgan?" I waited for him to face me and patted the bed. "Please come and lie down with me."

He hesitated, but after a moment, he resumed his position beside me. I ran my thumb along his cheeks and wiped the tears away. I stayed silent as he closed his eyes and his nostrils flared. A shuddering breath later, he spoke once again.

"I said things I can never take back. I didn't mean them." He choked around a sob. His anguish reverberated across the room.

I ignored the twangs of discomfort and moved so we lay touching from forehead to toes. I kissed his cheeks, took his hand, interlocked our fingers, and placed them under my nightgown against my heart.

"He knew, Morgan. Of course, he knew. You were eight. Whatever you said didn't matter to him."

He gaze flickered across my face.

"For the longest time, I blamed myself for their deaths." He squeezed my hand. "I don't anymore."

I pulled our hands to my mouth and kissed each of his knuckles.

"Logically, I know my aunt and uncle's death resulted from another distracted driver. But a part of me will forever wonder if I hadn't been mouthing off, if my uncle would have seen the car running the red light. I made a promise to him that day. I would never get emotional again. I learned to keep my guard up at all times. I didn't allow anyone to get close except for my family. I couldn't bear the pain of the loss. I told myself the fewer people I loved, the less the pain."

"You made room for Addyson."

He smiled at the mention of her name. "I did. And for you too."

Morgan shifted, dislodged his fingers from mine, wrapped his arm over my waist, and rested his hand on my lower back. He nuzzled my hair and kissed along my jaw and lower into my clavicle. He sniffed, causing goosebumps to rise across my skin.

"You smell so good."

I turned my head and placed my lips against his forehead. "You don't smell so bad either."

He chuckled.

"Think you can live with my surly ass for longer?"

"I'm not opposed to the idea."

He nodded and dug a finger into my side, making me laugh.

"You know if it wasn't for Susan, I would have never been prepared for you."

At my look of confusion, he snickered.

"Although we were friends before, Susan was the first person I let in after the accident and my promise. She put a crack in my walls. But then you came along and decimated them. I fought my feelings for you, but when you left the house, I couldn't breathe. I felt this horrible pain in my chest and then you called. But it wasn't you. All I could think was I lost you before I had you. That was my fault. I kept you at arm's length, but the reality is I didn't just make room for Addyson, I turned my heart over to you long before I was ready to admit it."

It was my turn to choke up and tears filled my eyes. I plastered my lips against his, gave him a kiss I hoped expressed my love for him.

He cupped my cheeks and nudged me away.

"Hey, hey. I didn't mean to make you cry. I'm sorry."

I laughed, my heart lighter than it's ever felt. "These are tears of happiness."

"I love you."

"I love you, too."

I threw my arms around him, buried my face in his neck and used his unique scent to ground me. He rubbed my back, and in that moment, I knew I needed to tell him my story. It was time for me to let go.

****

Morgan

Ann Marie pulled away. I waited, nervous but at the same time, lighter. I revealed my heart to her, and she hadn't run. I don't know how I got through it, but I told her everything. Things not even Pax or Caden knew. I never believed them when they told me talking about it would give me peace. They were right, not that I planned on telling them.

Giving Ann Marie all my truths liberated me. I was no longer alone facing a reality I couldn't control. All the years I buried my sense of hopelessness by controlling my behaviors came crashing down with my confession.

I lay on the too small bed with Ann Marie's body tucked against me. I counted and studied the different cadence of Addyson's low whimpers and discovered peace in them. With a shuddering breath, I let go of my role in the accident. The past may have shaped the man I became, but with Ann Marie and my baby in my arms I set my sights on the future.

"Thank…thank you for sharing that with me. I know it must have been difficult. I want to tell you about my past. I've never spoken of this to anyone. I've held it so close to my heart, and like you, I used it to build my wall."

"Sweetheart, please. Don't. I didn't do this expecting your secrets in return."

This time she palmed my cheeks, kissed my scrunched eyebrows, my eyelids, my nose, and ended with a soft press against my lips.

"I know. But I want to. Will you hear my story?"

"Of course."

She looked at the ceiling much like I had earlier.

"I dated my middle school boyfriend, Deacon, until I was sixteen. We were together for five years. We talked about getting married after we graduated, but our parents insisted we attend college first. We were so young and in love. Had everything going for us. We wanted to take our relationship to the next level. He planned a romantic evening. Borrowed his dad's truck. Filled it with blankets and drove us to a lookout point on Magnolia."

I gathered her closer to my chest. I had a feeling I didn't want to hear the rest but bucked it up for her. She lent me her strength. It was my turn to return the favor.

"It was both our first time." She laughed at the memory. I didn't share her sentiment.

"We fumbled, but in the end…well…" She rubbed her cheek against my chest, and I puffed it out, reminding her whose arms encircled her.

Mine.

I knew I was being ridiculous. This was her history, a time when we didn't know the other existed, and without a doubt, the guy was no longer in her life.

"We were insatiable after that. We found ways, places. Anything to be together. We weren't as careful as we should have been. I got pregnant."

I hugged her tighter as she shook against me. She hid her face in my shirt. Although I wanted to, I didn't force her to look at me.

"I was so scared. I knew I would disappoint my parents, but Deacon loved me and that was enough to get us through." Tears wet my shirt and all I could do was hold her as her heart ripped apart. I squeezed her and made a silent vow to help her mend. "He was so angry. Blamed me for entrapping him. Said he had a future, and a child was not a part of his plan."

My arms vibrated around her. Proverbial smoke wafted out of my ears. I wanted to go hunt him down and punch the shit out of him. But that wasn't what Ann Marie needed from me. I clenched my hand, dug my nails into my skin and used the pain to ground me.

"I was alone. Pregnant and too terrified to face my parents. I couldn't hide it from them after a few months. They noticed when Deacon stopped coming to the house. I told my mom, and she told my dad. He never said it, but I hated that I disappointed them. My parents were my rocks, regardless of how they felt."

I sighed, relieved she had a good support system. I thought of a young Ann Marie with a swollen belly and then it hit me. Where was the baby, the child, now?

"Mom took me to a doctor, and they told me my options." My heart thundered against my ribs and she lifted her head. Our gazes locked. "I didn't abort. I went through with the pregnancy. I chose adoption. My parents said they would help, but Mom had just gotten her diagnosis and she needed me."

I tucked her back into my chest. "The decision was yours. I'm not here to judge you. I'm here to hold you."

Tears welled in my eyes. Tears for the lost girl who went through a pregnancy alone. The young girl who gave up her child. The woman before me who's heart still hurt. She sniffled, and I held her, hoping it was enough.

After several minutes, she took in a deep breath. "I'm sorry. I must seem pathetic."

I lifted her chin with my finger. "Don't apologize. I'm in awe of you. Such strength. I wish I knew that girl, but I admire the woman she's become. She's strong, smart, beautiful, sexy as all hell, and crazy for loving me, and I'm glad her road led her to me."

She thumped my chest. "Stop it. You're going to make me cry again."

"Let it out. I got you."

She smiled at my words and burrowed further into me as her hands clutched my shirt.

"I too made a promise. I never held my baby boy. My mother did. But I couldn't hold him. I knew if I did, I would never give him up and deny him the life he deserved. My parents worked demanding jobs, mom was sick, I was a teenager in high school. I couldn't do that to him. But I also decided I would never let that happen to me again."

"I worked my ass off and became financially and emotionally independent. I made sure I never had to rely on another being. I hooked up, but never with someone with a potential for a future. After a while, it became easier to focus on my business. Sleep with men when I wanted sex. I didn't give them any place in my life."

I grew concerned the more she spoke.

"I didn't want to share my life with a man again. And then I met you. So alike we were. A tough exterior protecting our hearts. I wanted to shatter those walls surrounding you, but I think deep down I wanted you to obliterate mine. I goaded you into sex. It was shitty of me to use sex as a way in."

I laughed, took the breath I held, and felt the tension release. "I'm glad you did."

Her answering smile eased me further.

"Getting pregnant felt like my life was on replay."

"I'm not going anywhere."

"I know. I may have crumpled your walls, but you…Morgan, you restored my faith. And just in case you have any doubts, I want to tell you something." With her hand to the back of my head, she nudged me down. Her lips skated the shell of my ear. "I love you, now and forever."

Chapter Twenty-Seven

Ann Marie

If there was one thing the Anderson's loved doing was getting together for food. I think Mrs. Anderson lived for feeding her boys, and her baby girl as she was apt to call them. A week after Addyson's birth we were at Morgan's—now my—house waiting for the troops to descend for a barbecue.

Summer weather was at its peak. Sun warmed the deck as I sat in the shade under the awning while Addyson napped on my shoulder. The sliding door zipped open behind me, and Dustin and Parker stepped out. Dustin extended a gift bag to me.

"Wanna exchange? The baby for the gift?" His goofy smile could brighten the most depressed person.

"You can't keep her," Morgan said as he climbed the steps of the porch after setting up the folding chairs and cleaning out the fire pit for the evening's activities. We didn't expect this to be a quick gathering.

Dustin pouted and crossed his arms, making me giggle and waited for the foot stomp. He didn't disappoint.

"You promised."

"Promised what, brother?"

"Remember when I caught you playing tonsil hockey, and I didn't rat you out to Mom. You promised me your firstborn." He pulled open his unbuttoned flannel and revealed his shirt. I spewed out the water stupid me had just drunk. Dustin pointed at the top right corner of his clothes, and Morgan walked closer to us to read it.

Morgan chuckled. *"Hello. My name is Rumpleforeskin. I am here to collect.* Where the fuck did you get that shirt? And we didn't make that promise. Besides, you did rat us out."

Parker and Dustin laughed, shared a knowing look, and waggled their eyebrows.

"Seriously, hand the goods over. I am in need of hours of niece cuddles."

Dustin held Addyson close to his chest and gazed at her with a tear in his eye. He bounced her light on his feet. "She's getting heavier."

Without a doubt, Addyson's future held a lot of spoiling. Between Morgan, his brothers, cousins, and her grandparents, someone would always dote on her.

"Yeah. Went to the doctor's yesterday. She's growing and doing great. Preemie diapers are still too big, but at least we don't have to wrap the straps around to her back anymore."

Foster, Jesse, and Kate arrived, and they passed Addyson around from one eager family member to the next. I laughed when the last of the troops rounded the corner of the house. Mr. and Mrs. Anderson with Pax and Susan behind them pulling two wagons loaded with food.

"Mom spent all morning cooking," Pax said to my questioning look.

"She wanted nothing to infringe on her baby holding time," Susan added.

"Since everyone's here, can I get you all to gather around for a minute?" Morgan asked and my pulse sped. "Pax, Caden is on the phone." Everyone broke out in loud hellos at which Morgan chuckled. "He's promised to stay on and talk to anyone after, but I have something I want to tell you."

Nobody quieted, and the volume grew loud enough to attract the police for violation of the noise ordinance. With Addyson in Mrs. Anderson's arms and far away from me, my hands were free. I brought my fingers to my mouth and blew out an obnoxious whistle, stopping the commotion.

"Jeezuz, woman. Warn a guy before you do that," Morgan said and leaned down for a kiss to my temple. "Thanks."

"Give me the phone," Pax said and took it out of Morgan's hand. "Assuming you want me to hold it so he can see."

"Yep." Morgan stood beside my chair and took my hand in his. With the other, he pulled out an envelope from his back pocket. My heart stuttered and eyes grew wide. I knew what it was.

"Morgan? Are you sure you want to do this in front of everyone?"

He squeezed my hand, but instead of answering he addressed the crowd. "The results for the paternity test are in." Another uproar and shifting bodies spoke to the nervous tension riding in the air. "I was going to open it yesterday, alone, but decided not to. I want you all to know, especially Ann Marie," he looked at me then, "no matter the results, Addy is mine. I consider her my daughter, and I her father. Whatever is in here," he waived the envelope, "won't change a thing."

293

My vision blurred, but I blinked, keeping my tears at bay. I nodded and yanked at his hand. He leaned down, and I tugged until his ear was at my mouth. "I love you. Addy? Huh?"

He shrugged his shoulders.

"I love it. Baby Addy. She's lucky to have you as a father."

He straightened, let go of my hand, and ripped open the letter. For once his family was silent, all eyes on him as he read the contents.

A choked sob rendered the air, and Morgan sank to his knees. I wrapped my arms around his neck and pulled him to my chest. I couldn't tell from his reaction what the results were. He wept and his body shuddered against mine. All I could do was tighten my hold around him.

Jesse stepped up and took the paper from Morgan's hand and skimmed the contents of the page before he faced me.

"Morgan is Addyson's dad."

It was my turn to sob. Morgan shifted, so he was on his knees and his hips between my legs. We held onto one another and cried as his family hugged each other, then came and enveloped us in their arms. So many hugs and words of congratulations, but not once did Morgan or I lift our heads away from the other.

The pop of bottle caps echoed through the air, and a hand tapped me on the shoulder. Mrs. Anderson offered me a glass, and Dustin did the same for Morgan.

"A toast," he said, "To Morgan and Ann Marie." Hums chorused out. "Morgan, you lucky bastard." That earned him a smack from his aunt. "Wait, this is good, I swear it," which produced several snickers. "Morgan, you are the man. Growing up we looked up to you, Caden, and Pax. Whatever you guys did, us young ones wanted to do the same. Whereas Caden guided us with words, and Pax with teaching, you, Morgan, have always led by doing. Words were not your forte." Again, people snickered. "You were the first to ride and own a bike. First to walk away from a good job to work on his own. The first to buy a house. The best thing, though, is every time you did one of those things you somehow stayed Mom's favorite, which we all know irked the crap out of Pax. But by this one act alone, you have now permanently pushed Pax out of that ranking. Congratulations to you and Ann Marie, making adulting look easy. Salute."

Morgan chuckled.

"Oh, and before I forget, thank you for opening up a whole new world of slogan clothing for me. I've already started you off," he said and pointed to the gift bag on the floor beside my chair.

"You never need a reason to get new shirts, dipsh…" Parker began, then stopped and shot a glance at his aunt. "Sorry."

Mrs. Anderson nodded, but covered Addyson's ears. Dustin retrieved the bag and handed it to me once again. "Go on, open it."

I pulled out an array of rainbow-colored tissue and gave them to Morgan.

"Who wrapped this for you? A two-year-old?" he asked Dustin.

Dustin put his hand to his heart. "Man, that hurt. You don't think I can do pretty?"

Morgan squinted as he considered the question

before smiling. "Yep. That's what I'm saying."

Dustin pretended to stab himself and fell to the ground, making everyone around us either roll their eyes or chuckle.

"Is he always so dramatic?"

Morgan, still sitting between my legs, shifted so his back leaned against the chair. He gripped my ankle, almost like he needed to keep the physical contact between us. "He does have a flair for it. If you laugh, he'll keep trying to outdo himself. Haven't figured out if ignoring him or laughing at him is the best way to shut him up."

I reached into the bag and pulled out several onesies. "Dang it. He's making me laugh. What should I do?" I asked Morgan as I passed him the clothing one piece at a time. Morgan read each one, chuckled or shook his head.

"You are not using our baby to flirt," he said and held one up for his family to see.

It read: *If you think I'm cute wait until you see my uncle*.

"But then again, since she has six uncles, you're SOL."

Morgan continued reading them as I piled them in his lap. The last one brought a hitch in his breath. He turned to me, lifted it so I could see. "This one is my favorite."

That one displayed: *I'm adorable, Mom's hot, Dad's lucky*.

****

Morgan

I sat back with Addy nestled and sleeping against

my chest. I reveled in my family's enjoyment of the hot summer day. My heart stuttered each time I contemplated the paternity letter. Three hours later, and I still hadn't digested the news. I thought back to my life over the past eighteen years, and then focused on the recent eight months.

Ann Marie and Addy turned everything I believed on its head. They brought a lightness to my heart I hadn't felt since I was a kid. Ann Marie made me smile, laugh, love.

Now that was a word I never thought would enter my vocabulary.

Love.

Sure, I loved my family. But I showed them through actions not words. It was the best way I knew how.

Addy squirmed in my arms. She slept through the mayhem that was my family but woke hungry every hour. I stood and spotted Ann Marie talking with Susan. I approached them and the resonance of her laughter vibrated in my chest. Bending down, I kissed Ann Marie on the top of her head.

"Addy's getting hungry. Come with me?"

Ann Marie smiled and patted Addyson's back. "Sure."

She got up and took my offered hand. I led us to the dock. For what I had planned, I didn't want an overhearing audience. I waited for her to settle on a lounge before handing her Addyson. I sat on the lounge next to hers. Unexpected nerves coursed through my body.

Not because I wasn't sure, but because Ann Marie meant the world to me. She was my one. My everything. I was certain of my love for her and the place she had in my heart.

But I was still nervous.

I hoped my absolute certainty conveyed both in our everyday lives and in the special moments we shared. I hoped she didn't grow to hate what she loved about me now. I hoped she continued pushing me out of my comfort zone.

In my love for her, I came to realize I preferred to have loved and lost than to have never loved at all. Cliché? Yes. But it was how I felt. She was mine, and I was hers. The knowledge lightened the heaviness I carried in my heart for so many years.

In fact, I felt free.

"Hey," she said. "Share with me. What's making you smile?"

"Share? Do you think that's a strange word?"

Her eyebrows scrunched as she studied me and shook her head. "I've never thought about it. If you think about it though, we share something every day of our lives, don't we?"

I looked out toward the lake and the two jet skiers in the distance. "When my aunt and uncle passed away, I hated that word. Everyone wanted me to share my feelings. They wanted me to share my thoughts. All I wanted to do was shut down, hold everything inside. Give nothing away."

She reached out and placed her hand on my thigh. "They were worried about you."

"I know that now." I nodded. "Back then it felt like they were asking me to confess my fatal mistake."

"Oh, Morgan." She squeezed my leg, and I wrapped my hand over hers. I lifted her hand, turned it over, and traced the lines in her palm with my fingers.

I shifted my gaze to hers and smiled. "My family never blamed me, but I did. For years, I let the guilt rule my life. I was never worthy of my family. I let them down. I caused them heartache."

"And now?"

My stare flickered back and forth across her face. "I let go of the guilt. In its place, I invited love. Before you, I didn't know how to trust myself. I shut people out, shut the world out. I was scared if I gave any piece of me away, I would lose my tenuous hold on who I had become."

"Who you are is a result of that scared little boy. The man you've become…" Her breaths came out in short bursts. "The man you've become is a man I respect and love."

"Respect?"

She swung around in her seat and placed her feet on the floor in between mine. She held Addyson with one arm and took our interlaced fingers to her mouth. She kissed each knuckle while looking at me.

"You are so strong. You amaze me. Always there for your family. You were there for me. Made Addyson yours before you even knew. You never turned me away, even though I wasn't the easiest person to get along with. You supported me, gave me a way back to designing. Pampered me. Protected me. You did all this without ever once asking me for anything in return. I wish you could see yourself as they all see you. The way I see you."

"The way you see me now?"

"The way I always saw you, even if I refused to admit it."

"I never apologized for the way I proposed." Her gaze left mine. I nudged her to face me with my finger under her chin. "Looking back, I see my mistake." I dropped to one knee and pulled the ring box out of my pocket. "I may have screwed up, but this is me fixing it. Ann Marie, my heart, marry me."

"Is that the same ring from before?"

Never in my life had I used words to cover up my nerves, but there was a first time for everything.

"Yes, shit. I'm sorry. We can go pick out a different one. I wasn't thinking. Please, don't let my idiocy be the reason you say no. You're not going to say no, are you?"

A sparkle lighted her eyes and her smile weakened my knees. She cupped my cheek, leaned forward, and kissed me on the mouth.

"Don't return the ring. I love it."

She reached for the box.

"Does that mean you'll marry me?"

"I guess I have to if I want the ring. Or we can negotiate."

"No negotiations. Partners, parents, lovers for life. No rules, and a whole lot of strings."

She pulled me closer and looped an arm around my neck. She kissed me again then rested her forehead against mine, with Addy tucked between us. I wrapped my arms around both of them.

"I like the sound of that. All of it."

I growled. "Woman, I need to hear your answer."

"Is this growling going to continue for the rest of our lives together? Asking for a friend."

"I promise to growl, grunt, huff, kiss, lick, bite. I will do whatever as long as you answer me."

"Wait, what was the question again?"

Her mischievous baiting resonated in her voice. I loved her more for it. But I still wanted a verbal yes.

I sighed and looked up to the sky. "I can't remember. Guess we'll just have to wait until it comes back to me." I shifted to move away, and Ann Marie laughed loud enough Addyson stirred.

"My answer is yes."

I cupped my ear. "What? I didn't hear that."

"Yes."

I tilted my head. "Sorry, didn't quite catch that."

"Yes," she shouted and laughed. I jumped up, pulling her with me, and drew her into as tight of a hug as I could without hurting Addyson.

"Was that a yes? We couldn't hear her from all the way over here?" Dustin yelled from the back deck.

I pulled a fraction away from Ann Marie. We laughed as I slid the ring on her finger and turned to face my family as they rushed the dock.

Ann Marie raised her hand and showed off the ring. Hugs and back taps pulled us apart, and I felt the loss. I walked back to where she stood with Susan. I reached my arm around her waist, bringing her to my side.

She tilted her head and accepted my kiss. "I love you."

"I love you, too," I said, and with a certainty I never experienced before, I knew my heart was safe in her hands. I taught her to trust others. Trust herself. And without a shadow of a doubt, I knew she taught me the very same thing.

Rasha Selim

About the Author

Rasha Selim was born in Cairo, Egypt and was raised in both Cairo and Dubai, United Arab Emirates. She moved to the U.S. to attend college and pursue a career as a Forensic Psychologist. She left criminology behind to become the mother of three wonderfully active boys. Rasha has spent her life engaged with books and as stories of her own began to develop she knew that she had to get them down in print. She is extremely excited to be sharing her stories with the world. Rasha lives in upstate New York where she is blessed to be surrounded by her loving and supportive husband, children, great friends and incredible books.

~*~

Visit Rasha at

http://www.rashaselim.com

To Honor

Evergreen Point Book One

By Rasha Selim

Firefighter Pax Anderson has a job he loves, a family he cherishes, and a code of conduct he lives by. He should be on top of the world, but he's not. The one thing that would make his life perfect—the woman of his dreams—is his brother's best friend…and off limits.

Susan Hayes has had a crush on Pax for years, but after her mother's death, the Andersons became her surrogate family and she won't risk her relationship with them. Her thriving animal shelter helps keep her thoughts off Pax, but when he chooses her shelter for a fundraising event, her resolve goes up in smoke.

When a dangerous force threatens to drive them apart, Susan and Pax are put to the ultimate test.

Royal Snapshot
By Anya Sharpe

Gia Perrone is hired to fill in as famous photographer Scott Wainwright's assistant. The job entails documenting the life of Santoria's royal family and the prince's wedding. All work, no play, right? Wrong. Scott lives up to his reputation as an insulting bully of a boss until he makes his off-the-clock interest in Gia clear. Meanwhile, Prince Roman can't stop flirting with her, despite being engaged. Add in non-committal ex-boyfriend Jason Fortin begging for a fifth chance, and good grief, life in Santoria isn't just a job anymore. It's a conundrum of royal proportions.

Which one will win her heart? One she doesn't want. One she can't have. One she can have—maybe—but does she want him?

Thank you for purchasing
this publication of The Wild Rose Press, Inc.

For questions or more
information contact us at
info@thewildrosepress.com.